Rocky Road

Rocky Road

Rose Kent

Alfred A. Knopf　New York

THIS IS A BORZOI BOOK PUBLISHED BY ALFRED A. KNOPF

Grateful acknowledgment is made to Alfred Publishing Co., Inc., for permission to use the theme from *New York, New York,* music by John Kander and words by Fred Ebb, copyright © 1977 (Renewed) United Artists Corporation. All Rights Controlled and Administered by EMI Unart Catalog Inc. (Publishing) and Alfred Publishing Co., Inc. (Print). All Rights Reserved.

Visit us on the Web! www.randomhouse.com/kids

Educators and librarians, for a variety of teaching tools,
visit us at www.randomhouse.com/teachers

Library of Congress Cataloging-in-Publication Data
Kent, Rose.
Rocky road / Rose Kent — 1st ed.
p. cm.
Summary: Fashion-loving twelve-year-old Tess moves with her deaf younger brother and impulsive single mother to Schenectady, New York, where they open an ice cream shop and lead a campaign for urban renewal.
ISBN 978-0-375-86344-8 (trade) — ISBN 978-0-375-96342-1 (lib. bdg.) —
ISBN 978-0-375-89528-9 (e-book)
[1. Ice cream parlors—Fiction. 2. Moving, Household—Fiction. 3. Single-parent families—Fiction. 4. Manic-depressive illness—Fiction. 5. Brothers and sisters—Fiction. 6. Deaf—Fiction. 7. People with disabilities—Fiction. 8. Schenectady (N.Y.)—Fiction.] I. Title.
PZ7.K4197Roc 2010
[Fic]—dc22
2009022093

The text of this book is set in 12-point Goudy.

Printed in the United States of America
June 2010
10 9 8 7 6 5 4 3 2 1

First Edition

Random House Children's Books supports the First Amendment and celebrates the right to read.

To my daughter Kellyrose.
Love and ice cream forever.

Chapter 1

"Start spreading the news,
I'm leaving today.
I want to be a part of it,
New York, New York. . . ."

"Pleeeez stop singing, Ma. You're making me want to jump outta this car!" I called from the backseat. I would've, too, if it hadn't meant leaving Jordan. For three days and eighteen hundred miles, I'd been suffering in silence through Ma's

barn-owl screeching of the only New York song she knew. A broken leg had to hurt less than this ear torture.

"Thank the good Lord your laryngitis is cured, Tess," Ma said as we moved into the fast lane, passing a Volkswagen Beetle.

Laryngitis—ha. Staying silent as the falling snow outside was the only sane way of dealing with our latest hopalong adventure. I'd been around Ma for all twelve years of my life, long enough to know that presenting a sensible argument as to why we shouldn't move cross-country in the dead of winter without money or a plan wouldn't put a dent in her thinking. See, when Delilah Dobson makes up her mind, she leaps first and looks later. And sure as we were fishtailing in this freezing car on an icy highway, she hadn't done much looking.

I stared out the car window. A silver van passed with two little girls holding juice boxes and waving. *Now, where are they going?* I wondered. Grandma's? Ice-skating? A party? No matter, they each wore a brightly colored pom-pom cap and a plucky grin, as if they fully expected sunshine, lollipops, and welcoming smiles to greet them at their destination.

"I want to take up in a city that doesn't sleep. . . ."

"It's *wake up*, Ma. And we're not going to New York City," I said, though she didn't hear me over her own singing.

I have to admit I too caught the Big Apple fever that struck Ma on New Year's Eve when she announced her resolution was to "*re*fresh, *re*vitalize, and *re*locate us to New York."

Of course, I thought she meant New York City. Moving to the Big Apple might've been worth suffering through this long and freezing car ride. I read *Vogue* magazine every month, cover to cover (even the advertisements, *especially* the advertisements). Who wouldn't find living in the fashion capital of the universe irresistible? I daydreamed about passing celebrities on the streets of Manhattan, all of us decked out in designer wear like Dior and Stella McCartney. And I pictured myself strolling around the garment district on weekends, sorting through rich fabrics just asking to be made into snazzy outfits and home furnishings. Plus all those famous stores! Bloomingdale's, Barneys New York, Saks Fifth Avenue. And what's that jewelry store mentioned in movies? Tiffany's, that's it.

Sure wished Ma hadn't waited until the morning we left Texas to set things straight and tell me she meant *upstate* New York. No one would feel like chitchatting in a freezing car if they'd just gotten hit with that news.

"Now that you're speaking again, Tess, how 'bout sitting up front so we can have some girl talk?"

"Can't, Ma. I'll wake Jordan."

I rubbed the top of my brother's hood. He was sound asleep on my lap, with his sweatshirt pulled over his head like he was a turtle in its shell. I'd wrapped a fleece blanket around him too, tucking it tight under his sneakers to cut the draft. Looking down at his sandy brown bangs poking out, I realized that at times like this being deaf had its advantages for my eight-year-old brother. He didn't have to listen to Ma's wailing-siren singing or her ninety-miles-per-hour rambling about the whole new world awaiting us in a city called Schenectady.

Brr. It felt like an air conditioner was blowing straight into the backseat. My hands were throbbing, even though my fingers were crocheting furiously. I pushed the yarn to my side so it wouldn't bump Jordan's head. I was almost finished with a zigzag scarf like one I'd seen on a mannequin at the Gap. Not like that one, actually—far superior. This one would be softer thanks to an alpaca-merino-blend yarn with a stylish tousled fringe. It was turquoise, which *Vogue* declared the "hottest hue" this season. Jordan's doe eyes and puffy donut cheeks already drew smiles from women. Add this scarf to that sweetie-pie face and he'd resemble a mini boy-band singer.

"It's up to you, New York, New York. . . ."

The draft from the window was getting worse. Each time Jordan breathed out, it looked like he was puffing on one of Pop's Marlboros. I hadn't seen Pop in two years—since he stopped by to tell us he was taking that construction job in Galveston—but I still could predict his reaction if he knew what Ma had done. Sneering, head shaking, and beer swigging. "Sounds like another of your dumb-as-a-bowling-ball schemes, Delilah," he'd say, especially if he knew the heater was busted.

Thinking about the busted heater made me clamp up all over again. I'd told Ma she oughta fix it before we left San Antonio. "The Weather Channel says the Northeast gets colder

4

than a meat locker in the winter," I'd said. So what did Ma do before we left?

To affirm the *refresh* part of her New Year's resolution, she took our run-down car to Maaco Auto Painting. Our tired gray Toyota came back a tired and ugly lime-green Toyota, still with a busted heater.

Outside, the evergreen trees blurred like a green kaleidoscope. Then we passed what had to be the hundredth deer-crossing sign as we headed north on Interstate 87, this dreary highway that was sending us deeper into the New York section of Antarctica. Hail was smacking the windshield like frozen turds, and the chain pulling the U-Haul was groaning like it had a stomach bug.

I rested the unfinished scarf against Jordan's cool cheek, then touched his little fingers. Ice-cold.

"Jordan is getting frostbite!" I called to Ma over the rumble of a passing SUV. Having spent all my life in southwest Texas—where a fifty-degree cold snap causes a run on Walmart flannel pj's—I wouldn't know frostbite from fungus, but it got Ma's attention. First she whacked the heater. Then she pulled over to the highway shoulder, got out, and walked back to the U-Haul.

She returned holding two pairs of socks. "We've got three bins of your craft supplies, and two bags full of your brother's stuffed animals, but I can't find any doggone gloves or hats." She tossed the socks on my lap. "Put these on you and Jordan. Just a short ways to go."

I put them on Jordan's hands and mine, even though the look

was truly tacky. I wanted to finish this scarf, and I couldn't crochet if my fingers went numb.

"What about you?" I asked, noticing her bare hands. Ma's got no meat on her skinny bones.

"Can't grip the wheel with socks on," she said as we merged back on the highway. "Any more questions?" *Smack*—her knuckles whacked the heat vent again.

"Just one. Tell me again: How come we're moving to this sorry city, Schenectady? It's just asking to be spelled wrong." I knotted the aqua yarn and started chain-stitching in navy, but the socks made it impossible. I yanked them off.

"They've got good schools in New York, Tess. And there's a gold mine of business opportunities that I got wind of, thanks to Jimbo."

Jimbo worked in the produce department at Albertsons and was always shouting free advice over to Ma as she sliced meat behind the deli counter. He should've stuck to displaying fruits and vegetables. If he'd been so smart, he would've convinced Ma to stop with the spending sprees and get-rich-quick schemes. These past two years, that had only gotten us poor.

"What would he know about a business opportunity in Schenectady?"

"Jimbo's wife's cousin's stepsister lives there. Got herself a cushy job working for the New York Lottery. I've been e-mailing her on Jimbo's laptop during my work breaks, and she sent me listings of businesses that've gone belly-up in Schenectady. The upside of a slumping economy is plenty of leases to choose from at bargain prices. Sometimes life just calls for you to pick up and go. It makes me think about them immigrants who spent weeks at sea, only to arrive in New York Harbor and get welcomed by Gal Liberty, smiling and holding her big ol' torch."

"Nobody asked Jordan what he wanted," I said.

"Being deaf was no picnic for him back in San Antonio, Tess. He wasn't catching on in school. A third grader not reading? Nonsense. And you know how he fusses at me like the devil. New York's chock-full of smart special-education teachers. They'll get him on a straight and narrow path."

I didn't want to hurt Ma's feelings, but the teachers in San Antonio had nothing to do with why Jordan acted up. The reason he busted her chops was plain as the nose on her face. Jordan and Ma can't *understand* each other. Now, I'm not saying Ma hasn't tried to learn sign language since Jordan got the high fever as a baby and lost his hearing, because she has. When Jordan was littler and Pop was still around, Ma kept a sign-language dictionary propped open on the coffee table, and we'd all practice every night after supper, signing songs and silly rhymes. And she'd check signing videos out from the library for us to watch—that is, until our DVD player broke. Maybe it did have something to do with her being left-handed like she said, but for some reason, getting signs right was always harder for Ma. And then Pop's boozing got worse, and the money problems kicked in, and—well, right or wrong, mastering sign language fell to the bottom of Ma's priority bag. After Pop split for Galveston, she had to work longer hours at

Albertsons, so she started relying on me. I'd taken free American Sign Language classes at the Y, and truthfully, it came easier to me. "Tess, my interpreter," that's what she called me.

Ma's voice brought me back. "As for you, my crafty queen, I bet you a hog's curly tail that you'll take a shine to Schenectady from the minute we get there."

"Don't count on it," I said. "I'll be the new kid. Who wants to be the new kid in January?"

"Think about the possibilities. Northeast weather gives you more fabrics to work with for home and fashion design. You couldn't stroll down the River Walk in San Antonio in January wearing a full-length rabbit-fur coat, now, could ya? But you can in Schenectady. Like I said, a whole new world!"

"I wouldn't *want* to wear real rabbit fur," I told Ma, but I had to admit she had a point. I've always admired the bulky cowl-neck sweaters, pleated wool skirts, and shearling boots I saw in *Vogue* advertisements. That cozy look falls flat (and sweaty) on a seventy-degree winter day in the Southwest.

"Mark my words. Girls at the new school will appreciate your style *and* your warm heart. Folks say that New Yorkers act salty on the outside but they're sweet like honey on the inside, where it counts. That'll be a big change from those sorry witches back at your old school."

I couldn't argue that point either. The first half of seventh grade hadn't been worth the scuff on my shoes. That's because the girls at Navarro Middle School worshipped whoever had the coolest cell phone—*not* the neatest art project. Last October I'd overheard Kaylee, my science-lab partner, whispering about my "cheesy homemade vest" and setting off a chorus of snickers. Designing that black satin vest and embroidering those ghosts and pumpkins on the front lapels took weeks. And it looked nice—not "cheesy."

Ma looked back through the rearview mirror and caught me swimming in those mucky memories. "Don't fret your pretty face about those girls," she said. "That's yesterday's news. I see sunny skies and true-blue friends in tomorrow's forecast for you."

I smiled. Maybe Ma *was* right. Maybe there were other "crafty queens" in Schenectady just waiting for me to arrive with my yarn and paints and glue gun. Maybe, just maybe, my new school would even have an art club where we could hang out together and reveal our inner artists.

Bump. The car hit a pothole. Jordan opened his eyes, sat up, and pushed his hood back.

I put the crochet hook down and moved my hands. "Turtle Boy wakes!"

He stared out the window. "Where is new home?" he signed.

"We're not there yet."

"Hungry. Hungry." His hand moved quickly from his throat to his belly. As usual, his signing was sloppy. His fingers were clenched like a fist, which confused the meaning.

I took his hand in mine and corrected his fingers. My stomach growled too. Lunch was four hours and two states ago. Then I kissed his forehead. "What do you want for supper?" I signed.

"Chicken and ice cream."

Now, Jordan always got those signs right. *Chicken* looks like a beak, and *ice cream* is easy as licking a cone.

"Too cold for ice cream," I signed. Was it ever.

"Not too cold!" His fingers banged the air like he was playing drums.

Come rain, shine, or tornado, Jordan is always up for ice cream. No surprise. And he gets it whenever he wants. "Ice cream warms the heart, no matter what the weather." That's Ma's motto for a good life. Sure, it's silly, but I love ice cream too.

A road sign for Schenectady appeared an hour later, as daylight slipped behind the tall pine trees and gray horizon. Jordan was distracted, playing with his Happy Meal collection of zoo animals, but I noticed right away.

"Only a few miles to go. Time to check the local directions," Ma called. "Imagine folks like us from the Alamo City about to call New York home. Brace yourself, Schenectady— here come the Dobsons!"

Brace yourself was right, because as we entered the city, the truck in front of us swerved to avoid a pothole while Ma was looking down at the seat. She slammed on the brakes, lurching us forward and sending papers flying.

"Shoot balls of fire! That driver's not fit to steer a wheelbarrow!" Ma shouted. She kept looking at the seat beside her, shuffling through a folder. "I know I stuck that flyer in here. Son of a buck. Where is it?"

Suddenly she reached over for the papers that had fallen, causing the car to hit an ice patch and plow into the side of a parked car.

The driver had just opened the door and was about to step out when—*whack!*—Ma took his door clean off the hinges.

Clanky-clank, clanky-clank. The door scraped, wobbled, and banged the asphalt, then plopped against a sewer grate.

"Holy —————!" Ma let out a six-foot string of cuss-words that would've fried bacon.

I'd barely felt the bang in the backseat, but seeing that car door rolling was a real shocker.

Ma whipped her head toward us, I guess to see if we were dead or bleeding. Then she pulled over and glanced back at the car she'd hit. The driver was still sitting inside. His bald head was shaking back and forth like he was a robot.

Jordan looked at me to sign something, and I waited for Ma to say something, but she didn't. I rubbed Jordan's knee to calm him, and Ma scrunched her eyes shut like she does when she's thinking hard. Then she peeked in the rearview mirror and smoothed her hair.

"Could've been worse," she said, getting out of the car. "Doors are replaceable, right? That's why they got hinges. Stay here."

Back home, before we were evicted from the house, I used to tell little Juanita who lived next door that Ma did things up big like Texas. "*Hace grande*, that's what Mexicans would say about your ma," Juanita always said, her brown moon face giggling.

Juanita was three years younger than me, but I liked her better than just about all my seventh-grade classmates combined. And she was right about Ma. Arriving in Schenectady was another *hace grande* moment on this *hace grande* trip. Because as it turned out, Ma's wisest comment today was her warning Schenectady that the Dobsons were coming.

Our Toyota had a dent on the front passenger door, and the side mirror was cracked and twisted. Luckily the U-Haul had no damage, so we'd still get our deposit back. But no such luck for the car we hit, a gold Lincoln Town Car.

Yikes. Ma hadn't ripped the door off Mr. Nobody's car. This one had a custom license plate that said it all: MAYOR.

Chapter 2

Americans gulp down 1.6 billion gallons of ice cream per year, or twenty-three quarts per person. —*The Inside Scoop*

Two police officers showed up within minutes. One had a clipboard and asked Ma and the other driver questions. The second one redirected traffic and set flares along the road. Meanwhile, Ma tried to make small talk with the guy she hit. The cops called him Mayor Legato, and he really was the mayor of Schenectady. He wore earmuffs, and a pipe sticking out of his mouth made him look like Frosty the Snowman, only he wasn't jolly. Mayor Legato kept staring at his new car minus the door and shaking his head, disgusted. When he

spoke to the cops alongside Ma, his deep voice rolled right over hers, the way adults step on kids' words.

Jordan and I stood on the icy sidewalk with our teeth chattering while Ma tried to sweet-talk her way out of this mess.

"Can't imagine what came over me," she said as the tow-truck driver hitched a cable to the Lincoln Town Car's shiny front bumper. "Guess I was plumb excited about finally reaching the famous city of Schenectady. I've done my research, Mr. Mayor. I know this place saw plenty of action dating back to ol' George W.'s days—George Washington, that is."

"Quit jabbering, Ma!" That's what I wanted to say. She was playing her Texas twang so bad, she sounded like Yippee Coyote.

But the mayor didn't fall for Ma's flattery. As Pop used to say, it felt colder than hell with the furnace turned off. Mostly he kept scowling at Ma. And when she told the mayor that VIPs she knew personally said Schenectady might be the next washed-up city to turn things around, he exhaled a warm cloud and walked away without another word.

"Hush, Ma. You're making things worse," I whispered. Not that I was worried about Mayor Legato liking us—it was too late for that. Money was on my mind now. The police officer had already given Ma a ticket for something called driver inattention. And I knew insurance would be coming after her for all this damage.

Ma has a lot to say, but she never has a lot of money.

●●●●

Another hour and two stops later, we pulled into the Mohawk Valley Village. That's what Ma called it, anyway. It was too dark to read the sign.

"You and Jordan wait in the lobby while I find the rental office," she said.

The lobby of Building One smelled like stale potato chips. Its faded plaid wallpaper and coffee-stained carpeting reminded me of ugly "before" footage on my favorite home-makeover show.

There were no magazines, no toys, and nothing worth looking at in the waiting area, so Jordan started peeling leaves off a fake tree next to the love seat.

"Stop," I signed, and he growled back at me. Hunger is a surefire way of turning my brother into FrankenJordan.

Next thing I knew, he was pulling tissues from a box and flinging them into the air like a flock of seagulls. Kleenex soon covered the floor by my feet.

"I mean it, Jordan. Stop!"

He stuck out his tongue. "Tess no fun," he signed, and he charged into the laundry room just as Ma returned.

Ma said our apartment was four floors up—number 418. "The good news is they fixed the hot water. The bad news is we got one bedroom, not two like they promised, and the elevator's busted."

So I wrestled Jordan down from the dryer he was standing on, and up the stairs we climbed. By the third flight we were all huffing. My heart was feeling heavy like my feet, so I tried a positive-thinking exercise I read about in a magazine. In my mind I pictured Ma unlocking the apartment door to reveal a gorgeous suite with a plush leather sectional, a floral arrangement on a glass coffee table, and the soothing smell of lavender candles.

When we reached the door of 418, I stopped the mind-over-matter wishing. Who cared what the apartment looked like? It still beat sitting in a freezing car.

That night, Jordan and I shared the bed, and Ma slept in the living room on a futon that was pretending to be a sofa. Ma plumped the pillows that had been flattened from the car ride, dug sheets out from the U-Haul, and spread a down comforter she found in the bedroom closet on us. Warm under that soft, cozy blanket, we snoozed like ducklings in a nest.

The familiar smell of chorizo sausage, onions, and zucchini frying got me up around eleven. Ma's lunches and dinners are no great shakes, but when she's up to it, she's capable of whipping up better Tex-Mex breakfasts than any diner, and I've been to every one in Texas north of Raymondville. (The ones that let kids eat free, anyway.)

"Come and eat, Tess," Ma called, pointing the spatula at the kitchen stool. I thought she'd be wiped out from that long drive and our crash landing here in Schenectady, but she didn't show it. Obviously she'd been up early enough to make it to the grocery store. Her wavy black hair was pulled back neatly in a braid, even if the loose gray strands showed she was overdue for her monthly color rinse. (I clip the L'Oréal coupons and apply it for her. She'd let me cut and style too, but I consider hair a specialty best left to cosmetologists.)

Ma picked this apartment because Jimbo's wife's cousin's

stepsister recommended it via e-mail. They offered furnished units for dirt cheap, and Ma liked the dirt-cheap part. Ever since we were evicted from our last apartment, we'd been living on what she calls a girdle budget. Her grocery-store paycheck didn't stretch far, and she was always quick to add that no matter what the divorce paperwork stated, Pop didn't pull his financial weight.

"I get better support from ninety-nine-cent panty hose" is how she put it, but I didn't think she pushed hard either. Ma said Jake Dobson and responsibility were like oil and vinegar; they didn't mix. It was five years since the divorce, longer since Pop lived with us, though it didn't seem like that long to me. I still remember the night Ma kicked Pop out like it was yesterday. He wobbled into the kitchen late on a Friday night, smelling like his favorite Pabst Blue Ribbon and slurring his words, not much different than other Friday nights. Only this time, when Ma frisked his jean-jacket pocket, it was empty. He'd blown through his paycheck, and we were out of eggs, detergent, and hot sauce. That was the straw that broke the camel's back—Jordan and I put hot sauce on everything—and Ma told him to get packing. He stormed out of the house without so much as a goodbye to Jordan and me, and that made Ma even madder. Just as he reached the truck in the driveway, Ma ran upstairs, yanked their wedding picture off the wall, and flung it out the window. It smashed to pieces on the hood of the truck as he backed out, with Ma shouting, "Good riddance, ya cockeyed cowboy!"

I knew the only real money we had was in a trust fund my grandmother set up back in Texas, but so far Ma hadn't touched it. She called it the Ditch Fund, and many times she told me the story about how her mama and paw spent a lifetime earning that cash the hard way: breeding horses. "With my right hand resting on a tub of horse liniment, I swore that I'd save that chunk of change for when things hit bottom. And then I'd come up with a sound plan to dig out of that ditch."

"If you didn't touch the Ditch Fund, then how can we afford to move here?" I had asked during the ride.

"I sold my engagement ring and wedding band, and I put in all that overtime at the Albertsons deli counter, remember? I knew we'd need a furnished place."

Ma was right about needing furniture. We had close to nothing besides the odds and ends in the U-Haul and a set of beat-up southwestern patio chairs that Ma inherited from her parents' ranch years ago. Sometimes I wondered if Ma thought Pop had a contagious disease, what with all his stuff she threw out. She even pitched the rattlesnake boots he won in a card game, and I bet *they* cost a pretty penny.

Ma scooped meat filling into the tortillas as I looked around at what the Mohawk Valley Village brochure called a newly renovated kitchen. The cabinets were freshly painted like they said, though that must've been one farsighted painter. Brush bristles were stuck to the puke-green cabinet doors, and the walls had spots missing paint. And the sink was cracked, like someone had whacked it with a cast-iron pot. The kitchen had a counter with three wobbly stools with ripped cushions. At least there was a microwave, even if the door handle was broken.

Ma poured me a glass of juice. "Jordan still sleeping?"

I nodded.

"Good. He needs the rest." She refilled her mug. Ma drinks her coffee with the socks on, meaning plenty of cream.

"Better add batteries to the shopping list," Ma said, pointing to the wall clock. It was stuck on 2:25. Beside it was a frayed poster of a horse race titled "Saratoga, Top of the Stretch."

I sipped the juice. "We've got to find a craft store. If the home-fashion police saw this place, we'd be under arrest. We need new curtains, throw pillows, and a gallon of paint primer, and that's just for starters."

"Decorating can wait, my crafty queen. First thing this morning, I'm calling to get you registered to start school tomorrow. And I'll ask about the best school for deaf kids. They must have a good one nearby."

My mouth dropped open. "What do you mean, they must have a good one nearby? You said that's why we moved here!"

" 'Course they got a crackerjack school for deaf kids, Tess. I just haven't seen it yet. How 'bout you give me twenty-four hours before quizzing me on local geography?"

Ma put a chipped yellow plate in front of me with two breakfast tacos and a pile of apple slices sprinkled with cinnamon sugar. A newspaper called the *Daily Gazette* rested beside it.

"I've been studying the classifieds," she said, pointing to the paper. "Trying to find the best place to hang a shingle. I'm fixing to meet Jimbo's wife's cousin's stepsister on her lunch hour when you're at school tomorrow to hear more about this city. More to come, but I'll give ya a preview like they do in the movies. Something sweet is calling for Delilah Dobson in the world of retail."

The world of retail? I didn't like how that sounded. "Something could've called you back in Texas, and we would've saved a lot of gas," I said. For one, we had no money; two, we knew nobody in New York; and three, aside from slicing ham and scooping ranch-style beans for deli customers, what did Ma know about retail?

Then, as if it would make me feel better, Ma rubbed my back. "Trust me, honey. I've got a plan."

My whole life I've wanted to trust Ma, but that's impossible if you're around her more than an hour. Know that guy Murphy, whose law always predicts the worst? Ma lives by the Dobson Doctrine, which promises sunshine and lemonade— but we end up with rainstorms and spoiled milk.

I finished off my first taco and spooned hot sauce onto the second. "What kind of business are you talking about?"

"The kind that wipes away sadness the way an antibiotic clears an infection."

"Selling what?" I asked, chewing. The suspense wasn't killing me, but it was getting on my nerves.

Ma started singing. "I scream, you scream, we all scream for ice cream. . . ."

I gulped down a mouthful of spicy sausage. "You want to buy an ice cream truck?"

"Heck, no! The mayor would never approve that license after my tango with his car door. I mean an ice cream *shop*."

I stared at her long and hard. "Here? Now? It's *freezing*. People don't buy ice cream when it's cold."

"It won't be cold forever," she said, refilling her coffee again. "And some white powder falling from the sky is no reason to squash a celebration. Why, we've already got three half-quart containers stocked in our freezer and we just pulled into town! You know our family motto: 'Ice cream warms the heart, no matter what the weather.' "

Ma started rattling off reasons why an ice cream business might save the day for us. Stuff about how the shop would mostly be open when Jordan and I were in school, and what a good fit this was, what with our family's "passion for the products." She was going to bring to the business the same mind-set and rituals we used at home: every day is an ice cream day deserving special bowls and spoons, plenty of scrumptious flavors, and enough wild and wonderful toppings to make a kid belt out, "Yahoo!"

For a few minutes my mind took off in a delicious daydream, imagining Ma's exotic ice cream shop might even make Willy Wonka jealous that he hadn't looked beyond candy. No mother in San Antonio ever gave a kid's birthday party with more belly-jiggling laughter than Ma, never mind tasty frozen treats and fun-blasting games.

But then a cold wind rattled the windows, and I remembered where we were. Who we were, and what might be happening—Shooting Stars. The seesaw moods that struck every so often and made Ma sleep little, spend too much money, and do crazy things at a turbocharged pace. In the beginning she soared, full of energy and grandiose plans. But like a shooting star, she eventually burned and crashed to earth—to bed, actually, unable to do much but sleep, stare at the ceiling, and cry.

Ma's Shooting Stars got us into money trouble. They caused Pop to escape in his beer, which caused her to send him packing. Right now I wondered what I always wondered: Was this spur-of-the-moment New Year's move because of a mood swing? And if so, how long would she fly high—and then, how soon till she crashed?

The bedroom door opened, and out shuffled Jordan. He stopped in front of the living-room window and started giggling and clapping and bouncing up and down like he was on a pogo stick.

"What's going on?" I signed.

He paused in thought and then raised both his hands, cupped them, and brought them down, all the while wiggling his fingers.

What's he signing? Maybe he's describing those old-fashioned musty drapes. "Yes, silly curtains. Downright ugly, if you ask me," I signed, making my best "Yuck" face.

"Don't worry, Tess will make new ones," Ma said.

Jordan read Ma's lips, shook his head, and kept pointing out the window. And then he did a handstand, flipping over and smashing into the futon, still wearing an electric smile that lit up the whole apartment.

"What is it? What's he saying?" Ma asked.

"Don't understand," I signed to Jordan.

Squealing now, Jordan rushed over to the kitchen counter and grabbed my arm, knocking my fork to the floor. Then he yanked me off the stool.

"Hold your horses!" I signed and spoke, laughing as he pulled me toward the living room.

It hit me—I knew what had come over him. The reason was falling outside. "Snow, Ma! Jordan sees snow!" I shouted.

We all stared out the big window, suddenly speechless at the whiteness that lined the world like tissue paper.

Ma picked Jordan up, kissed him, and spun him around. "Hooray for Jordan! 'Let it snow, let it snow, let it snow!' " she sang at the top of her lungs, shaking her right hand to sign *joy*, one of the few signs she knew.

I wiggled my straightened fingers as I moved my hands down in front of me so Jordan would get the sign right. "Snow."

Jordan watched and then copied the sign over and over, giggling all the while. Seeing him snow-struck like that made me laugh too, for the first time in weeks.

"So, what're we waiting for, Christmas?" Ma shouted, untying her apron.

Jordan dashed to the closet for our coats. "Hurry!" he signed. "Snow!"

Down the stairs we flew, out through the potato-chip-smelling lobby to the snow-dusted parking lot. Snow tickled our faces, landed on our hair like white confetti, and filled our noses with jolting freshness. *If New Year was a fragrance*, I decided, *it would smell like this*.

Jordan scooped his sock-covered hands into the fluffy whiteness and threw a snowball at my pajama leg.

Giggling, I molded one with my cold, bare hands and nailed him on the back of his jacket.

Ma stood beside us, twirling like a ballerina and laughing. "Get a gander at this winter wonderland," she said. "This here's a welcoming omen, Tess. Good things are happening for the Dobsons. Ice-cold good things."

For a second I thought of Pop, how he always rolled his eyes at what he called Ma's Pollyanna proclamations. "Death and taxes are the only things a man can count on," that's what he said. But then I looked at Jordan, standing next to me with his tongue stretched out as far as it would go, watching snow dissolve on it.

Just a month ago, on a muggy December afternoon in San Antonio, we'd seen *A Charlie Brown Christmas* together. Jordan had been mesmerized as the *Peanuts* gang caught snowflakes on their tongues.

"Me do that," he signed, pointing to the TV, but I explained that we didn't get snow in Texas.

Now he got his turn.

My better judgment was telling me to exercise caution before inviting hope to this sorry city, Schenectady, but watching Jordan catch snowflakes and seeing Ma's ballerina dance got the better of me.

"Woohoo!" I shouted, and I stuck out my tongue and tasted white magic too.

Chapter 3

The savvy ice cream retailer understands curb appeal.
You *can* judge a book by its cover and a shop
by its entryway. —*The Inside Scoop*

Uh-oh. 8:14. I'd hit OFF instead of SNOOZE. I'd be late on my first day of school here in Antarctica. No wonder—I hadn't fallen asleep until past two. Ma says insomnia runs in our Dobson blood. So do morning grumpies. Jordan was still sleeping as I jumped from the bed and wiggled into my jeans with a ten-pound chip on my shoulders.

"Bus is coming, Tess. Git your motor in overdrive!" Ma shouted from the kitchen.

"Big deal if I'm late," I growled to myself.

Ma handed me my lunch and an envelope as I scrambled out the door. "Take these registration forms. Bus picks up a block south, by the fire hydrant. Hurry!"

I tried, but hurrying on snow-covered ice is no walk in the park, especially without winter boots. Just a few steps from the lobby door I slipped and fell. Then I flopped again near the apartment-complex entrance, right where the snow plows had dumped a pile of gray, sludgy snow.

As I got up and brushed dirty snow off my jeans, I saw the big wooden sign. The sign that I missed when we arrived after dark: MOHAWK VALLEY VILLAGE—INDEPENDENT & ASSISTED SENIOR LIVING.

The words struck like a cane to the head. This place was for *old people*! What was Ma thinking, moving us here? But I had no time to let it sink in. The bus pulled up and I ran to catch it.

By the time we reached Ottawa Creek Middle School, my hair was messy, my jeans were damp, and my sneakers were soaked. I wanted to find the girls' room and peek in the mirror to check if my big ears were poking out or if my neck was covered with nervous blotches. No time. A bell rang, so I hurried to the main office.

They sent me to guidance.

"Have a seat, please. I'm Ms. Hockley. Is Tess short for something?" the guidance counselor asked matter-of-factly as she escorted me to her office, which faced the reception area.

"Just Tess," I answered. She was the tallest woman I'd ever

seen. Way over six feet. With a deep voice too, like a Texas prison warden. (Pop once told Ma and me that Texas has the toughest prisons in the country, though he never explained how he knew this. Years later Ma admitted that between his thirst for booze and his crummy driving record, she had a feeling he might've had firsthand experience with those wardens.)

"Fine then, Tess. Let's get down to business so you can get to class."

Out in the reception area a skinny boy with orange curly hair was staring back at me, making goofy faces. Our eyes met and I looked away.

Ms. Hockley thumbed through my registration papers. "Based on your records, I think we should place you in grade-level math, period three."

"I was in advanced math back in Texas," I interrupted.

"Yes, I noticed. But New York has a challenging math curriculum. Grade level is the recommended starting point for most out-of-state transfers."

Years back, Pop used to brag to his work buddies about how fast I worked numbers in my head. For fun I used to memorize square roots. Once when I was in first grade, Ma took me to visit Pop on a construction site and he called out, "Go on, Tess, tell these guys what the square root of 1,225 is." Without skipping a beat I shouted, "Thirty-five!" That got them all raising their eyebrows approvingly, which doesn't happen every day around men in hard hats pouring concrete.

No matter, I didn't want to take advanced math to please Pop. He hadn't called or sent a single letter to Jordan or me in two years, and I didn't expect an "Attagirl" now. I wanted to take this class because I knew I could handle it.

"Really, math's my best subject," I insisted, sitting up straighter.

Ms. Hockley looked up from behind her glasses. "Give grade-level math a try, and we'll see how things go," she said.

Case closed. So much for the new kid's opinion.

Then she ran down a checklist of questions.

"Do you play a sport, Tess?"

"No."

"Dance or act in school plays?"

"No." I stared at a shelf behind her desk that held dozens of fancy Pez candy dispensers. Beside them was a sign: PLEASE DON'T TOUCH.

"What about band or orchestra?"

I shook my head and peeked out into the reception area. That orange-haired boy was still making goofy faces. Was he trying to be funny, or was he making fun of me?

"Any interest in student council?"

My head was still shaking.

"How 'bout the Go-Green Gang, our environmental club?"

"No thanks." I had a hard enough time getting Ma and Jordan to stick the pop bottles in the recycle bin, never mind policing others.

I rubbed my ice-cube hands. The heater in this school didn't work much better than the one in Ma's Toyota.

Ms. Hockley's down-turned mouth said it all. She'd sized

me up as a do-nothing slacker. Well, tough beef jerky. *I don't even like your freezing school, Prison-Warden Lady.* I looked out the window. It faced an empty warehouse with broken windows. Icicles hung down from the gutters. I wanted to open a window, grab one of those Pez dispensers, and toss it at those icicles.

"How 'bout chorus?" she pleaded, desperate to write something.

I shook my head. Been there. Done that.

I joined chorus in sixth grade after Ma nagged me about not getting involved enough at school. "A baby coon can't sit in the den and learn to catch frogs," she said. "Be a joiner!"

I *was* involved: those ASL classes at the Y after school met three times a week. If Ma had given it a hard try, she would've known: learning ASL took concentration and lots of practice. But chorus, well, that met on Tuesdays during lunch. I could do that.

My short-lived middle-school chorus career ended on a flat note. Shooting Stars struck Ma right in the middle of the spring concert. As we sang "Singin' in the Rain" onstage, Ma started crying in her seat—loud boohoo bawling like someone died. Later she said that watching me on the auditorium stage hit a nerve. All the emotion of the years passing by for me without Pop hit her like a ton of bricks and sent her into a crash. All the kids, teachers, and parents just kept staring at Ma sobbing, and wondering what on earth was wrong. Three days later, when I returned to school after taking care of Ma, I quit chorus. I couldn't go back to those questions and stares.

"Is there *any* extracurricular activity that interests you?" Ms. Hockley asked, sighing.

I perked up. "Do you have an art club?"

Art was my favorite special back in elementary school. Mrs. Menendez, the art teacher, let us play our favorite CDs as we worked, and we made all kinds of masterpieces, as she called them. We turned old nuts and bolts into wind chimes, we made modern-art sculptures out of crushed Coke cans, and we created salt-dough potted-plant people to give our moms for Mother's Day. She always asked me to float from table to table to help other kids since I usually finished early, and that was the best part of class. Art disappeared when I got to middle school because of budget cuts.

Suddenly the thought of art club was warming me up.

"Sorry. We don't have an art club."

Figured.

A tall, skinny girl blew into the office just as we finished talking. She had bushy eyebrows and she wore a red basketball jersey. I barely came up to her shoulder, but I sure outweighed her in the hip-and-thigh department.

"Ellie will be your meet-and-greeter," Ms. Hockley explained. "Meet-and-greeters help new students find their way. And she'll sit with you at lunch."

Ma tells me not to act like the soda pop is always flat. Still, I knew right away I wouldn't click with my meet-and-greeter.

And I was right. Ellie kept dribbling an invisible basketball and talking about the "big game against Shen" later. She played forward and led the team in points because she wasn't afraid to shoot threes. Shed has a zone defense—tough to penetrate, she explained. Like I had a clue.

Ellie led me down the seventh-grade hallway and stopped at room 228. "Here's your English class. I'm off to French, which is *très ennuyeux*," she said, cupping a pretend yawn. "Four more hours until tip-off. Can't wait!" She took off down the hall, then turned around and shouted, "Oh yeah, I sit in the back of the cafeteria with the rest of the team. I'll save you a seat."

The morning went just as expected. Lots of kids staring at Tess the new kid. Teachers giving me beat-up textbooks needing covers, and what-you-better-do-in-my-class-or-else handouts. And just like I predicted, grade-level math was forty-two wasted minutes of figuring out percentages that I learned two years ago.

I stopped at the lockers before lunch. Ms. Hockley had written my locker number and combination down for me, but there hadn't been a minute to find it earlier. I'd been carrying my backpack around all morning, and I wanted to unload some of the heavy books.

My stomach rumbled as I searched for locker 226, though I wasn't sure if it was from nerves or hunger. There it was, in the middle of the blue row, with a big dent in the middle like someone had kicked it hard. The window was cracked open nearby, and the breeze made me shiver.

Would I fit in with Ellie and her basketball friends? The only hoop I cared about was the kind that holds needlepoint. Worrying about it made me mess up the combination.

"Hee-haw to you, San Antonio gal!"

I turned around. Ugh. That redhead from guidance was standing nearby with two other boys. He must've been eavesdropping. I pretended I hadn't heard him.

"Hey, little lassie. Word at the water fountain is you're from the great state of Texas!" he called over, looking back to impress his friends.

"Lassie's a dog," I mumbled softly as I twirled the lock knob.

"C'mon, let me hear that southwestern drawl," he pleaded. "I love that drawl—and jalapeño peppers!"

What, like he *didn't* have an accent? Maybe Texans stretch words out like taffy, but New Yawkers have their own speech quirks. Like dropping *r*'s off words that have them, and adding *r*'s to words that don't.

I kept ignoring him, trying to open my locker. So far nothing was working. This thing looked so old, I bet it was rusted shut.

"You think I'm joking, but I'm not. I swear in another life I was riding horses and rustling cattle on a ranch in Texas. I've watched every cowboy movie ever made, especially the ones about the Alamo. Right, guys?" He had a birthmark on his cheek that moved up and down when he spoke, and his breath smelled nasty, like cheese.

The two other boys with him laughed. One said something about him looking more natural riding a circus elephant.

I wasn't listening anymore. I was fed up with the Texas jokes. Sure, San Antonio has the rodeo and the buckaroos with their cowboy hats and silver studs, but it also has military bases, sunny skies, and more Hispanic flair than this city could ever hope for. But I knew lecturing this kid would be like talking to a tree stump. I kept trying the lock.

The boy elbowed one of his buddies and turned to me again. "I'll prove you're not dealing with no dumb Yankee here. You know the Lone Star song? I do. Let's sing it together!"

Was he for real? I didn't even look at him, even though he started crooning.

"*There's a bullet in the heart tonight in the heart of Texas. . . .*"

I turned my body away from him. Round and round I twirled the knob: 24-26-6, that's what the paper said. Why wouldn't this blasted thing work?

One more time I pulled with all my might and finally it flung open. I started unloading my books and lunch bag from my backpack.

"Why so quiet? Is this a front, or do you always act deaf *and* dumb around new people?" he said, facing me and then turning to wink at his buddies.

That did it. Nobody sticks *deaf* in the same sentence as *dumb*.

"Watch your mouth, Pumpkinhead!" I shouted, and without even thinking, I pulled a pear out of the lunch bag in my hand and threw it at him. *Smack!* It hit hard, right between his eyes.

"Ouch!" he yelled, grabbing his nose.

No sooner had that pear left my hand did a lady in a shaggy

striped sweater grab my elbow and yank me to the center of the hallway.

"Where do you think you are, prison?" she roared. All the hallway traffic stopped as kids watched the new girl get grilled.

Miss Shaggy Sweater turned out to be a social studies teacher. She must have missed the lesson about the Bill of Rights, though, because she sent me to the main office before I could speak out in self-defense. And she didn't make the red-headed jerk come along. He got sent to the nurse's office for an ice pack, as if it was a steel pear or something.

Without even thinking, I stuck my lunch bag in my locker, slammed it shut, and walked to the main office, where I waited fifteen minutes until Mr. Godfrey, the assistant principal, returned from eating *his* lunch. At which point he took me in his office and rambled on about his "zero-tolerance-for-violence policy."

The lecture lasted six minutes and thirty-five seconds. I know because I stared at a clock shaped like a New York Giants helmet above his desk the whole time. Pop hated the Giants. "Any day that the Cowboys kick the Giants' teeth in is a good day," he always said.

Mr. Godfrey kept asking for my version of what happened, but I said little. I knew who was the insider here and who was the outsider. Besides, having a deaf brother has taught me how much is said without words.

Then he asked if I wanted to resolve this conflict in something called peer mediation.

I shook my head, not even interested in hearing what that meant.

About now I was expecting Mr. Godfrey to dole out a hefty punishment, but instead he said he was giving me a one-time-only do-over at my new school.

"Pete is a decent kid but he does have a way of sticking his foot in his mouth, so I'm going to assume that's what happened. At a bare minimum, I'll expect you to apologize to him. And from now on, keep your nose clean and quit throwing fruit," he advised.

That was it. No call home and no detention. I'd gotten off easy, and I knew it. I thanked Mr. Godfrey and gave him my best "this won't happen again" face, and then I bolted.

Back in the hallway I actually got my locker open on the first try. The secret was to pull hard. Really hard, as if your life depended on it. But by then I didn't have to worry about finding a seat near Ellie in the cafeteria. Lunch was over.

Chapter 4

After school I returned to discover the apartment door locked, with no sign of Ma or Jordan. My eyes were tearing from the wind, my nose felt like a frozen cherry tomato, and my big ears felt as if they'd snap off and shatter on the ground like china plates. More than anything, I wanted to jump onto the futon with a bowl of chips and salsa and click the remote to the Home and Garden Channel.

But I couldn't, so I went back downstairs to the lobby.

It was deserted, with staticky music playing and washing machines rumbling in the nearby laundry room, sending a bleach smell floating through the air. I sat on the love seat and dug into my backpack for something to eat, only to realize that I'd left my lunch in my locker after I'd gotten in trouble. Sure wished I had my crocheting so I could work on Jordan's scarf.

I pulled out my math homework, which took all of two minutes. So much for Ms. Hockley saying out-of-staters couldn't hang. Then I read a chapter in my social studies text about the Erie Canal. When I finished, I put my feet up on the coffee table and looked around.

Yuck. Who decorated this place? Wicker furniture typically gives a breezy tropical feel. But upholstered in brown corduroy and up against faded, red-striped wallpaper, this wicker only made the room feel Jekyll-and-Hyde weird! The windows were smudgy and the garbage can was overflowing. On the floor by my feet, somebody had dumped a tray of fast-food trash. Greasy fries and ketchup smells lingered.

With nothing else to do, I played my favorite mind game. Tess the Fashion Fairy Godmother, that's who I became. I imagined all the ways I would transform this room with my mighty invisible wand into something extraordinary, worthy of elegant people. A modern skirted sofa covered with ivory heart pillows and a set of triangular mirrors mounted behind it. Stiffel lamps with antiquey shades and a bamboo rack stacked with magazines—with *Vogue* front and center, of course.

Wham! In the midst of my magic makeover, the automatic doors flew open. In shuffled an old man with a limp. A gust of frosty air followed.

The man wore a fur-lined hooded parka, zipped up to his chin. Watching him reminded me who lived here: old people. *Really* old. And if Ms. Hockley was the tallest woman in Schenectady, he was one of the smallest. Almost as small as Ma, and she says she's two pinkies short of five feet.

The man sure had a strange walk. His right leg was stiff and swung in a small circle with every step. As soon as he got through the doors, he picked a wrapper off the floor.

When he saw me, his eyes darted down to the messy tray. "This place sure could use a field day," he said sternly.

"Field day?" I asked.

"That's navy lingo for scrubbing and cleaning up your mess here on deck," he said, pointing to the floor.

"I didn't leave that," I said.

He glared at me like I'd cursed. "What if we all ignored trash, young lady? This place would be crawling with roaches and spreading germs to folks who already have weak immune systems!"

He pushed down his hood. His hair was buzzed in a crew cut, the color of a dull coin. He started reaching for the trash, but I bent down and grabbed it first. "I'll clean it up, but it's not mine. I swear."

"Thank you kindly," he said, sounding neither grateful nor kind. "Who are you here to visit?"

"I live here," I mumbled. Even I still had a hard time believing it.

With that, he twisted his face and walked over to the mailboxes, swinging his bad leg with each step.

An hour later Ma and Jordan still hadn't returned. I started writing a letter to Juanita, describing the bumpy trip to New York and my first day in school (equipped with a tall prison warden, a lousy locker, and a bigmouth redhead). But Juanita was sunshine in sneakers. I could just see her shiny lips beaming as she ripped open the envelope, and I didn't have the heart to deliver gloomy news about the car accident and my embarrassing trip to the assistant principal's office. I stuffed the letter in my backpack.

That's when I looked up and saw them. White Hairs. Talking loud, laughing, teasing each other, and sporting trendy coats and accessories like they shopped in the juniors' section at Target. One woman with glasses was wearing a glittery gold pompom hat and matching mittens. A thin Hispanic lady had on a sporty tweed peacoat with disco-style boots that came past her knees. Yet another old lady clomped in wearing a beret and the longest fake eyelashes I'd ever seen. That grouchy old guy with the limp was back, holding the door open as more of them arrived.

As I took in this senior fashion parade, a hefty black woman in a cheetah-print coat squeezed beside me on the love seat.

"Love those bracelets!"

I looked up. She was staring at the trio of brightly colored lanyard braids on my left wrist. I smiled. "Thanks. I made them."

"Then you've got talent *and* good taste," she said in a husky voice, like we'd been chatting for hours. "I heard Chief fussing at you before, from down the hall. Don't mind him— that military stuff flows in his veins. Old nurses like me would code him a PIA, a pain in the—oh, you know what I mean."

She had wide-set eyes that took everything in like a camera. Her plump cheeks were dusted with freckles.

"Chief?"

"Senior Chief Petty Officer Fred Morrow. Retired U.S. Navy. But just shout, 'Yo, Chief!' and he'll hobble in your direction. He lost a leg in a snowmobile accident ten years back, not that it slows his step much."

"Does he work here?"

She grinned. "You'd think so, wouldn't ya? No, they've got staff, all right, though never when you need them. Chief just likes to help. Volunteering is in his blood, I guess. If he's not picking up trash, he's planting daffodil bulbs by the parking lot or running errands for neighbors. Stubborn as a rusty pump, but he means well."

The lobby doors flew open again, and in came a man wearing a white smock, pushing a woman in a wheelchair who was holding a sleeping cat on her lap. The woman handed a key to Chief, who walked over to the mail center.

"Isn't she a beauty?" the lady beside me whispered, pointing toward the wheelchair. "That's Catherine. She's over in Assisted

Living, and that's her aide, Jack. Thirty years ago Catherine was hot stuff on Broadway. But with the MS eating away at her muscles, well, she's trapped in that wheelchair, poor soul."

The lady stood up and called, "Over here. What's shakin', girlfriend?"

Catherine smiled and waved. She had a milky, thin face with high cheekbones. Her hair was pulled back crisply in a bun. The cat on her lap opened its eyes and purred. Loud too. I could hear it from across the room. Right away I thought of Jordan.

"Are pets allowed here?" I asked. Back home Jordan had a turtle named Bandito. But Ma wouldn't let him come along to New York. She'd read somewhere that officials didn't take kindly to crossing state lines with reptiles that could carry diseases not native to the region. So the day before we left, we drove up to the Texas Hill Country and set Bandito free by a creek. Jordan cried and kicked the back of Ma's seat the whole ride home.

"Official policy says no pets allowed. I say what harm is it for an old lady who can't walk? Besides, if the manager made Catherine get rid of Rudy, why, he'd have a mutiny on his hands. Folks at Mohawk Valley Village aren't your zipped-lips, rocking-chair kind of seniors." She pointed toward two women and a man in the far end of the lobby. "Cal over there runs Tuesday-night poker in the lobby after the staff goes home. And Jessie and Veronica beside him lead a kickboxing class in the community room on Thursday afternoons. I hear it's a real gut buster, not that I go. I've usually got an appointment with a bowl of ice cream around that time."

I smiled. Ma would enjoy hearing about her passion for ice cream.

Maybe it was the lady's pillowy body spread beside me, or the crowd filling up the lobby, but for the first time all day, I felt warm. She smelled cinnamon-sweet too. Like potpourri.

She lightly touched my knee. "What's your name, pretty girl?"

"Tess Dobson. Just Tess."

"Pleasure to meet you, then, Just Tess. I'm Winnie Lincoln. No relation to the president, but I like his politics," she said, grinning. "You waiting for a relative?"

"No, ma'am. We just moved in. From San Antonio. My ma and my little brother and me."

"You moved in *here?*" she said, shaking her head and making her purple earrings bobble.

I frowned.

"Forgive me, Tess, didn't mean to make you feel bad. We're delighted to have you and your family. And you'll grow to enjoy this place."

"You like it here?" I asked, staring at a thin crack in the window.

"I'd vote to knock this sorry old building down and build a new one, but the residents here, they're good as gold. I've called the Mohawk Valley Village home since I retired from nursing twelve years ago, and there hasn't been one dull day. Hollywood could make a reality show smack-dab in this lobby, with all the quirky characters we've got. Bet it would get high ratings, too!" she said, winking.

I wanted a place to call home too. But not this drab one decorated with zero style—and not with that Chief character as a neighbor.

Suddenly Winnie stood up, stuck her pinkie fingers to her mouth, and whistled.

"Listen up, gang! This sweet face belongs to Tess Dobson. Her family just moved in, and don't anybody give 'em any grief. We'll take a hearty welcome, though!"

Dozens of old folks looked over at me with curious expressions. Then they started clapping: soft, thumping claps on account of their gloves and mittens.

"What, you want to give Tess the impression that we've got low blood sugar or hypertension? Try that again, but with feeling!"

After a few laughs the lobby filled with applause. And cheers. And a loud, ear-piercing whistle like you hear at a rock concert—that came from Winnie.

I waved back, like a celebrity on a parade float.

Only one person didn't clap. That crazy Chief.

A shrill gears-grinding sound came from outside, and soon all the seniors shuffled through the lobby doors.

"Better go. That's the five o'clock Burger King–and–bingo bus. Last week's winner took home an iPod Touch. Week before it was a giant plasma TV." Winnie smiled and pulled her purple pocketbook strap over her shoulder. "Remember, Tess, old Winnie lives in number 132. Should you ever get locked out—well, you just buzz me."

"Thanks, Mrs. Lincoln," I said.

"It's Winnie. The only person I made call me Mrs. Lincoln was a pesky HMO administrator. And Lord knows I can't say what I called him."

"Okay. Winnie," I said softly with a grin.

Through the window I watched Chief help the bus driver load Catherine's wheelchair, all the while swinging his artificial leg in circles.

Chapter 5

Late winter is an optimal time to launch an ice cream business,
just in time for returning snowbirds and folks struck
with spring fever. —*The Inside Scoop*

"Tess, make your brother quit that fussing, will ya? That shrieking is splitting my skull!" Ma yelled from the kitchen later, as she fixed supper. She had to yell. Jordan was jumping up and down on the futon, wailing like someone stuck his foot in a blender.

"No fair! No fair!" he signed when I walked near.

"Enough already!" Ma barked.

Ma's edginess surprised me. Jordan was acting like a pain in the drain, but usually it didn't rattle her this much.

I walked over to the futon-sofa and touched his arm. "Shush, Jordan," I signed, pointing to the wall, where I could faintly hear a TV. "Someone else lives behind there."

He kicked the coffee table. "Meanies! Yucky school!" he signed.

Thump. A pillow hit my head. *Thanks a lot, FrankenJordan.*

Facial expression counts big-time when you're signing to deaf kids and when they're reading your lips, so I furrowed my brow and signed, "We *don't* throw!"

He paused, stuck his tongue out, and started bouncing again.

"What happened today?" I called to Ma. "He sure is grouchy."

"We saw a stray dog out back behind the apartment building. Jordan begged me to let us keep him, but I said nothing doing," she shouted over Jordan's shrieks as she joined me in the living room. "We're both worn to a frazzle from visiting his new school all morning and getting him set to start tomorrow. And we spent the afternoon walking around downtown and talking to retailers. Jimbo's wife's cousin's stepsister canceled on me. Turns out she got herself transferred to the New York Lottery office in Buffalo. Barely had time to tell me that."

Figures the Jimbo connection was a bust, I thought, frowning.

Immediately Ma spoke up. "Put away that duck-in-a-desert troubled face. Nothing's changed as far as our plans. I'm still going full steam ahead with this business opportunity."

Ma's voice warmed when she said *business opportunity.* Not me, though. The words made me shudder slightly, like seeing lightning off in the distance.

Ma has used those words plenty of times since we got evicted from our house and bounced from one apartment to the next. She called the cutlery franchise that she bought into two years ago a cutting-edge business opportunity, pun intended. But the only thing those overpriced knives cut through was our savings. And she said Cats in the Cradle, the cat kennel she opened six months later, was a business opportunity that capitalized on the fact that cat owners were frequent travelers. We blew through two thousand dollars on that one—mostly on pet crates and giant sacks of cat food and kitty litter. Then Shooting Stars struck, and Ma took to her bedroom for three days straight, only she forgot to mention there was a Siamese cat boarding in the kennel, which was twenty miles away from our apartment. Miraculously Gatsby survived, but Ma's business reputation didn't. I still remember that hysterical lady holding a weak and droopy Gatsby and threatening to get Ma arrested.

Tonight I didn't feel like talking about a "business opportunity." That only led to another fancy term: *financial crisis*. I turned my attention back to Jordan.

He'd stopped jumping. "Good boy," I signed. Then, remembering Winnie's friend Catherine, I told him I'd seen a cat in the lobby earlier. "Maybe we can find out where he lives and visit him," I added.

"Go now!" he signed sloppily, but I signed, "Can't. We go another day."

With that, he started kicking the armrests on the futon. They were frayed down to cross-threads, and I knew his shoe might rip through. I made a note to myself to crochet a couple of doilies to cover them. We could use some to cover the scratched furniture tops too.

I let my fingers do the yelling. "Quit that right now, mister!"

I had a feeling that Jordan's fussing wasn't just about a stray dog or visiting a cat. He kept signing "Meanies!" and "No go!" I let him know he was acting like a crybaby, which made him toss his stuffed turtle at me.

In the kitchen Ma unloaded more groceries. Bags were scattered all across the floor and the counter.

I spotted a familiar package sticking out of a bag and pulled it out. Chocolate pinwheel cookies. Yum. I ripped open the package and dug in.

"Not too many," Ma said loudly, still trying to drown out Jordan's wails. "Chicken potpies are in the oven."

Ugggh. I hate chicken potpies, especially the store brand Ma buys. The crust always burns, and the vegetables taste like they've been soaked in glue.

The Jordan volume had lowered temporarily, but then his shrieks returned. It's funny how people think deaf kids are soundless when they can bark louder than a hundred sea lions.

I poured a glass of milk and looked at Ma. "Why is he talking about meanies at school?"

Ma shook her head. "Jordan didn't get off on the right foot with his new class."

"What did he do?"

"The class was spread out on the floor building a Happytown milk-carton village, and Jordan wasn't watching where he was going and squashed the police station flat like he was King Kong.

The kids got really mad, and the teacher asked Jordan to apologize, and I guess he felt like they were all ganging up on him."

"What did he do?"

"He uprooted Popsicle-stick trees from Happytown and tossed them at the kids. The teacher had to put him in time-out."

Whoa. The Dobson kids were two for two for bad behavior today. At least I didn't destroy property.

"What did *you* do?" I asked.

"The teacher's the captain of the classroom ship, Tess, and she handled things just fine. Personally I think Jordan couldn't understand those kids. They talk faster in New York, so it's hard for him to read their lips. He'll get used to it, though."

Ma's reaction amazed me. Wouldn't most mothers be humiliated if their kid terrorized Happytown? Not Ma. She acted la-di-da. I wanted to tell her that we shouldn't rely on Jordan reading lips. A sign-language instructor once told me that people only get thirty percent of the spoken meaning by looking at lips. And I wanted to tell her that she had to handle Jordan's brat attacks better—but I didn't. Words always fail me with Ma.

"Jordan's new school looks super, Tess. It's a regular ol' public school, with plenty of special-needs kids—three others are deaf. They all looked happier than armadillos digging grub worms."

The apartment suddenly felt calmer. FrankenJordan's roars had subsided to whimpers. Ma checked the oven, and I swiped another cookie.

"Did you tell the teacher what a hard time Jordan has reading?" I asked.

"Didn't have to tell her anything. She's an educator."

Reading is hard enough for deaf kids because they can't hear the sounds. But in San Antonio I sensed that the teacher knew Jordan's trouble wasn't what he didn't hear, but what *Ma* didn't hear. She needed to sign more herself and not give in to his fuss fits. It reminded me of a movie I'd seen about Helen Keller and how she used to throw tantrums before she met her teacher Annie Sullivan because she had no other way to express herself.

I peeked in the oven. The potpies looked bubbly and mushy, and the crusts were already starting to burn.

"Hey, Ma, did you know this apartment complex is for *old* people?"

Ma set three plates on the counter. "You mean *seniors*, and of course I know. The way I see it, we could benefit from their seasoning."

"Then you haven't met the old navy nut."

"Chief? Why, he saved the day this morning. Jordan was sprawled on the lobby floor, banging his fists and screaming 'cause he wanted to watch TV and skip the visit to his new school. Putting socks on a rooster would've been easier than getting him in the car. Just when I was about to give up, Chief limped over to help. He's a good-hearted fella."

"*Good-hearted fella?*"

"You bet. He showed Jordan his whatchacallit, leg prosthesis. Jordan got to pull it apart and snap it together like he was assembling a real live robot."

Ma stuffed the empty grocery bags in a drawer and looked at me. "Tell me about *your* day."

I gave her a thumbs-down since my mouth was still full.

"Did you make any friends?"

"No, but I might've earned myself a new enemy," I said as Pete's face flashed in my mind.

"What happened?"

"Nothing important."

If Ma heard about my visit to Mr. Godfrey's office, she'd start in how I had to resist that type of feisty behavior that was in my genes thanks to Pop. How I had to count to ten more and not let others get under my skin. Maybe Pop shouldn't have slammed doors and punched holes in the walls after a few beers, but that wasn't me, and I didn't like her always bringing it up.

Ma started massaging my shoulders. "I heard on *Oprah* that it takes a whole year to get your life back after a move, honey. Give Schenectady a chance."

Ma's fingers felt nice rubbing my tired muscles. All those years slicing meat behind the deli counter had left her with strong hands.

"I'm trying to give this place a chance," I said. "But I think you should give Jordan and me a *choice* the next time you drag us cross-country."

"Leaving San Antonio made a lot of sense, Tess. I'm not about to wrap all my yesterdays in a fluffy blanket, and neither should you." Ma sighed and rubbed her eyes. "How about a cold drink while we wait for the potpies? I'll tell you all about the ice cream shop I'm fixing to buy. It's got the cutest banana-split sign you ever did see, blinking in the window. And an old-fashioned counter with one of those shiny chrome shake machines!"

We didn't have enough money to get the car heater fixed. Or to live in a normal apartment building with other people below age seventy. Buying this ice cream shop felt all wrong. Why hadn't Ma learned her lesson from the past business flops, never mind the evictions from our house and the two apartments?

Well, I wasn't up for her pie-in-the-sky plans and talk tonight. Not after the day Ottawa Creek Middle School dished out.

I grabbed two more cookies. "Sorry, Ma. I'm skipping dinner," I said as I left the kitchen.

No wonder the apartment felt calm. Jordan had dozed off on the futon with his head resting on his stuffed turtle. I unlaced his sneakers and covered him with a throw blanket I'd knitted years ago.

In the bedroom I pulled out my bag of lanyard and started braiding a two-tone belt, light blue and dark blue. All blue, like how I felt. Here I was in a new state, a new apartment, and a new school, but déjà vu feelings kept running from my heart to my head like a ticker tape. Nothing had changed, except the weather, and that had taken a nosedive. I tried to imagine how it might feel to be stretched out on a tropical beach with a warm breeze blowing, surrounded by friendly kids sipping refreshing smoothies and talking to me.

Without Ma's latest business scheme. Without money worries, and far away from the slippery snow in Schenectady.

●●●●

Two hours later I awoke, surprised that Ma hadn't come knocking on the bedroom door insisting I eat dinner. My stomach was rumbling, so I walked into the kitchen. Maybe I'd nibble at the chicken-potpie crust.

Ma was sitting on a stool, slumped over with her face resting on her forearms on the counter. The three potpies sat on plates, untouched. She was out cold and snoring.

I should've seen it coming: Shooting Stars. That's the only time Ma snores.

With my arms hooked under her armpits, I dragged her out of the kitchen—past Jordan, who was still asleep on the futon—and into the bedroom. I tried my best to be gentle, but I knocked a small lamp over in the living room as I passed. I lifted her up onto the bed, took off her shoes and socks, and covered her with the blanket.

I left my backpack by the nightstand, grabbed a blanket and pillow from the closet to spread on the living-room floor, and shut the door behind me, fully knowing I wouldn't need my backpack tomorrow.

I wouldn't be going to school.

Chapter 6

Think twice before launching a retail endeavor with family. Business partners need to share a vision and a work ethic, not necessarily the same DNA. —*The Inside Scoop*

Ma spent the next four days in bed, sobbing, and ruing the day we got stuck with her for a mama. She wouldn't eat and only drank coffee with the socks on, but caffeine didn't even get her engine going. I walked a sleepyhead Jordan to the bus stop on Friday. But I couldn't go to school—I wouldn't be back to watch him by the time the bus dropped him off, and besides, I had to look out for Ma.

Seeing Ma crashed and useless again made me frustrated.

She was the one who moved us cross-country when she was flying high. *She* was the one who said Schenectady would be a fresh start. And *she* was the one who was gunning to open this ice cream shop in the middle of a freezing winter. I wanted to burst into her bedroom, yank the covers down, and shout, "Pull yourself together, Ma!" But I didn't. That would be as helpful as spanking a sick puppy.

Shooting Stars was predictable in its usual ugly way. Back in San Antonio it struck Ma about twice a year (or more, before the divorce, when she and Pop fought a lot). She wouldn't talk to anyone about it. I guess she was embarrassed.

With Ma unable to function, Jordan and I spent the weekend cooped up in the apartment watching cartoons, eating microwaveable meals, and playing old maid and war with an old deck of cards. I finished some crocheted doilies too, including a pair to cover the ripped futon, and I did some touch-up painting in the kitchen and rearranging of pillows and knickknacks to give the living room a fresher look.

I'd check on Ma in the bedroom every hour or so, and Jordan would deliver her meals on a tray, not that she ate much. I could tell by his pouty face that it bothered him to see Ma lying in bed with a zombie look. I couldn't understand it and I was twelve; Jordan was barely eight.

Ma got out of bed for the first time Tuesday morning. She slipper-shuffled over to the kitchen counter in her bathrobe with her hair looking like a bird's nest. I fixed her a poached egg and a buttered tortilla. Then she started weeping again, saying how truly sorry she was to be such a good-for-nothing parent. But then Jordan jumped on her lap and wiped her eyes with a napkin, and she stopped crying. And when I got back from walking him to the bus stop, she was in the shower.

"You dressed for school?" she asked as she strolled out of the bathroom with a towel wrapped around her hair.

"That depends. Are you through hibernating?"

She paused, then nodded. "Reckon so. You know me, tougher than a cast-iron washtub."

Nothing about Ma seemed tough. She looked pale and skinnier than her usual one hundred pounds. Her collarbone stuck out like a hanger.

I tried to talk to her about what happened. "You can't keep doing this, Ma. You gotta get help," I said. But she answered in the same way she always did.

"I know you mean well, sugar, but I've told you before. I don't have a screw loose in my thinking gear, if that's what you're hinting at. I just inherited my paw's energy bursts and patches of blue, God rest his soul. Once I ride this out, I'll be back to my usual strong-as-a-bull self."

Then Ma grabbed the TV remote and clicked on the morning news and tuned me out.

So back I went to Ottawa Creek Middle School. It was my second day there, but my first one running the Cafeteria Gauntlet. Anyone who's been the new kid knows that the bus ride, the locker scene, and classes are just the warm-up. The true test begins at lunch, with that sea of unfamiliar faces drinking from flavored-water bottles. I wasn't looking forward to that, even though I'd packed my favorite smoked turkey and cheese piled high on butter-crust bread. And I hadn't made any friends on the bus or in my classes.

At least I had someone to sit with—thank goodness for the fine print of the meet-and-greeter contract. Ellie sat at a long table of chatty girls who were laughing and sharing snacks. They all smiled when Ellie introduced me, and they seemed friendly enough. Then a lunch aide came over and told Ellie that Coach McGregory was looking for her, and she took off. So I ate my lunch, listening to the jock girls moan and groan about what drills they would do later at practice and how many suicides Coach would make them run if they missed their free throws. All this basketball talk made me think about Jordan, and how he must feel when he's surrounded by hearing kids who don't sign.

When I got up to throw out my trash, I noticed a bake-sale table by the side doors. The sign taped to the table read: GIVE PEACE A CHANCE: SUPPORT PEER MEDIATION.

Peer mediation. I remembered Mr. Godfrey mentioned something about that in his office after I'd tossed the pear at Pete. I walked over and stared down at the table packed with brownies, cupcakes, donut holes, mini muffins, slices of pound cake, and my favorite: giant M&M cookies. A white boy covered with pimples and a black girl with red glasses stood behind the table. The girl was counting the money. The boy was looking down at his notebook.

I picked up an M&M cookie and gave the girl two quarters. She studied my face. "Hmm. I've never seen you before," she said, grinning. She had wild, curly hair that shot out like tangled wires and a gauze sleeveless blouse. I was cold just looking at her.

"I'm new," I explained, and I told her my name.

"Welcome, Tess. I like *new*." She poked the boy next to her. "Ritchie and I are co-presidents of the Peer Mediation Club, which also likes *new*. As in new beginnings, new agreements, and new members. My name's Gabriella Danes—Gabby for short. I'm a tiger."

I laughed. "A *tiger?*"

She nodded. "The Chinese zodiac. Tigers find pleasure in the unpredictable and, contrary to their image, can be just as calm and warmhearted as they are ferocious. Which is why I do Zen archery *and* peer mediation."

More kids started gathering around the table. Gabby was scrambling to keep up with sales, and Ritchie was still glancing down at his notebook.

"Need some help?" I asked him.

Ritchie perked up at that. "Thanks. I forgot I had a Spanish quiz next period, and I gotta study."

I squeezed between Gabby and Ritchie and began taking money from kids and passing them napkins.

A boy biting into a donut hole pointed to me. "Hey, aren't you the one who punched Pete Chutkin?"

I felt splotches spreading across my neck like spilled red ink. "I didn't punch him; I threw a pear—oh, never mind."

"Pete's a loser anyway," he said, spewing powdered sugar from his mouth. "I've seen him picking through trash at the city dump. He lives with his dad in a trailer without indoor plumbing. Swear to God!"

"Excuse me, but could you take your toxic talk *away* from our bake sale?" Gabby said with a looks-can-kill glare. Then she turned to me. "So what's your month and birth year, Tess? Are you a tiger like most seventh graders?"

When I told her, she said being slightly older made me an ox.

"Figures," she said, nodding. "You act like an ox."

I felt my face redden. "Huh?"

"Relax. I'm not dissing you." She reached for the bag of napkins under the table and put some beside the donut holes. "The ox is serious, loyal, responsible, intelligent, and good with her hands. Which leads me to ask, did you make your belt?"

I looked down at my lanyard rope belt and nodded, smiling.

"Very stylish. Oxen also make true friends if you can overlook their worrywart tendencies. But don't mess with them! They take things *very* seriously! Maybe that's what happened between you and Pete? At least now you're helping like a dependable ox, and you're even wearing green. Obviously the ox loves an earth-friendly look."

A small girl with a freckled face came up to the table and greeted Gabby.

"Sorry I can't help, Gabby. I've got a meeting with the reading teacher. But I have enough time to buy a treat." She started counting pennies in her hand. "Just my luck, I'm short ten cents. And I'm a peer mediator," she said, frowning.

I gave her a dime from my pocket.

"Thanks. I'm Kim," she said, all smiles, before picking out a brownie and leaving.

"So where did you move from?" Gabby asked me.

"San Antonio, Texas."

"Wow. Us upstaters get excited when someone moves here from Long Island, and you come all the way from *Texas*. So what's there to do back in San Antonio?"

"Plenty." I told her about the River Walk, the fiesta celebration, and the annual rodeo. "And I lived seven miles from Sea World. They've got the best dolphin and whale shows. You even get to feed the dolphins."

Gabby shook her head. "Don't get me started on Sea World. They exploit animals just to make a buck."

I shrugged. "The fish looked happy to me."

"Whales and dolphins aren't *fish*. And would you be happy trapped in a concrete tank if you belonged in the ocean?"

I got the picture. Gabby, Zodiac Girl with a Cause. Now I knew why she was in peer mediation.

With five minutes left, most of the cookies and brownies were gone, but we still had half a table full of donut holes and cake.

Gabby wasn't pleased about that. "This is the last lunch period. That means we're going to be stuck with all these leftovers. And we really need to raise money to buy team shirts."

Back at Albertsons deli, where Ma worked, the manager used to run a BOGO special on whatever ham or turkey was close to its expiration date. That meat always moved. Ma said folks never pass up a bargain.

I turned to Gabby. "I've got an idea. How 'bout announcing a buy-one-get-one-free sale?" I pointed at the front of the cafeteria, to a microphone propped on a stand.

Gabby's eyes flashed approval from behind her red glasses. "Brilliant idea, Texan!" She jumped up and made the announcement, and before you knew it, the table was swamped with eager customers.

The bell rang, and I said goodbye to Gabby. Ritchie pointed me toward the computer lab for my next class.

Halfway down the hallway I felt a tap on my shoulder.

Gabby again. "Here," she said, handing me something wrapped in a napkin. "I saved the last one for my new friend. Tess the ox."

Another M&M cookie. I'd save it for after school. I smiled at her. "Thanks."

"Thank *you* for using your Texas smarts. We sold thirty-two dollars' worth of baked goods because of you. That will help cover the cost of team shirts. Hey, Ritchie and I were talking. We think peer mediation could use your creative persuasive skills. You interested?"

I shrugged.

This Gabby was strange, but I kind of liked her.

Chapter 7

"**I**'ll take black and you be white," Ma said as she plopped the backgammon game onto the kitchen counter. It was a lazy Sunday afternoon, and the three of us were still lounging in pajamas, sweaters, and scarves on account of our igloo apartment. And as if it wasn't freezing already, the TV weather lady said an arctic blast was headed our way. With windchill, the temperature would hit twelve below zero.

I set up my backgammon pieces opposite Ma's, tossed the dice, and took a piece of beef jerky out of the bag. Jordan sat cross-legged on the floor at my feet, making animals out of the Play-Doh he'd found in one of my craft bins. Already he'd made enough creatures to fill a zoo, although they sure weren't ordinary-looking, especially the lion with an elephant trunk and the monkey with two tails.

Ma's turn. She tossed the dice and then threw me a question. "Remember how tight money was back home? How we always had to count nickels just to have enough for ice cream?"

I nodded. All our money problems seemed like just yesterday. Come to think of it, it *was* yesterday.

"From here out, your cup and Jordan's runneth over with ice cream," she said, all grins. Ma folded her skinny arms across her baggy cardigan sweater. "You're playing backgammon with the soon-to-be owner of an ice cream shop on State Street in Schenectady, New York."

I groaned on the inside. Not this again. I had figured this business scheme faded away after the last Shooting Stars episode sent her to bed. "You're serious?"

She nodded. "Serious as a snakebite."

"What do you know about running an ice cream business, Ma?" I moved my piece six spaces. *Or any business*, I thought. Not that I wanted to keep rehashing mistakes, but facts were facts: she'd only sold one set of steak knives from her cutlery franchise—and that was to Juanita's grandparents. Cats in the Cradle lasted a month, and we almost got slapped with a lawsuit. The only jobs Ma ever kept were farmhand at her parents' horse ranch when she was a teenager, and more recently, at Albertsons in the deli. She was good at slicing meat:

friendly, efficient, and—as she liked to brag—one of the few workers who hadn't cut off a finger. Kids liked how she always gave out free samples too.

With no horse ranches in downtown Schenectady, my vote was for her to apply at the grocery store.

"Ice cream isn't rocket science, Tess. And thanks to the *Inside Scoop* here, I'm learning a lot," she said as she passed a thick magazine my way. "Check this out. I just read that the profit on a single-scoop cone is a whopping hundred and fifty percent!"

I picked up the dice and rolled a one and a three. Not my best roll, but it still enabled me to bump Ma's piece off the board. Drats. Ma came up with doubles and got her piece back.

I glanced at the *Inside Scoop*. It had an ice cream sundae on the cover, piled high with whipped cream, nuts, and hot fudge. *Who would actually buy this magazine?* I wondered, noting the price was pretty steep, the same as *Vogue*.

"It's not a magazine. It's a training manual," Ma said, as if she read my mind. "For folks serious about scooping their way to financial freedom."

Ma pointed to the middle of a section listing guiding principles for achieving success in a retail ice cream business, and she started reading business suggestions. Dairy Dips they were called, and they sure sounded dippy to me.

"'Number Forty-two: Go beyond vanilla. Reach out to your customers with dramatic flavors and attention-grabbing novelty items. Remember that ice cream is indulgent entertainment for the masses. Number Forty-three: Humor the calorie counters with some lighter varieties, but weigh heavy on the good stuff. Americans gladly dump their diets at the door of an ice cream shop.' "

Then she pulled out a brochure from the Schenectady Chamber of Commerce with instructions for new business owners. "Says here this city is all but bribing ladies to throw their hats in the business ring. They're offering tax breaks for women only."

But not for business owners with Shooting Stars, I thought as fear clawed at my throat. *Especially those bursting with drive and determination one day, and crashed in bed the next.*

"No more," Jordan signed to me, holding the empty Play-Doh can. Dozens of bright, funky animals were gathered at his feet.

"Sorry," I signed.

He pouted, and then shuffled into the family room, scuffing his footie pajamas along the way. A few minutes later he returned and threw the TV remote on the backgammon board. Pieces fell to the floor.

"Jordan!" Ma yelled and I signed.

He was trying to sign "Not working," but he was doing it wrong. Gently I formed his hand in the A shape and thrust it forward from his chin for "not." Then I moved his S hand up and down on top of his fisted left hand for "working."

Ma and I followed him to the family room. The remote control wasn't working. I kept pressing buttons, but nothing helped.

The same question whirled around in my head like a

Hula-Hoop. What was Ma going to buy the business with? I'd peeked at her checkbook on the counter after she'd returned from grocery shopping the other day. There wasn't enough to fix the car heater. But she spewed on with her business plans. How the shop was located in the heart of bustling Schenectady, at the corner of State and Lafayette streets, between a shoe-repair place and a pizzeria, with a bus stop right out front.

"The owner, Jerry Breyers—no relation to that grocery-store brand," she quickly pointed out, "gave me the full shop tour. Place was built in 1926, and it's got a charming old-fashioned marble counter and backsplash, and brass light fixtures like the drugstores had back then. You're going to love it, Tess. With your style and decorator know-how, we can turn this place into the talk of the town!"

Ma said the shop had been turning a decent profit for the past twelve years—in spite of a downtown business slump running longer than the Mohawk River—but Jerry's arthritis was flaring up so bad this snowy winter, he'd decided to pack it in and move to North Carolina.

"He calls his shop Van Curler Creamery after the city's founder, but I've got another name picked out," she said, grinning.

"What? Tell me," I said, my arms crossed over my sweater.

"Not so fast. I didn't announce you'd be a Tess till you made your appearance, and the same goes for my business baby. But don't you fret. It's the perfect name."

Finally, after fiddling with the remote buttons fifty different ways, I tried changing the batteries. That did the trick. I gave the remote back to Jordan, with closed captions turned on. He smiled and plopped down to watch a cartoon.

Ma and I went back to the kitchen. I rubbed my cold hands together and suddenly felt like a temperamental ox.

"Once the business is mine, I'm getting our old sewing machine repaired," Ma said. "I was hoping you'd make curtains for the front display window. Nobody's better at prettying up a room than you, and this shop is just asking for a cutesy old-time café look."

If there was a shred of good news in all this, it was hearing Ma was getting the sewing machine fixed. It sat in the hall closet broken, just like it had been back in San Antonio for six months. I missed being able to make clothes and accessories.

I reached for the dice and looked up at Ma. "What does that training manual say about an ice cream shop's chance of making it in the snowbelt? Nobody eats as much ice cream as we do, Ma, especially not when the weather is colder than ice cream."

"The *Inside Scoop* says there are plenty of four-season consumers around here," Ma answered. "It all comes down to the 'razzle-dazzle factor': making our shop an entertaining experience for everyone who walks through the door. And we'll offer prepacked products too, so folks can grab and go when they're freezing their patooties off."

"You think it's that simple?"

"Nothing's simple, Tess. It'll take a lot of elbow grease. And the *Inside Scoop* says we gotta stay ahead of the trends. That's how those fellas Ben and Jerry got rich, right?"

Ma quoted the *Inside Scoop* like it was the Bible. I imagined a chorus of ice cream shop owners kneeling before the hot-fudge dispenser, their hands clutching scoopers and their hearts filled with the divine Spirit of Frozen Creamy Sweetness.

I heard Jordan giggling as he watched TV. Peanut butter is his all-time favorite flavor. It's hard to find, but Ma knew exactly where to get it back in San Antonio—at a drive-in stand ten miles north of the city. Once when Pop was still with us, and Jordan was a toddler and teething, we'd been out running errands when we passed the stand. I remember Ma shouting, "Pull over!" Rain was pouring fast and furious, the way it does in southwest Texas in late spring, and Pop was yelling that Ma spoiled us, and for God's sake who needs ice cream during a monsoon?

But she insisted, saying ice cream would ease Jordan's gums. So Pop pulled over, and Ma dashed out. She tripped on a tree root coming back to the car, but she held on to those plastic cups piled high with whipped cream and the works.

Ma started humming a country song as we finished up the backgammon game. I was one turn away from victory when she rolled double sixes. That moved her last four pieces off the board to beat me.

Grrrr. I hate losing at board games, especially to Ma, who doesn't take them seriously. Pop used to say that God looks out for kids and drunks, but I think he gives Ma special breaks too.

"Where are you going to find money to buy this shop?" I asked.

"Got it figured out," she said, arranging her pieces for a new game.

Ma didn't offer more details, and I didn't ask, even though I'd figured it out too. She'd be digging into the Ditch Fund—the last bit of money we had standing between us and being homeless on the cold streets of Schenectady.

Just as I rolled the dice to start the next game, Jordan leaped onto a stool and, standing, started swinging his arms across his body. Both hands were shaped in a Y. "Party!" he signed.

Party, our code word for ice cream. Back and forth his arms swung with urgency. "Party! Party!"

"Careful," I signed, holding his legs steady as the stool wobbled.

Ma laughed at Jordan's excitement and glanced up at the wall clock. "It's five-thirty, close to suppertime, though that never stopped us from having a party before. Let's git to it."

With that, I pulled down our special red heart-shaped bowls and matching red spoons from the top shelf. Ma put on her cherry-print apron and warmed the fudge sauce while Jordan took out as many candies, nuts, sprinkles, sauces, crumbled cookies, pretzels, cereals, fruits, and mini marshmallows as he could find in the pantry to pour into custard cups.

Within minutes the counter was transformed into an ice cream smorgasbord, with oodles of tempting toppings just begging to be had. Jordan started first, scooping ice cream, spooning candy and nuts, ladling toppings, and squirting whipped cream like he was a culinary artist.

"Don't forget a cherry on top!" Ma said like she always says just before we dig in, holding the maraschino-cherry jar up.

Jordan read Ma's lips that time perfectly. Next thing he did was stick his finger deep in the jar and pull out a cherry by its stem. Then he tossed it way high, wiggled his hips, and maneuvered his bowl to catch it centered on his whipped-cream-covered sundae. He quickly set his bowl down on the counter, then signed, "I did it. Jordan is the MAN!" That set off a laugh attack in both Ma and me.

I didn't admit it out loud, but I had to agree with Ma. Ice cream does warm the heart, no matter what the weather.

The first person I saw when I walked into school on Monday was Kim, the tiny freckle-faced girl I'd met at the bake sale. Only now she was wearing a pirate bandanna and an eye patch.

"I'm not weird. Today's Hilarious Hat Day," she said when she caught me staring.

"Ahoy, mate," I said, and we both laughed.

I wished I had something covering my head for another reason. The Mohawk Valley Village had a power outage that morning, and I hadn't been able to blow-dry my hair. I was wearing my favorite shirt—a magenta henley with pretty silver buttons I'd added myself—but my stringy hair was matted to my head, and my big ears stuck out like Frisbees.

At the lockers kids paraded by wearing all kinds of freaky hats. I saw a sparkly chicken that clucked, a chef hat, a killer shark, a beanie with a propeller, and an Abraham Lincoln tall hat on a kid with *stilts*.

I ran into Gabby in the bathroom before homeroom. "Festive!" I said, giggling at the plastic fruit bowl piled high on her head.

She was sticking bobby pins into her hair to keep a red apple from drooping. "My father wore this for his law firm's Halloween party last year. It's called 'Got Fruit?' " Then she reached into her backpack and handed me a baseball cap with a pink flamingo on top. "Here you go. Luckily I brought a spare."

"No thanks," I said, smiling. "I'll pass." It's rough enough being the new kid. I couldn't stand everybody looking at the new kid with a freaky bird hat.

She grinned. "There's that workaholic ox again, not taking time to play."

"You don't really believe all that Chinese astrology stuff, do you? I mean, you're not Chinese."

Gabby's face tightened. "I bet you like pizza, but you're not Italian, are you?"

I shook my head.

"We can't stick each other in categories, you know. Chinese astrology helps me understand my life patterns."

"I guess you're right. Sorry," I said sheepishly.

She pushed back a banana that had flopped between her eyes. "I mean it about thinking you're right for peer mediation. Chinese astrology suggests the ox is no bull in a china shop. She is dependable and steadfast, and we need more of that since most of our classmates are tigers. And besides, everyone knows you don't mess with Texans, which could help when mediations turn rocky."

I laughed.

"C'mon, Tess. Peer mediation is a blast! Where else in school do teachers let kids call the shots? We meet on Wednesdays. And our teacher-rep brings homemade chocolate chip cookies. Say you'll come."

Cookies sounded good, and hanging around with Gabby was appealing. You never knew what she would say or do. But I wasn't so sure about peer mediation. I could use my own live-in mediator at the apartment to deal with Ma.

I looked at Gabby. "Aren't you forgetting something? I was the kid who tossed a pear at Pete Chutkin."

She adjusted a wobbly banana by her ear. "That's *exactly* why we need you. You get it, you understand disputants."

"Disputants?"

"Kids who have issues with each other."

"I'll think about it. See ya," I said, and I waved goodbye.

In the hallway, Pete Chutkin was leaning against the fire extinguisher. He wore a speckled jester's hat with jingle bells.

I pretended not to notice him, but he came right up to me.

"Hey, Tess. Did you know that I met your family at Walmart?" he asked, walking beside me.

"No," I said, coolly thinking he was *my* disputant. Of all the people for Ma and Jordan to meet!

"Your mother was wearing a 'Find Yourself in San Antonio' sweatshirt, so I told her about the awesome Alamo clay model I built last year. She told me about you, and I said we'd sorta 'met' already."

I rolled my eyes. "We sure did."

"Don't worry, I didn't tell her you threw a pear at me." Suddenly he pulled his jester's hat off and stuck it on my head.

"Get away!" I swatted the hat, and it flew across the hall. *Not again*, I thought. Not another trip to the assistant principal's office. Mr. Godfrey would give me detention for sure this time.

Pete picked his hat off the floor, put it back on, and caught up with me. "Wait—I was just trying to help. Really. You get a free snack in the cafeteria today if you're wearing a hat."

As Ma would say, he had to be shuckin' me. Did he actually think I'd embarrass myself for a bag of pretzels? But the thing was, he looked serious—and sorry, like Jordan when he's making nice after a temper tantrum.

"I bring my own snacks. And you did me a big enough favor making fun of me and getting me in trouble," I said with a steely-eyed glare.

"Really, I was just kidding around. I didn't mean anything bad. And I swear I didn't know your little brother was deaf. But it's true what I was telling your mom. I'm a *huge* Texas fan. You heard me singing 'The Lone Star Song'! I bet I know more about the Alamo than you. 'I shall never surrender nor retreat!' "

"Never whatever," I said, turning into homeroom and hoping he'd disappear.

But he followed me in, with his jester's hat jingling, and he was *loud*. "C'mon, Tess. I'm not leaving until we 'resolve our conflict,' like my court-appointed social worker always says."

Sleepy kids slouching in their chairs perked up when they heard *court-appointed social worker*.

Then he leaned over my desk and stuck his hand out to shake. "Apology accepted?"

His breath still smelled like cheese. But I could also see clear into his golden-brown eyes. There was no meanness.

I shook his hand. "Apology accepted, and I'm sorry too— about throwing the pear."

The homeroom bell rang.

"Since you're from Texas, I'll grant you an unconditional pardon. I better scram. The grim homeroom reaper will thrash me!" Pete shouted as he took off.

Just before he reached the door, he whirled around. "Hey, Tess, one of these days remind me to show you my Alamo model. I got a B. Remember the Alamo!"

I'll remember you, *all right,* I thought, rolling my eyes as he jingled out the door.

Chapter 8

Take time to prepare a business plan. Running a retail operation
without a business plan is like building a house
without a blueprint. —*The Inside Scoop*

What's going on? I wondered as I walked into the lobby of the apartment building later that afternoon. "You Ain't Nothin' but a Hound Dog" was blasting from a boom box, and the space was wall to wall with seniors eating ice cream, chatting, and filling out forms. Snow was falling outside again, and the lobby was drafty. Old men and women dressed in coats and scarves and boots filled the room, swaying to the music and eating.

"Hey, sweetie pie!" Ma blew past me, wearing her cherry-covered apron and carrying a tray full of ice cream in small Styrofoam bowls. "Can't talk long. Conducting market research."

"What's market research?"

"Business homework. Neighbors have kindly offered to test-market ice cream and give me their two cents on flavor, texture, and presentation. So far this crowd gives fudge ripple four stars and rum raisin two thumbs down. And in case you haven't noticed, they're wild about Elvis, just like me."

I walked toward the mailroom, where even more White Hairs were sitting in a circle, talking and stretching back lazily in chairs like it was summertime. Those chairs looked familiar. Ma's parents' old patio chairs! And nearby, I noticed she'd arranged the end tables from the bedroom where Jordan and I slept. They were pushed together and covered with bowls of toppings, as well as hot fudge and cans of whipped cream and nuts.

"Hey there, Tess!" Winnie called, waving a spoon in the air. Two older black men sat across from her, and Catherine was parked beside them with a bowl on her lap. Something squeezed right beside Catherine in her wheelchair was wiggling. I thought it might be Rudy the cat, but it wasn't.

It was Jordan.

"Look, Tess. Peanut butter ice cream!" Jordan signed to me, smiling with a tan mustache.

"Your brother just polished off his third bowl," Catherine said, patting his head with her trembling hand and smiling.

Winnie introduced me to the men, Melvin and Sam, "fellow music bandies," she said. Melvin had wavy gray hair gelled back in a flip. His eyes twinkled when he told me that Winnie was the real star of their act.

"How's the ice cream?" I asked.

"Never had better," Melvin said, scraping his spoon against the bowl.

"And you can't beat the price," Sam added.

Winnie dabbed her mouth with a napkin. "I must admit I tossed my diet out the window when Delilah offered me seconds. Peppermint ice cream is my weakness, and this brand just melts in your mouth like a cloud. I predict your mom's shop will be a gold mine, Tess. No wonder she's in a hurry to buy it on Wednesday."

Wednesday?

"Attention, all hands," Chief shouted from the lobby. "Last call to turn in your survey. And Delilah says don't hold back with your opinions. Good, bad, or ugly."

"No need to worry about that with me, Chief," Winnie said, reaching for a pencil.

I could tell which people were from the Assisted Living building. Their hands shook more than the other seniors', and a few aides in white smocks stayed nearby.

Ma came over as Winnie and her friends finished writing and handed me a bowl of ice cream. "Here you go, Tess. Rocky Road, your favorite," she said.

I stared over at the tasty toppings spread out on the end tables. I felt torn about eating ice cream right now. For one, the lobby was downright chilly, and my ribbed-jersey henley wasn't keeping me warm enough under my jacket, even if I did like the look. More importantly, I wasn't sold on Ma's new business. Last year she'd tried to butter me up when she bought the cat kennel too, saying in no time we'd make enough money to go to Disneyland. Within two months we took a trip, all right—out the door of our apartment to a fleabag motel, where we had to stay for a month until Ma scraped up enough money to cover the next apartment's security deposit. The carpet smelled like pee, and the women who lived downstairs hardly wore any clothes.

Eating this ice cream could send the wrong message. But . . . I *was* hungry, Ma sure had this lobby looking festive, and Rocky Road was hard to resist, what with all the chocolate ice cream, marshmallow bits, fudge, and nuts swirled together and staring up at me.

"Thanks," I said, and I dug in. And while Ma continued peppering seniors with questions on their ice cream preferences, I moseyed on over to the toppings table and loaded up with extra nuts and fudge sauce.

Tug. Jordan yanked at my jeans. "Me too. More!" he signed.

I shook my head and moved my fingers. "You'll get sick." Too many times I've seen Jordan overeat and end up driving the porcelain bus, as Ma calls vomiting.

He stomped his foot. "More now!"

My head shook again. "No!" I signed firmly.

So he ran over to Ma and signed that I was no fair, but Ma didn't understand, and she was too busy talking to seniors to concentrate. That made Jordan even madder, and he charged back to me at the toppings table, grabbed the fudge jar from my hands, and stuck his tongue in.

"Ugh!" One of the ladies seated nearby groaned.

I grabbed the jar from him, shaped my hand like a claw, and circled it on my stomach. "Disgusting!"

"Tess meanie!" he signed back. Then he swiped the whipped cream can and took off.

"Get back here!" I yelled, no matter that he couldn't hear me.

Round and round the lobby Jordan galloped, all the while grinning and aiming the can at seniors he passed, who looked horrified, like he was pointing a machine gun.

I kept trying to grab him, but he was speedy—probably on a high from all that sugar. Then he ran past me with the whipped cream can pressed between his lips like a baby bottle.

I reached out and caught the tail of his shirt. "Gotcha!"

Psssst. Whipped cream sprayed everywhere. On the carpet. In my hair, on my jacket, in my face, even up my nose.

"Brat!" I roared—I didn't know that sign. I wiped cream from my eyes. I could feel the heat on my face from the seniors' disapproving stares. Jordan sat on the floor beside me, covering his eyes with messy hands, looking embarrassed.

Chief hobbled over with paper towels and started wiping the mess. "This behavior is unsat. Somebody's going to fall and break a hip," he growled.

Ma appeared, her arms full of papers. "Take him upstairs, Tess," she pleaded. "Jordan's going to run customers off before I even own the shop."

"Okay, okay," I said. Then I grabbed Jordan's hand in a huff and headed over to the elevator.

Jordan went straight to the bedroom when we got in, and he

stayed there. He was wise enough to stay clear of me. I knew the FrankenJordan episode was only partly due to his being sugared up. He was overwhelmed by all the change in our lives too. He had a new home, a new school, and a new life—and with Ma, who knew what would hit next. I wanted to talk to him, to set him straight that things would settle down, but the words weren't there. And I was tired too.

Ma returned to the apartment an hour later, her arms full of leftover ice cream and toppings. Her nose was red like she'd been outside. "Phew, conducting market research requires active listening! My ears took in a boatful about ice cream likes and dislikes. These seniors sure aren't a bland vanilla bunch. The funkier the flavor, the higher they rate it, with Mississippi mud and turtle cheesecake tying for the top spot."

"Have you been serving ice cream this whole time?"

"No. Afterward, Chief talked me into snowshoeing with his friends. I couldn't turn 'em down since they helped me out. A sporty ol' gal named Veronica had an extra pair of snowshoes, and we clomped our way through a two-mile trek behind the apartment complex. Chief keeps a speedy pace. He's better at snowshoeing with one leg than I am with two!"

I stared at her hard. "You didn't tell me you were buying that ice cream shop on Wednesday."

"Must've slipped my mind," she said, sticking the whipped cream in the fridge. "Tell ya what, I'll make it up to you. You're about to be the first person in Schenectady to hear the name for our new shop. Drumroll, please. . . . Introducing A Cherry on Top!"

"Cute," I said. I did like that name, but I still didn't like the idea of buying a business.

Ma wiped the messy hot-fudge jar with a cloth. "Glad you mentioned about Wednesday, 'cause I need you to watch Jordan after school so I can go back downtown for the closing. There'll be lots of paperwork for me to sign at the bank."

But Wednesday was Peer Mediation Club. I'd been thinking about Gabby's offer a lot. Maybe she was right; I might be good at peer mediation. It was worth a try. "I can't do it on Wednesday," I said. "I've got plans."

Ma wasn't listening. Her work papers were spread across the counter, and she was talking to herself using business lingo about advertising and promotions.

"Ma, I'm busy on Wednesday. I'm joining peer mediation, and that's when it meets. You're always saying I should get involved."

"This is a family priority, Tess. You saw your brother running hog-wild today. I'll never get through the closing if he's there."

"Why can't you get a job at Thrifty King?" I asked. "You said yourself deli pays the best in a grocery store, and you've got experience as a meat slicer."

"Been there, done that. Working for a fat-cat corporation that doesn't give a hoot if I slice off my finger isn't my idea of the American Dream. Owning my own shop is. I've got six weeks to come up with a plan to make this shop the best thing that hit Schenectady since General Electric opened its factory."

Ma's eyes flickered like she was a kid about to jump on the merry-go-round. She showed no fear about messing up again. But

I knew plenty of reasons to pass on this ice cream shop. I'd read the headlines in the *Daily Gazette*. Nobody shopped downtown Schenectady anymore. They went to malls like Crossgates and Colonie Center. Vacant buildings were scattered everywhere, just like the trash in the streets. And families were tightening their belts on account of the economy.

Besides, what would happen when the next Shooting Stars sent Ma soaring and then crashing—who'd scoop ice cream *then*? We'd end up broke, homeless, and frostbitten. I thought about Pete and his dad. I bet they never imagined life's winds would blow them into a trailer without indoor plumbing.

Ma didn't seem to notice my six-foot scowl. She was tying a bag of trash. "Take this down the hall to the Dumpster, would ya?" she asked, handing it to me.

I flung the bag over my shoulder and stomped across the room without answering. My throat burned. Outside the window, the frozen tree limbs swayed slightly like old people dancing.

When I returned, she gave me another job. "Go draw Jordan's bath so I can study my training manual, okay?"

Smoke was practically shooting from my ears as I walked into the bathroom and turned the tub faucet. Jordan was standing by the tub in his undies, holding a plastic frog.

The water poured out cold. I waited for it to warm up. But it didn't.

"There's no hot water!" I shouted in my grouchiest, it's-all-your-fault-Ma voice.

"Again? I'll boil water," Ma shouted back, not even noticing.

Three pots of water, two capfuls of bubble bath, and a bucket of toys later, the bath was ready. Jordan splashed carefree in the soapy water, but fury bubbled beneath my henley. We were going to get kicked out of this drafty apartment, just like in San Antonio.

I stormed into the kitchen, carrying the empty pot. Ma was holding her mug and reading the *Inside Scoop*.

"You drink too much coffee!" I mumbled.

"Guilty as charged," she said, chuckling without looking up.

Nothing here felt funny to me. I wanted Ma to know how scared I was. I wanted to stop her from wasting whatever money we still had in that Ditch Fund too. The only thing this ice cream shop was going to serve up was disaster.

Ma started humming. It reminded me of the last time we got evicted, from that apartment on Wurzbach Road. Kids watched us from the second-floor-apartment window as we crammed all our stuff into the Toyota. All the while, Ma hummed some silly old country tune.

The same thing would happen once Ma blew through the Ditch Fund on this shop. Only this time would be worse. There'd be no backup money and no place to go.

I followed Ma into the bathroom, still wearing oven mitts on my hands.

She was kneeling beside the tub, rubbing a washcloth behind Jordan's neck. Jordan's eyes ping-ponged back and forth from Ma's relaxed smile to my worrywart frown.

I couldn't hold back one more second. "Don't do this, Ma.

Please!" I said. Tears flooded my eyes. I wanted to rattle off a laundry list of reasons this business would bring us to utter ruin, but I couldn't. It was hard talking with Ma about all our past problems, never mind Shooting Stars. And even if I did try, I wouldn't change her mind. She was the worst kind of stubborn: Texas stubborn—determined, unyielding, and willing to go to the mat for what she believed was just cause.

"Bath's over," Ma said, only she signed, "Bath's open."

Jordan looked at me, confused, and I showed him what she meant. He got out of the tub.

After Jordan passed, Ma grabbed my hands and pulled them to hers like we were praying. "Listen up, Tess. I reckon I've made my share of mistakes—big mistakes. But that's done and over. Chin up, little lady! It's a brand-new day in Schenectady for us Dobsons. And I'd be deeply obliged if you'd consider helping me with Jordan on Wednesday."

Ma's big brown eyes shouted, "Give me a chance! Give me a chance!"

And I wanted to. I really did. But my whole body shook. Convincing words struggled to get free from my mouth and put the kibosh on this doomed plan, but they lost the fight when I looked into Ma's hopeful eyes.

"Okay," I said softly, looking at the plastic frog sitting near the tub drain. "I'll do it."

Chapter 9

Hire hardworking employees, and show appreciation for their efforts. A pat on the back is only a few inches up from a kick in the pants, but when deserved, it's more soothing to the bottom line. —*The Inside Scoop*

*K*nock. *Knock.*

Winnie's plump cheeks and dangling earrings greeted us when the door opened.

"We were out playing in the snow, and I lost my apartment key. Jordan has to go to the bathroom—*really bad*," I said as he squirmed in his boots beside me.

"Step right this way," she said, taking Jordan's hand.

When Jordan came out a few minutes later, Winnie invited us to stay. "You two have Rudolph the Red-nosed Reindeer looks going. Let me make you a cup of Chocolate Heaven."

Chocolate Heaven. Hmm. That sure sounded tasty. I turned so Jordan could see my hands move. "Want a hot drink?"

"Yes! Yes!" he signed, pumping his fist in the air.

So while Winnie disappeared into the kitchen, Jordan and I gazed around her apartment. There was so much to take in, and it sure looked wild and exotic. A giant aquarium spanned the back wall and was filled with all sorts of colorful fish. A zebra-patterned couch in the center of the room was sandwiched by end tables with carved-wood animal-hoof legs. Metallic birds swung from the ceiling, and a silhouette of Kokopelli, the flute-playing god of the Southwest, hung near the door.

Wow. I didn't think New Yorkers even *knew* about Kokopelli.

But what stood out the most was a red piano in the far corner with "Music of Angels" painted in swirly letters above the keys.

We sat on the zebra sofa while Winnie prepared the hot drinks. Jordan kept jumping up, trying to poke the metallic birds and make them fly.

"Here you go!" Winnie called as she carried out two steaming mugs and rested them on the coffee table.

Jordan took a long swig and his eyes lit up like lightbulbs. "Mmm!" He licked his lips.

"No need for me to translate what that means," I said, smiling.

Winnie gave a husky laugh. "I got the recipe for Chocolate Heaven from a fellow nurse I worked with thirty years ago. It uses a secret ingredient, but you couldn't zap it out of me with a defibrillator."

I nodded and looked up at Kokopelli again. "I'm into fashion and interior design, and this place has personality."

"Thanks. I could tell you know fashion, what with how polished you always look."

Suddenly Jordan slammed his mug down, spilling some, and dashed across the room to press his face against the aquarium.

"Sorry. My brother loves fish. Reptiles too," I said, wiping the mess and watching as Jordan's finger moved across the glass, following a yellow fish shaped like a pancake.

She laughed. "No apology necessary. Curiosity is a good thing." Then she turned to me. "So are you settling into your new home?"

I gave a polite half smile. I couldn't tell Winnie that the odds that Schenectady would be our forever home were slim as that pancake fish.

Winnie saw right through me. "I think I understand how you might be feeling, honey," she said. "Landing here in the dead of winter. Must seem like hard times."

I sipped silently, watching Jordan try to play peekaboo with the fish.

"Life in upstate New York must be worlds apart from Texas. I had a cousin visit from the Florida Keys last winter, and Lord, did she have a hard time with our weather. Her body ached for seventy-degree sunshine and warm breezes, never mind Key lime pie."

That made me laugh. "You know what I miss? Tapatío sauce. My ma can't find it around here, and Jordan and I sprinkle it on everything."

"Oh, we've got hot sauce if you know the right place to shop," she said. Then she paused before adding, "But loved ones, well, you can't replace them."

The mug trembled slightly in my hand. I missed Juanita and her grandparents. It was hard to say I missed Pop—it had been so long since he'd been a real part of my life, so long since he behaved like a pop, as Ma always said. On second thought, I *did* miss Pop. I missed the sweet way Ma says he was back when I was first born, even if I couldn't remember it myself.

Winnie smiled softly. "I'd like to share something with you, Tess. My husband died when my son was just a little tadpole. That was over forty years ago, and I still remember Elston's longing look when we'd see boys playing ball with their fathers in the park. We named him after the first black Yankee, Elston Howard—what a fine catcher he was. And wouldn't you know, my Elston was a natural behind home plate! We'd throw the ball around every night when I finished my shift. But no matter how I tried, my love couldn't fill that hole. He missed his father."

I swallowed hard. Winnie barely knew me, and besides, my father wasn't dead. He was just distracted. Forever distracted.

"Now on top of that, there's a new city, a new school, and putting up with us old-timers. Never mind temperatures that must lead you to believe you've been tossed in the bottom of a freezer!"

I looked away.

And then the past few weeks of headache and heartbreak gushed out like a busted fire hydrant. "It's hard to be homesick around Ma," I explained. "She moved us here at lightning speed without even asking how we felt." I was glad that Jordan was still staring at the fish. I didn't want him to see my tears.

Winnie leaned toward me, all ears.

"Schenectady is like this giant do-over for her. She's erased our whole lives back in San Antonio. And now she wants me to get excited about her ice cream shop, and I want to, but I'm scared."

"Your ma seems like a shrewd businesswoman to me."

"She *is* smart," I said, remembering all the times Ma won employee of the month at the grocery-store deli for her ideas on improving the operation and reducing waste. "But Shooting Stars comes—I mean, mood swings—and that ruins everything."

"What kind of mood swings?"

"Sometimes Ma gets turbocharged. Super Delilah, I call her, racing a hundred miles a minute and hardly sleeping. Nothing seems impossible, and she's full of ideas and plans.

But it doesn't last forever. Eventually, like a shooting star, she crashes, landing in bed, sad and empty."

"How long has this been going on?"

"Four or five years. And when she's Super Delilah, she blows through money and runs up bills, which gets us into even more trouble."

"Tess, your mom sounds like she could be sick," Winnie said, resting her hand on mine.

I told her I thought so too, but Ma didn't agree. "She says that she's prone to rough patches and ups and downs."

"When did your ma last have a checkup?" Winnie asked, sounding like the retired nurse she was.

"I can't remember. She avoids doctors. She calls them overrated bearers of gloom and doom."

"The mind and body both need regular tuning. Thirty years in nursing I dealt with folks who paid a heavy price for avoiding doctors." Winnie rubbed my shoulder. "Sickness, death, divorce, it's all different but the same too, in how it leaves you wounded. Part of your mother taking on a new business might be how she heals. After I lost my husband, I practically turned my home into a shrine, insisting everything had to stay put like before Carl passed on. After six months of living like that, I put Elston to bed, called in sick, and crawled under my comforter. I didn't wake until noon the next day, to the sight of my little boy at the foot of my bed eating out of a cereal box. But I'll tell you what: I changed from the caterpillar into the butterfly. Ready to get on with the business of living for Elston's sake. Maybe your mom's still in the cocoon."

I sighed. "Ma's gotten us evicted from three cocoons so far. It's not fair."

"My mama used to tell me that life ain't fair, but to lace up my ugly boots anyway. Lord, I hated those words—and those boots! But she was right."

Winnie walked into the kitchen and returned holding an opened tin. "Here. You and Jordan have to try my homemade peanut brittle. Get your mind off your troubles," she said, handing pieces to me.

I thumped the floor to get Jordan's attention. He turned around and came over. We both bit into the crunchy candy.

"Like peanut butter!" Jordan signed approvingly, and I nodded.

I told Winnie about our move in the freezing car and taking off the mayor's car door.

"Driving cross-country like that, knowing nobody, and now going solo in business. I'd say your ma's got true grit fitting a Texan," Winnie said.

"Pop used to say Ma had more guts than you could hang on a fence."

Winnie let out one of her hearty laughs. I giggled too.

"Is your pop back in San Antonio?" she asked, and I explained about him moving to Galveston and how he didn't write much. Truth was he never wrote, but I didn't say that.

Winnie crossed her arms over her sparkly sweater. "Sounds to me like your mother's been pulling double parent shifts for a while now."

Bang! Bang! Bang!

Jordan was hunched over the piano, smashing the keys with his hands.

"Too hard," I signed, running over and lifting his fingers.

Winnie sat on the bench beside him. She took his palms and pressed them against the wooden side of the piano. "Tell Jordan to keep his hands still. Right here."

She started playing what she called classic Motown. And she sang, swinging her shoulders and making her bangle bracelets jingle. The music bubbled in my heart like a bottle of cherry cola.

My favorite song was "Stop! In the Name of Love," especially when Winnie raised her hand high like a traffic cop and shook her fanny.

"If I didn't know better, I'd swear this child hears the music," Winnie said, grinning as she watched Jordan raise his hand too.

As Winnie played song after song, I glanced at the framed pictures resting on the piano. In one, she was standing with four older men with their arms wrapped around each other. They all wore sequined vests. On closer look I recognized Melvin and Sam from Ma's ice cream test-market session.

"That's our band. The Salty Old Dogs. Melvin and I are the lead singers," she said.

I bit into the last piece of peanut brittle. "Is Melvin your boyfriend?"

She let loose a laugh. "Us seasoned sisters don't have boyfriends, but you could call us a twosome. That sounds more sophisticated, doesn't it?" Jordan was sitting on Winnie's lap now. She was pushing his fingers as if he was playing.

"I bought this piano the very first day after I retired, and then taught myself how to play," she said, rubbing the side of the piano after finishing a song. "All those years seeing so much pain and suffering in the ER, I swore one day I'd play the music of angels." She stretched her back and laughed. "Ow-wee. Even with my built-in padding, these old bones don't take kindly to benches anymore."

I looked at the piano bench, already forming my craft plan. I would sew a patchwork bench cushion and double-stuff it with batting to make it extra comfy. I'd use a black trim border outlined in white lace, to complement the sofa. Each patch would reveal a different side of Winnie, like music and nursing. Maybe even Motown, though that might be tricky.

The wall clock chimed. Five-thirty. Ma would be home from signing the business papers any minute.

Winnie let out a yawn. "Excuse me! I'm overdue for my afternoon nap. That's one of the advantages to being a card-carrying senior. Best you two run on because I get cranky without it."

"Yes. Thanks for the snack," I said, tugging Jordan and walking toward the door.

"We're friends now, honey," she said, sticking some peanut brittle in Jordan's pants pocket.

I put our mugs in the kitchen sink and noticed a bag of potatoes on the counter. Winnie saw me looking.

"That's for Catherine. I'm bringing meatloaf and mashed potatoes over to her later. Having MS makes cooking hard," she said. "Am I guessing that Texans like meatloaf and mashed potatoes too?"

"As long as you leave the skins on and sprinkle hot sauce in the gravy," I said.

"And it better be Tapatío sauce, right?"

"Right," I said, all grins.

Chapter 10

Doing everything required to launch a business can feel like *Mission Impossible*, but do *not* be deterred! Order takeout, drink plenty of coffee, and chip away at that to-do list. —*The Inside Scoop*

The weeks from January to mid-February blew by hard and fast, like the cold wintry winds that rattled the apartment windows. From Monday to Friday, Ma and I started having what we called Jordan handoffs. She would spend all morning at the shop fixing things up, then rush back to the apartment before Jordan's bus arrived in the early afternoon. Then as soon as my bus got in an hour later, she'd return to A Cherry on Top for another work stretch.

Ma decided the Grand Opening would be on Sunday, April 15. Tax day. (Getting your taxes done, she reasoned, gave folks a good reason to treat themselves.) I'd fix Jordan's dinner and help with homework and bath time. Most evenings Ma didn't get back to the apartment until long after he was fast asleep. She always came in with her bag crammed with business papers. Sometimes she'd be holding a toolbox, looking worn and greasy like a mechanic. Once she showed up wearing her old deli smock, covered in blue paint. Her eyes always had charcoal shadows under them, but she never complained about being tired. She'd fix a pot of coffee and plop down on the futon for a few hours of studying the Inside Scoop and taking notes. She'd always pause after a while, look up, and ask, "How's school?"

"School's school," I'd say, shrugging.

I didn't tell her that I had straight A's in my classes, including math. (Take that, Ms. Hockley!) Or that Pete and I played Texas hold 'em in study hall, and I beat him just about every time. And I didn't tell her that Gabby and I had gotten to know each other better and that I didn't mind her strange ways so much. I'd even confided in her a little about Ma's new business and my worries about it. Gabby was a good listener. She kept encouraging me to join peer mediation, saying I'd get as much out of it as I gave, that I was exactly the kind of mediator who would "keep it real." But because of Ma's long workday, it would never happen. I had to take care of Jordan.

No, Ma and I didn't talk about my life at school much, and I sure didn't ask about the shop, even though I knew she wanted me to.

One drizzly Wednesday afternoon Winnie stopped by after school. I was slicing apples for Jordan's snack, and she invited him to play in her apartment. "Just Jordan," she said, winking at me. "Big sister here deserves a break."

Jordan loved the idea, and off they went. Alone for the first time in weeks, I jumped onto the couch to watch a home-makeover show and work on a patch for Winnie's piano-bench cushion. I was embroidering a nurse's cap in mother-of-pearl thread using a scrap of white linen that Juanita's grandmother gave me from an old skirt of hers.

But after an hour of embroidering, my hands started cramping and my chain stitches started looking sloppy. I got fed up with the show too, which was all about remodeling a bathroom on a shoestring budget. The host kept telling the money-strapped homeowners to retile, but personally I think stenciling and a fresh coat of paint give you more bang for your buck. That sure gave our run-down bathroom a fresh look on less than twenty dollars, and it only took a couple of hours to finish.

So I roamed over to Building Two—which was identical to Building One, even down to the fake tree missing leaves—and then on to Building Three, Assisted Living. Now *that* lobby was appealing. It had contemporary maple furniture with teal cushions and a set of sunflower paintings, even if it did smell like a hospital. The place was hopping with staff and residents. Next to the lobby was a hair salon, a game room with a Ping-Pong table and giant TV, a library, and a cafeteria where residents ate their meals.

I sank into a rocker by the front window of the lobby just as Chief walked in, pushing a metal cart stacked with grocery bags. Lots of them.

"Hi, Chief," I called. He still had my vote for Schenectady's oldest oddball, but I didn't want him to think I was rude.

"Young lady," he said as he passed, saluting with a brush of his hand to the fur trim around his parka hood.

The elevator opened and he pushed the cart in, but a wheel got stuck. He pushed it again, but it wouldn't budge.

I jumped up to help, and together we wiggled it into the elevator. Before I knew it, the doors closed and we were headed up.

"This can't all be yours," I said, pointing to the groceries.

" 'Course not. Plenty of folks around here can't get out in winter, especially in Assisted Living, so we give them a hand."

The doors opened, and I pushed the cart out. Chief followed. I could tell steering the cart on carpeting was hard for him, what with his prosthesis.

An aide passed beside an old man. The aide was telling a joke as he helped wheel the old man's oxygen tank.

"Doesn't the staff help with groceries?" I asked.

Chief looked annoyed at my question. "They only make deliveries once a week, so we supplement with a midweek run. A week's a long time to wait if you run out of something, don't you think?"

I nodded. Chief kept saying *we*, but he was the only one here besides me.

From one apartment to the next, we canvassed the second floor, delivering drug prescriptions, shampoo, cold medicine, and aspirin, as well as candy bars and all sorts of snacks. Chief double-checked each order before we made a delivery, and he chitchatted with everyone. He took the job seriously, that's for sure, until we headed to the third floor.

Then his face lit up like a kid getting presents. And just as we stopped at apartment 333, he ran a comb over his crew cut and popped a mint into his mouth.

Boy, was I curious who lived behind *that* door.

A tiny lady in wool slacks and a bright red turtleneck slowly opened the door, releasing a soapy scent into the hallway. She leaned on a walker and grinned through cherry lipstick when she saw Chief. "At last, my prince arrives!"

"You look sweeter than Vermont maple syrup, Adelaine. How's rehab helping that hip?" he asked.

"I'm up and moving. Even if I am a slowpoke," she said.

"The turtle beat the hare. That's what I say," Chief answered, serious like he was dishing out deep psychological wisdom.

"I've been looking forward to your visit all day. I gave my last cookie to my granddaughter when she stopped by earlier."

Chief turned to me. "Look for the bag marked 'Heisey.' Adelaine Heisey," he whispered.

"Mine has cookies, dear," she said. "Sugar-free cookies. I'm a diabetic. I go through a bag a week."

I held out the package for her, but Chief grabbed it first. "We're full-service, Tess. We don't let customers with walkers lift heavy bags." He scowled as he walked into her apartment and put the bag on the kitchen counter.

Adelaine handed me money. "I saw you at your mother's ice cream sampling party, but I don't remember your name. I've never been good with names."

I smiled. "I'm Tess Dobson."

"Nice of you to help, Tess. Isn't Frederick wonderful? I call him the Good Samaritan of Schenectady."

I could think of better nicknames for Chief, but I didn't tell Adelaine that.

Chief blushed like a teenager. "Aw, no trouble at all," he said, kicking his good leg against the cart before he kissed her hand and "bid her farewell." My oh my, Adelaine's face turned as red as her turtleneck.

It took us two hours to make all the deliveries. Most of them were for Assisted Living folks, but we brought some to the other two buildings too. We had to go back up to the fifth floor in Building Two twice, being that Mr. Gulden in 529 was blasting opera music and didn't hear us knock. And there was a mix-up with a lady in 305 who thought her prescription was filled incorrectly. Chief had to call the pharmacist, who explained that she got the generic version. It was the same drug but with a different name, and he had to tell her four times before she finally believed him.

"Same drug, same drug," Chief whispered to me after we left her apartment, and I grinned.

The most unusual customer was the guy wearing a leather bomber jacket and smelling like he'd been dipped in aftershave. He practically sprinted past us in the lobby of Building Two.

"Got an order for ya, Cal!" Chief called to him.

"Leave it next door with Jessie. I'm running late," he said. I recognized the Oakley sunglasses on top of his head. As in hip-hop-happening and pricey.

"Will do. Everything okay?" Chief asked.

"Never been better. I'm meeting the 1956 Miss New York for coffee at Starbucks. Match.com says we could be soul mates!"

Making deliveries wasn't the end of Operation Homebound. That's what Chief called it too, like it was a military mission. After we stowed the cart in the basement, we returned to the building lobby to stuff "chits" (order forms) in the mailboxes for next week's run. Had I been the boss, I would've tucked the flyers in the delivery bags, but Chief didn't take too kindly to having his authority questioned. Last but not least, he posted the supermarket sale sheet and the Seniors' Special flyer from the Chinese takeout on the bulletin board: "General Tsao's chicken, rice, egg roll, miso soup, and a fortune cookie: $8.99 plus tax."

I thought the staff here must love having a stubborn take-charge guy like Chief around. Sure saves them some work.

Afterward, Chief insisted on walking me back to Building One since it was dark out, even though I said it wasn't necessary. My stomach was growling like a grizzly bear. And I still had to get Jordan from Winnie's apartment.

When we got to the lobby, he reached into a bag, pulled out a bakery box, and handed it to me. "Payment for services rendered," he said.

An angel food cake.

"Thanks but you keep it," I said, knowing it was his.

"I insist. Nobody accuses Chief Morrow of not paying his crew."

There was no sense arguing with the commander in chief of Operation Homebound. I thanked him and took the cake.

As I turned toward Winnie's apartment, Chief called my name. "We get under way every Wednesday at 1630 sharp."

I could see myself enjoying doing this every week. Winnie was right about all the colorful characters in this place. One guy had shown me his collection of Civil War relics, including a letter written by General Ulysses S. Grant before the siege of Vicksburg. A lady with a British accent told me she spoke seven different languages, including Dutch, which she picked up when she aided the underground resistance in Holland during World War II. I had to admit there was far more to these White Hairs than met the eye. And I liked how excited they got when I handed them their favorite snacks.

Still, something stood in the way of my accepting this job, no different than it was with peer mediation: Jordan. I had to take care of him.

"I can't make it," I said.

Chief's weathered face looked confused. "If it helps, I can talk to your mother, explain about Operation Homebound."

I didn't want to get into it with him about Ma and her new business and my watching Jordan. "Sorry, I just can't," I said, and I walked away.

Jordan was feeding the fish when I got to Winnie's apartment. It smelled spicy and meaty-delicious inside, and I was dying to peek in the oven.

"Sure hope you did something pleasant for yourself with your free time, Tess," Winnie said as we both watched Jordan sprinkle fish food in the water.

I told her I did some embroidery, which always makes me happy. I sure wasn't going to tell her the cushion I was working on was for her.

"Nice to know someone with design flair. If you ask me, folks around here get stuck in their old ways, including fashion and home decorating," Winnie said. "Well, Jordan and I had ourselves one blow-the-roof-down jam session. If you and your ma don't mind, I think he and I should spend every Wednesday together. It's good for me to have an audience while I'm rehearsing for my band gigs. And he does a nice job feeding my fish. They smile back at him."

My eyes got big. *Every Wednesday?* That would mean I could go to peer mediation! And if I took the late bus, I'd still be back in time to help Chief with Operation Homebound afterward. Of course Ma would approve. Winnie was a nurse, an entertainer, and a soulful fairy godmother wrapped in one. I looked over at Jordan. He was staring into the fish tank again, with his cheeks puffed and his arms moving like flippers. He loved it here.

"Winnie, that's the best plan I've heard in a while. Thanks!"

As we headed out the door, Winnie gave me a grocery bag to take with me. "Hold it from the bottom and don't peek until you get in," she said.

As soon as we got back to our apartment, I put down the cake from Chief and pulled the foil-covered tray out of the bag from Winnie.

A note was taped on top:

> Dinner's served just like the San Antonio patient ordered, with skins on the taters & Tapatío sauce sprinkled in the gravy. Nothing's impossible when you know where to shop!

Chapter 11

"Watch out, world. The great state of Texas just brought us their best mediator!" Gabby shouted as I walked into the peer-mediation conference room the next Wednesday.

All the kids standing near Gabby flashed welcoming smiles my way, and I felt my neck get blotchy like a giraffe's. Living with Ma for twelve years, I've got tons of experience facing problems—but judging from my parents' past shouting matches and our ongoing money troubles, I can't say I own bragging rights to solving any of them. I wondered, too, if kids had heard about that pear I'd tossed at Pete. Thinking about that made me feel out of place here in peer mediation, like a drunk sitting front and center at Alcoholics Anonymous guzzling a beer.

"Hey, Tess!" Ritchie called.

A large oval table filled most of the room, and there was a desk in the back. Ritchie and Gabby and six others were standing near the desk, hovering over a tray of chocolate chip cookies. Right away Gabby introduced me to everybody. They were discussing what kind of team shirt would best represent peer mediation.

"I say one with a collar so we look slick," Ritchie said.

"I vote for a casual T-shirt in a cheery color, to put everyone at ease," Gabby said.

"I don't care as long as it's baggy," Kim said. "I love baggy shirts!"

Watching them, I was struck by how different they all looked. Kim was tiny and freckled. Gavin was Asian and "into skateboarding," as he explained. Devin, a skinny black kid who rode the same bus as me, always carried a violin case. Malika, who sat in front of me in social studies, always wore a scarf over her head. Yesterday the social studies teacher asked the class what infamous general contributed to the colonists' victories at the battles of Ticonderoga and Saratoga in the Revolutionary War, and hers was the first hand up. ("Benedict Arnold, the traitor!" she answered quickly like she was on a game show.)

A teacher walked into the room and greeted me. "Hello,

Tess. I'm Mr. Winecki, but this group has given me the notable nickname Mr. Win."

Ritchie shoved a cookie in his mouth, chewed, and then began speaking. "Yup, our motto is, 'Win-win solutions please Mr. Win.' "

I half expected a peer-mediation advisor to look stern like a judge, but Mr. Win didn't come across that way. He reminded me of that sweet, innocent guy in the movie *Forrest Gump*, fully expecting life to be like a box of chocolates. He wore suspenders, and he kept a pencil tucked behind his ear.

"Gabby has probably told you that we like to think of ourselves as advocates for peace in progress," he said, reaching for a cookie from the tray.

"Peace sounds good to me," I said, smiling.

"Spoken like a true mediator. I like that southwestern accent of yours. Disputants will pay attention when you speak."

Don't count on it, I thought.

Mr. Win gave me a thick folder labeled "Peer Mediation Training" to take home and read. "For today, observe what goes on in the session and how the mediators respond. Mediators don't judge who's right and who's wrong. Two mediators guide the process along to a win-win outcome; the rest of us will be non-participating observers, sworn to confidentiality. The ultimate objective of the peer mediator is to empower the disputants to resolve their conflict themselves—"

"Nothing personal, Mr. Win," Gabby interrupted. "But you're making us sound like a bunch of boring guidance counselors."

Pointing to Ritchie and the others, she added, "Mind if we give Tess the skinny on what this is really about?"

"By all means," he said with an amused grin as he tightened his suspenders. "We have about ten minutes."

Mr. Win closed the door, and we gathered around the table. Gabby sipped from a water bottle, then began speaking in a no-nonsense tone. "Ottawa Creek Middle School might look like a picture postcard for tranquil, cooperative learning, but don't be duped, Tess. This place is a war zone. Enemy combatants launch strikes in the lunchroom, in the hallways, and even in the restrooms, inflicting pain and causing destruction. Our job as peer mediators is to: one, help heal the emotional wounds; and two, get to the root of each conflict to resolve it and prevent further explosions."

With that, Ritchie and the others described the problems that bring kids to peer mediation: rumors beings spread; taunting and teasing about everything from who couldn't do a single pull-up in gym class to whose iPod has better tunes; nasty boyfriend-girlfriend breakups; and the occasional shove in the hallway or on the school bus. It sounded like the same type of troubles back in my old school. The difference here was that kids involved had some say-so in how things got resolved. As long as the conflict wasn't violent and didn't involve drugs or weapons, teachers could recommend that students attend peer mediation rather than have their fate decided by adults. (Or students could request peer mediation on their own.) And if they didn't want to, that was fine too.

"Peer-mediation training helps you understand how all

conflict goes back to the same tainted well," Kim said, giving me a handout titled "Basic Human Needs." "We all want similar things out of life, such as to be treated with respect, to do something well, to belong to a group, et cetera. When someone else gets in the way of those needs being fulfilled, fireworks erupt."

I nodded. Made sense to me, but what I didn't get was how I could possibly help *fix* problems. In my family, trouble had a way of tangling up so badly that even when I wanted to help, I couldn't. I got caught too, like a bug trapped in a spider's web.

"Peer mediation sorta follows a script," Devin explained in a husky voice. "One at a time each disputant explains what he or she thinks is going on. Then one of us mediators repeats what was said, using facts and restating the feelings."

"Disputants have to be willing to agree to ground rules— no put-downs or interruptions, and they must be open and honest," Kim added.

After storytelling, Malika said, came brainstorming solutions. "Mediators restate the problem and then encourage the disputants to come up with a solution together. It works better if *they* figure it out. But be prepared. This part gets messy."

"Messy, heated, and stuck," Gabby added.

Mr. Win jumped in. "During the brainstorming phase, we're deep in the weeds of the problem. Egos kick in, and disputants are often reluctant to admit mistakes or look for another way through the conflict. That's when our mediators earn their big bucks by encouraging, prodding with more questions, and sticking with the resolution process."

"All that's true except the part about us earning big bucks. We work for cookies," Ritchie whispered beside me.

Then Kim explained the last step. "Once a fair, specific, and *do-able* solution is found that both disputants can live with, we write it all down, and everybody in the room has to sign the agreement. After that, we thank them for coming, and the mediation ends."

"Nicely explained," Mr. Win said. "Anything else, team?"

Gabby spoke quickly. "We almost forgot. Watch for the hidden agenda."

"What's that?" I asked.

"Usually there's more to the problem than meets the eye. Something else might have been said or done that led to their dancing the trouble tango."

Mr. Win nodded. "Indeed. Thanks, Gabby."

Knock-knock.

"Speaking of dancing the trouble tango, our disputants are here. I believe Malika and Devin are our designated mediators today. The rest of us will move to the back and take an observational role."

A boy and a girl walked in the room. The girl had a kerchief over her long, thick hair. She towered over the boy and wore raggedy, old-fashioned clothes. The boy wore a leather cap and a fake scraggly beard.

"We just came from dress rehearsal for the musical," he explained.

Devin welcomed the disputants and asked them to sit down and introduce themselves.

The girl scooted her chair as far away from the boy as she could.

"I'm Sophie and I play Golde in *Fiddler on the Roof*," she said, frowning as she crossed her arms over her apron.

"I'm Justin and I play Tevye," he said. Pointing toward her, he added, "Tevye is married to Golde. Poor milkman."

Immediately Malika stated the ground rules, emphasizing the bit about no put-downs. "The musical director suggested you two come to peer mediation after an incident took place at Monday's practice. Please tell us what happened."

With that, Sophie and Justin took turns speaking, without looking at each other. Sophie said they'd been rehearsing an important scene in Act One and practicing "The Wedding Dance."

"Justin kept stepping on my toes and twirling me at the wrong times. He wasn't taking it seriously. All he wanted to do was flirt with Brooke—she plays my daughter. And when I complained to the director, Justin pointed to the papier-mâché cow backstage and shouted, 'I'm dancing with a cow!' The whole cast started laughing, and that's when I threw the milk pail."

Justin gave his version next, which sounded a lot different. He said he'd been doing his best to keep up with the dance. "You think Sophie would help, but noooo. She acted all mean and witchy, just like Golde is to Tevye!"

"No put-downs, Justin. You agreed," Devin interrupted.

Justin continued. "Okay, okay. I admit I was messing up on the footwork—it was tricky. But Sophie kept rolling her eyes and mumbling, 'Matchmaker, matchmaker, make me a match—only find someone who can dance.' And then she ran to the director saying *I* wasn't taking it seriously. I guess I snapped. But she had it coming."

"Well, *you* deserved that milk pail hitting your fat head!" Sophie shouted.

Once again, Devin reminded them about the ground rules. Then Sophie got up and said she'd had enough, and Justin said it figured, but Malika gently coaxed Sophie back.

When they'd calmed down, Devin continued. "Okay, let's restate the problem. Sophie, you are upset that Justin made a joke about you that hurt your feelings. Justin, you are upset that Sophie insulted you and told the director you weren't taking things seriously, which hurt *your* feelings. Is that correct?"

Sophie and Justin both gave slight nods. Beside me, Mr. Win jotted down a note and passed it to me: "Notice the body language."

I studied the disputants. Sophie's legs were crossed and she kept picking at her cuticles. Justin's face was red under that fake beard, and he wouldn't look at her either. I felt myself drinking in their toxic emotions, as Gabby would say.

"Brainstorming time," Malika said. Turning to Justin first, she asked, "What can you do to solve this problem?"

"Nothing. Sophie's never going to change," he said.

I thought, *Poor Devin and Malika.* This mediation seemed harder than running track!

Malika kept prodding. "What can *you* do, Justin?"

He paused for a long stretch, then spoke more softly. "Maybe I could avoid comparing her to a cow. That is kinda low."

Sophie didn't offer much initially, but then she said she could stop throwing props. It was hard to tell if she was serious, since she kept looking down at her fingernails.

"What else can you do now, Justin?" Devin asked.

He shrugged. "I guess I could apologize for what I said. But heck, it would be easier to dance with a cow than with you, Sophie. A cow would be more patient."

Sophie turned to him, then jumped up and started moving her feet. "If you paid attention to the pattern—hop two, step two, twirl two, stomp-stomp-stomp—you'd get it. The only thing you pay attention to is Brooke's dumb giggle!"

Gabby leaned over and whispered in my ear. "Hidden agenda. She's got a crush on ol' Tevye."

With that, Justin turned to Sophie. "Easy for you, what with all that ballet training you've had. I've never had a single dance lesson. And you always act like you *expect* me to mess up. Remember when we did *Grease* last year? You told the makeup crew that I danced rock and roll like I had rocks in my sneakers!"

Gabby tapped my shoulder this time. "Hidden agenda number two. He feels inferior," she whispered.

Devin turned to Sophie. "What can you do to help Justin feel more confident as a dancer? You're the stars of this show. You have to support each other."

Sophie turned to Justin. "Hmm . . . I could stay after and practice one on one with you. And I guess I could be more patient. You're not *ruining* 'The Wedding Dance,' Justin. You just need to slow down. You sing 'If I Were a Rich Man' perfectly—jiggly, sweet, and funny, just like you'd expect from a milkman."

Justin sat up straighter in his chair. "Really?"

Sophie smiled. "Really. You mean Brooke hasn't told you that?"

"As a matter of fact, no," Justin said, smiling back.

The rest of the mediation went smoothly. Both disputants agreed that in the future they would stop airing their issues publicly and instead talk privately, and they apologized to each other. Then, after signing the agreement, they left together, practicing "The Wedding Dance" footwork all the way down the hallway.

Mr. Win complimented Malika and Devin afterward for not letting the mediation get derailed. "You kept hope alive, even when things were headed south," he said. Then, as kids started leaving, he turned to me. "Any questions on what you observed, Tess?"

I shook my head. I had to admit I was impressed with Malika and Devin. I might have thrown in the towel back when Sophie and Justin were raging at each other.

"Alrighty then," Mr. Win said. "Study that training booklet, 'cause next month is *your* debut, though not in a musical."

"Mine?"

"That's right. You'll be in the mediator's chair beside Ritchie."

What did I know about getting people to get along? A month—I needed six months, maybe six years! Worry pinched at me beneath my sweater. *I shouldn't have joined Peer Mediation Club*, I thought. *I should've stuck around the apartment and made another patch for Winnie's cushion.*

Waiting outside for the late bus, I told Gabby I was having second thoughts on being a peer mediator.

"Don't give in to your inner fear," she said, patting my back. "Read through the materials once, and you'll be fine. Trust your persistent ox instinct."

Just as I was about to come up with another excuse, Gabby pointed out that: one, I was exactly the kind of mediator Ottawa Creek Middle School needed, and two, the kids in Peer Mediation Club were a lot of fun.

"And from what I see, you could stand to ramp up the fun in your life," she added, winking as the bus pulled up.

I grinned, waved goodbye, and climbed onto the bus. I didn't exactly agree with Gabby, but something about the way her tangly wild hair bounced when she spoke wouldn't let me set her straight.

Chapter 12

Back at the apartments, Chief and I set a new record by finishing Operation Homebound in one hour and twenty-five minutes. And that included a pit stop in Building Two, apartment 209—to provide a design consultation for a Mrs. Jankowski. She had dinner guests coming, and she wanted to give her living room a snazzy look. Winnie had raved about my decorating flair, and Mrs. J. was so pleased with how I rearranged her end tables, candlesticks, and antique picture frames that she insisted on tipping me with a ten-dollar bill.

Afterward, I picked up Jordan at Winnie's and started making grilled cheese-and-pepper sandwiches for dinner. But I got distracted helping a grouchy FrankenJordan solve his subtraction problems and burned the bread, and I was too tired to make anything else. So we ate mixy cereal instead (half Cheerios, half cornflakes). Later, we looked at *Ranger Rick* magazine in bed until I saw that his eyes were closed, and I got up. I felt sleepy, but I wanted to wait for Ma to return.

She got in close to midnight. Even the man next door had turned off the war movie he was blasting by then. And when Ma finally arrived, she sounded like she was dragging a sack of bowling balls.

I got out of bed to investigate.

"Whatcha got there?" I asked, squinting in the dark room.

"An old friend who's missed you something awful," she said, brushing her gray-streaked hair from her face and lugging something heavy up onto the kitchen counter.

I flipped on the light switch. Our old sewing machine! It looked polished and shiny and, well, better.

"Lady Kenmore's got a new drive belt. The Sears service guy says she's good for another five years or five hundred yards of sewing, whichever comes first."

I touched the machine's arm shaft, then lifted the presser foot like I was about to slide fabric underneath. Perfect. Now

I'd be able to sew the rest of the patches for Winnie's cushion much faster.

"This *is* good news," I said, smiling.

For a minute we both stood silently with our arms folded, admiring the sewing machine like it was a marble sculpture in a museum.

Ma spoke first. "I figured you've been missing your craft work something awful, Tess. And I've got a project to get started on myself."

I was about to tell Ma all about peer mediation and how I'd be co-mediator for the first time soon. That and about Operation Homebound and how Chief actually complimented me on my customer relations. Ma and I had hardly spoken two words lately, and I missed talking.

But now she had me curious about her project. Ma and sewing mix like orange juice and diesel fuel. Once she accidentally slip-stitched the crotch closed on a pair of her shorts. Another time she hemmed Jordan's dress slacks inside out.

"What are you making?" I asked.

"Curtains for the display window of the ice cream shop," she said, reaching for a shopping bag on the floor. "I picked up this darling fabric today. I'm going for a cozy café look."

She pulled out a lightweight chintz with red and yellow flowers along the top and bottom edges. The middle was covered with stemmed cherries with a mint-green background. It would need a lining to blend all those colors, for sure.

"Have you measured the window?"

"Naah, I eyeballed it," she said as she walked over to the sink and started filling the coffeepot with water.

"You know the saying, Ma: 'Measure twice, cut once.' Are you adding a valance?"

She shrugged. "I can hardly say *valance*, never mind make one. Plain curtains will have to do."

I stared at Ma. Her face looked worn like a crumpled lunch bag. Sleep would do her good.

I picked up the sewing machine from the kitchen counter and carried it out to the living room.

"Where are you going with that?" she asked.

I moved the lamp off the desk facing the big window and put the sewing machine down.

"I sew better with natural lighting. Valances aren't hard for me and they're worth the extra time. They give tab tops a finished look, and that's how you'll get the cozy café atmosphere."

Ma smiled bright like the North Star. No, even brighter. The North Star's North Star. "Does this mean you'll make the curtains?"

"I'll make them once I have good measurements. But only if you go to sleep, Ma. You look really tired."

"Hands down, I've got the best daughter in Schenectady—with the finest decorator know-how too!" Ma shouted, hugging me. Her skinny bones poked out from beneath her sweater.

"I'm still not sold on the ice cream shop," I said. "But there's no sense wasting a nice chintz fabric."

"The *Inside Scoop* says a healthy skepticism is an advantage to an entrepreneur, so you've got a leg up in this business." Ma turned off the light. "Let's hit the hay. I'll bring you the window dimensions tomorrow."

I shook my head. "I do my own measurements. You take Jordan with you to the shop tomorrow. After school I'll catch the bus downtown and bring my tape measure."

Chapter 13

The menu is the treasure chest of the ice cream shop. Ensure it leaves customers ecstatic, duly agonizing as they choose from an array of sinfully sweet frozen treats. —*The Inside Scoop*

"Well, howdy-do, interior designer!" Ma shouted down from a ladder as I walked into A Cherry on Top the next day. A drippy piece of wallpaper was hanging over her arm. Half the shop was covered in wallpaper that looked like a sea of smiling yellow ice cream cones.

I smelled Murphy oil soap as I dropped my tape measure on the counter, next to a big box of sugar cones, a case of toppings, and an opened can of Dr Pepper. I stared over at the giant bow window with crown molding, which poured light in from the street. There was plenty wrong about this ice cream shop, but Ma was right about something. That window *was* an eye-grabber, just begging to be dressed up.

Jordan dashed out from behind the counter, wearing his favorite yellow shirt, a server's paper hat, and a devilish grin. "Ice cream?" he signed.

"Two scoops, please," I signed, and he pretended to serve me. I handed him make-believe coins, then licked my imaginary cone and peeked down at the freezer.

"How come the freezer's empty?" I called over to Ma.

"It's called a dipping cabinet, and filling it comes later," she said, smoothing the wallpaper with her hands.

"I don't get it. Equipment and supplies are everywhere, but no ice cream. What's an ice cream shop without ice cream?"

"I'm working off a business plan, Tess. And I'm up to the part that says, 'Get your shop in tip-top shape before investing in product.' "

Who was I to argue with the Ice Cream Gospel According to Delilah? Still, I thought we should have at least a half gallon in stock. Truth was, this curtain installer was hoping to take measurements and be rewarded with some Rocky Road.

I looked around. The shop *did* feel quaint and old-fashioned, what with its long marble serving counter and checkered-vinyl swivel stools. I personally wouldn't have opted for that goofy cone wallpaper, but the bright color scheme worked. And the mirror behind the cash register was outlined in lightbulbs that gave a retro, funky look, like it belonged on the vanity of an old movie star.

I walked into the storage room in the back. It was sky blue and smelled freshly painted, and I remembered when Ma returned to the apartment with her deli smock splattered with blue paint. One of the pillows that belonged on the apartment futon was on the floor, and the shelves over the sink were stacked high with supplies: nuts, bags of candy, plasticware, napkins, sauces, and a whole case of maraschino cherries.

Jordan followed me in, plopped down on the pillow, and turned on the TV. A McDonald's commercial came on, and he pulled his hand down from his chest to his stomach, signing "Hungry."

"Jordan the hungry hippo," I signed back. The sign for *hippo* uses the Y hands to show a wide mouth opening and closing. I like how it resembles the real animal.

"No hippo. Turtle," he signed, sliding his thumb from under his other hand for *turtle*.

I tickled his belly. "Jordan Dobson, do you ever stop thinking about turtles?"

He shook his head. "Hungry," he signed again. "And happy! Happy, happy!"

"How come?"

He pointed back at me and then signed, "Tess here."

"Yes, here." I smiled and looked away, out the back window. I didn't want him to see my teary eyes. He wouldn't understand why I'd been avoiding this place.

Out back in the alley, a man wearing a stained white apron was throwing garbage into the snow-covered Dumpster. I figured he worked next door at Bianco's Pizzeria.

I felt a draft from the door and discovered it was open a crack, so I pushed it shut, but it wouldn't lock. Then I turned back toward Jordan, whose eyes were glued to the TV. I tapped him on his shoulder and signed, "I have to help Ma. Then we'll eat pizza, okay?"

Jordan's head moved up and down like a puppet on a string. "Pizza *and* ice cream!" he signed.

It took five late nights to make the window treatments, but they were well worth the fuss. I chose a lemon-yellow valance to complement the wallpaper and added a fringe with red dangling beads that resembled cherries. The fringe alone took two days because my stitching was crooked the first time and I had to rip it out. (Guess even crafty queens can get out of practice when they're away from their equipment.) I was most proud of the lining. It was a matching yellow satin that I got on sale for $3.99 a yard, but it looked elegant, like Chinese silk.

Ma was tickled pink with the curtains—so much so that she asked me to make matching tablecloths for the dining area and skirts to hang beneath the sinks in the restrooms to cover the rusty pipes. I told Ma too much cherry fabric in those tiny bathrooms would make customers feel like they were trapped in the Hi Ho! Cherry-O board game. But Ma said looking at fruit sure beat looking at rusty pipes any old day.

One Saturday morning I loaded up my power drill and

tools, and Jordan, Ma, and I piled into the Toyota and drove to the ice cream shop. Snow was starting to melt, and marbled, muddy slush was piled against the curbs. A fog covered State Street like a wet washcloth. My face felt damp just from the walk in from the car, and Jordan kept sniffling.

Right away I began installing the curtains, but the plastic hardware cracked as I started drilling. Ma told me there was a hardware store a few streets west on State Street and then across Broadway.

"I come too!" Jordan signed when he saw me leaving. He was sitting on the serving counter, arranging his tiny plastic animals around a lion that ruled from the top of a stack of ice cream cones.

But Jordan's nose was running, and he'd been sneezing all morning like he was coming down with something. "It's raining. Stay here and play," I signed, handing him a tissue.

He stuck his lower lip out and tossed an elephant at my feet. "Tess meanie!"

The walk to the hardware store took about ten minutes, but I practically had to hopscotch-jump the whole way, with all the smashed pop cans and fast-food wrappers on the sidewalk. It was still drizzling, and I kept my sweatshirt hood on so my hair wouldn't get wet and frizz.

One building after the next had empty stores and windows sprayed with graffiti. It smelled, too, like gasoline on one corner, trash on the next, and then like soup as I passed a diner (I didn't mind that one).

I kept thinking about what Ma had read in the *Inside Scoop*, how a retail shop was all about location, location, location. Well, *this* location was the pits. Who'd want to eat ice cream on a dirty street? Why were we fussing to create a cutesy café when it was sitting right smack in the slums?

Seeing the hardware store, I crossed the street and went in. When I came back out, the rain had stopped. I noticed a woman with torn clothes sitting on the curb, with steam coming from a thermos bottle in her hand. Beside her was a shopping cart overflowing with recycled cans and a paper cup with "Donatiens" scribbled on it. I tossed the change from my purchase into the cup and she thanked me.

"That you, Tess?"

I turned around. Pete Chutkin was in the distance, riding on a bicycle built for two—only he was riding solo.

"What are you doing here?" he asked when he caught up and stopped his bike beside me. An old-fashioned camera with a chip on the base was strapped around his neck.

"Running an errand. My ma's opening up a business nearby. What're *you* doing here?"

"I live here," he said, pointing behind him to a small cluster of trailers poking out between the buildings. "I'm taking pictures. I got a nice one of a little girl eating a donut at the bus stop on Erie Boulevard, and a dog sleeping on a sewer grate. You never know what you'll find in Schenectady."

I stared at his bicycle. It was white with rust patches everywhere like a spotted cow. The seats had rips, and the handlebars were wrapped in duct tape.

"Want a ride?" he asked, oozing pride as if he was driving a BMW.

"No thanks," I said, beginning to walk away, but he pedaled alongside me.

"I bet you've never been on something like this. It's called a tandem bike, and it rides like you're steering a telephone pole! Hop on. I'll give you a tour of the city."

I kicked a rotten apple core. "From what I see, I don't want the tour."

"Oh, we've got plenty of stuff worth checking out in Schenectady. And I know a place you'll love, you being from Texas and all. It's not far. C'mon!"

Don't ask why, but he had me with that bit about Texas. I hopped onto the backseat and away we went, bump-bumping along, over potholes and cracks in the street. A car beeped when we turned around suddenly because a wind gust made my shopping bag blow off the handlebars. It *did* feel like we were steering a telephone pole. Riding the tandem bike reminded me of the train game I used to play with Jordan. He'd grab my waist from behind me and we'd choo-choo, chug-a-chug around the kitchen.

Pete played tour guide as we pedaled, telling me how Schenectady was originally the land of the Mohawk tribe, and how in 1690 its Dutch settlement was attacked by the French and their Indian allies in a brutal massacre.

"Later they used to call Schenectady 'the city that lights and hauls the world,' on account of Thomas Edison starting his company here, which became General Electric. And American Locomotive Company was here too, and they once made all the steam and diesel trains in the country. Back in those days the streets of Schenectady were paved with gold. Not so anymore, but we're working on that," he said.

We rode down Liberty Street all the way to Eastern Parkway, and then kept going until Pete stopped the bike on a side street near the entrance to a park.

"This is Central Park. New York City is such a copycat naming their park after *ours*," he said, grinning. He pointed to a huge plot of scraggy bushes muffin-topped with snow. "That's the famous Rose Garden. Every color and type of rose in the rose alphabet blooms here. In the summertime, this place is filled with wedding parties getting photographed and lots of 'garden angels' pruning the bushes."

Pete asked me to stand beside the white trellis arch leading toward the bushes, and he took my picture. Then we followed the stone maze through the garden, and he photographed a sparrow perched atop a bench.

He was right. This place did remind me of Texas. "I love roses," I said, thinking out loud. Back at our house, years ago, we had a pink rosebush next to the driveway. I loved getting a whiff of that heavenly scent every time I got out of the car. The bush had a hollowed-out shape on account of the fact that Pop hit it with his truck after a night out. I remember Ma yelling at him when it happened, furious that he'd taken the wheel when he was what she called three sheets to the wind.

Back on the bike, we pumped hard up hills, cutting through

a playground and looping past a soggy field to a body of water called Iroquois Lake with a stone fountain in the middle. The fountain wasn't working, probably because the lake was partly frozen. We parked the bike on the grass and walked down to the shore so Pete could get more pictures.

The air was still, except for the melting ice on the lake, which crackled like Rice Krispies in milk.

"How long have you been taking pictures?" I asked Pete.

"Since I found this little beauty at the city dump last year," he said, touching the camera strap. "This is an Olympia—top-of-the-line brand. How lucky am I!"

"Why would somebody throw out an expensive camera?"

"My dad says, 'One person's trash is another person's treasure.' He's got an eagle eye for uncovering all kinds of good stuff. He pulled this bike out from under a moldy mattress, and he found a gas grill that only needed a few bolts tightened, hardly used otherwise. And yesterday I struck gold myself: a giant inflatable lawn Santa. Betcha no one else in our trailer park has one of them next Christmas!"

We got back on the bike and started pedaling, until Pete stopped suddenly in front of a monument. A soldier holding a rifle horizontally was perched on top of a gigantic boulder and surrounded by a wrought-iron fence. The statue was huge. It stood about fifteen feet off the ground.

"Schenectady doesn't have an Alamo, but we've got hometown heroes," he said. I followed him over to the statue, where I read the bronze plaque. The statue was dedicated to locals who served in the Spanish-American War. Its copper had weathered to a pale green. I liked the expression on the soldier's face: serious and determined, but kind.

Suddenly Pete handed me his camera. "This would make an awesome photo, what with how the sun is fighting its way through the clouds behind the soldier's back. Stand here and take my picture, okay?" Then he hopped the fence and started climbing on the rock.

"You sure about this?" I had a feeling that climbing on giant slippery statues wasn't on a list of suggested park recreation.

But he didn't answer. He kept trying to pull himself onto the rock and slipping back down because it was covered with ice patches. But neither common sense nor fear of broken bones was stopping Pete. Within a few minutes he was standing on the rock, beside the soldier, who was twice his size, pretending like they were having a conversation.

"Should I take your picture now?" I asked, but he shook his head, and then he started climbing again. This time up the *soldier*.

My heart raced. "Pete, stop. This is crazy. You're going to get hurt!"

Why had I come with this nutty redhead? Ma would call Pete crazy like an outhouse rat. If he slipped, he'd hit the rock, or worse, fall way down to the ground. We hadn't seen a single person in the park to get help. I hardly knew Pete, and I might have to do CPR on him. I didn't even *know* CPR!

Pete waved his hand at me. "Quit worrying. Just take the picture when I say 'Cheese.'"

Now he was halfway to the top, resting his sneaker on the soldier's elbow, and pulling hard to get up higher. The wind kept blowing snow flecks down from the evergreen branches onto Pete's head. His face grimaced and his eyes strained like he was a gladiator.

"Be careful!" I shouted.

Then there he was on top, his legs straddling the soldier's head, wobbling and beaming like he'd just scaled Mount Everest. "Cheese!"

Click. I took the picture, and he lowered himself quickly off the soldier, down to the rock, and then to the ground, like it was easy doing. Like he'd been climbing on a little tyke's jungle gym. Like he was an average seventh grader with ordinary, everyday hobbies.

On the ride back, Pete gushed with excitement. "I can't wait to develop this roll at Photography Club. I'm calling that last picture 'Standing on the Shoulders of Giants.' Maybe it will get picked for the school magazine. How lucky was I to be there today!"

"You're lucky you didn't end up with a concussion," I said, but I smiled, thinking of his Mount Everest grin when I took the picture.

As we neared the downtown shops, Pete asked me what kind of business my mother was opening. I told him about the ice cream shop.

"Ice cream whenever you want, wow! Mind if I become your new best friend?"

We turned back on Broadway, and I told him to drop me off near the diner. I had enough money to bring soup back for Jordan to help fight his cold.

"You know what, Tess? If it wasn't for you, I never would have gone to Central Park today and taken that picture. I told you, I'm the luckiest kid in Schenectady!"

Then he waved and rode away, toward the trailers.

For the rest of my walk, I couldn't stop thinking about Pete. How he talked up Schenectady like it was a first-rate place. He never once tried to hide that he lived in a trailer, or that he got stuff from the dump. He called himself the luckiest kid in the city, and the thing was, he believed it.

I thought about how I couldn't even bring myself to get excited about Ma's ice cream shop. How I'd turned up my nose at the surrounding neighborhood. And how I'd never used the word *lucky* to describe moving into Mohawk Valley Village, where we *had* running water and friendly neighbors.

Maybe Pete was the one taking photos this morning, but he'd opened my eyes to a different way of looking at things too.

Chapter 14

It was close to one o'clock in the afternoon when I got back. Ma was holding the door open as two deliverymen carried in a long cardboard box.

"You had me worried. I thought you got lost," Ma said, and I explained how I met up with Pete.

The TV was blasting from the storage room, so I knew where Jordan was.

After the deliverymen left, Ma grabbed an X-Acto knife

and opened the box. "I've been waiting for this baby to arrive," she said.

I stared at what looked like an ordinary chalkboard. "What's it for?"

"Our menu board. Where we'll post one-of-a-kind, to-die-for ice cream specials in big, bold letters, just like the good book suggests."

"What are these one-of-a-kind specials?"

Ma's face lit up. "Glad you asked. For starters we've got the Yankee Doodle Dandy—two scoops of strawberry ice cream topped with blueberry sauce, covered with red, white, and blue sprinkles, and slathered with whipped cream. That should sell big with upstate conservatives—and liberals love it too!"

That did sound tasty. "What else?"

"Next up: the 'I Loved Him Tender' Banana Royal. Fit for the King himself."

I rolled my eyes. Why can't Ma keep her Elvis obsession to herself?

"That packs a whole pint of vanilla ice cream between Nilla wafers, nuts, and banana chunks—thick and creamy, the way the King loved his pudding."

"Ma!"

"Shore 'nuff, you know I loved that boy from Memphis," she said, clasping both hands to her chest and exaggerating her Texas drawl.

Ma listed off more wacky specials that had me giggling. And then she announced one would be R-rated, adults only. My eyebrows jumped up, eager to hear about *that*.

"I call it 'Having a Bad Day' Brazilian Coffee Malt, and what grown-ups haven't had bad days?"

"What's in it?"

Ma's voice dropped to a whisper. "One cup of Brazilian coffee, three scoops of specky vanilla, soda water, shaved ice, and a bonus ingredient that's strictly between me and the person having the bad day."

Bang! Bang! Machine-gun sounds from the storage room startled me. Yesterday I'd found a note in Jordan's backpack from his teacher, encouraging more signing at home, more reading, and less TV.

I pointed back toward the storage room. "I think you should take the TV out of there. Jordan will never get better at signing if all he does is veg out."

"Aw, every kid loves TV, Tess. Even you got hooked on *Project Runway*." She leaned against the dipping cabinet. "Besides, it keeps Jordan from getting in trouble around here."

I didn't agree. But I knew I wouldn't change Ma's mind, so I didn't try. I grabbed the drill and climbed up the stepladder to get started on the installation.

The metal brackets I'd bought felt more secure than the plastic ones. The left one mounted quickly, so I moved the ladder to the other side of the window. But first I took off my sweatshirt. The shop had an old radiator heater, and no matter how many times Ma tried to lower the temperature, it felt hot.

When I finally got the curtains up, Ma dragged a small dining table and two wooden chairs over and centered them underneath the window. "This place looks straight out of a

Norman Rockwell painting," she said, clapping. "Can't you see starry-eyed lovers slurping their shakes with those frilly curtains framing the picture?"

I gazed at the window and grinned. Not bad. Not bad at all.

I hadn't even unplugged my drill before Ma handed me a paintbrush. "Okay, Artsy Annie. Now that you dolled up the windows, how 'bout dressing up the walls with ice cream art?"

Ice cream art? Now that sounded right up my alley. "Where?" I asked, looking around at the wallpapering.

"A spot guaranteed to get traffic, the bathrooms," she answered, pointing toward the back.

"Bathrooms are bathrooms. Can't we leave them be?" I asked.

"Where's your selling spirit? We leave *nothin'* be. I want a sundae on the men's room door—covered with nuts; Lord knows men in my life have made me nuts—and a milk shake on the ladies' room door. Inside, you design whatever floats your boat, as long as it sends what the *Inside Scoop* calls a subliminal message."

"What's the message?"

"Buy more ice cream!"

I looked over at Ma, amazed at the way her mind worked. How had she managed to sucker me into doing all this when I voted "heck, no" on the business?

Yet this *was* an artistic challenge. The narrow space in the bathrooms above the hand dryers would be perfect for painting a slender ice cream soda glass with two straws sticking out.

136

And near the ceiling, I could stencil a wraparound border of kids holding hands and licking ice cream cones. Wait . . . make that *cartoon animals* smiling and eating ice cream! Giraffes, kangaroos, tigers, even turtles. Customers might like that even better. I knew Jordan would!

"I'll start with the doors. Just keep Jordan's little hands away for a while," I told Ma.

"Will do. You think you'll finish by later this afternoon?" Ma asked.

"Not a chance. You can't rush art," I said. If I was signing my name to this creation, it would be something noteworthy. *That* couldn't be rushed.

"All right, you just bought yourself some extra time. After all, you're no two-bit artist. You're the Venus de Milo of Schenectady."

"That's a statue with missing arms! And I'm *not* from Schenectady." I had to laugh. Ma was *serious*.

"Whatever. She's an original, just like you," Ma said, offering me a sip of her Dr Pepper, which just so happens to be my favorite pop too.

I walked back to the storage room to get more paper towels. My mind was bubbling with ideas. I would add an octopus to this parade of animals eating ice cream—kids would love how it could hold eight cones. And I was considering painting catchy quotes below the animals, like "We're Wild for Ice Cream!" and "Dessert Brings Out the Beast in Me!" It didn't get more subliminal than that.

A cold draft from the storage room caught my attention.

The back door was open again, and a juice box lay in a purple puddle. A cartoon blasted from the TV, but Jordan wasn't here. Where was he? I dropped my paintbrush by the slop sink and looked outside.

"Jordan!" I shouted, as if yelling did any good. The wind whipped through the alley, and I smelled pizza, but I saw no one. My hands and legs started shaking, partly from the damp cold, and then I heard a screechy noise. A garbage truck was backing up toward the giant Dumpster. Suddenly a yellow flash caught my eye. Jordan! He was standing on a chair up against the garbage bin, perched on tiptoes, trying to pull himself up to look in.

I rushed over, grabbed his waist, and yanked him down. I couldn't recall the sign for *dangerous*, but I looked straight at him and mouthed the word as clearly as I could, shivering.

He jumped, startled. "Want big box," he signed, jerking back toward the Dumpster.

"You could fall in!" I grabbed his cold hand and pulled him away, just as the garbage truck stopped in front of us and the driver gave me a dirty look.

"No going near garbage. You almost got hurt!" I glared with wicked eyes.

"Want big box for . . . for . . . Want box! Want box!" Jordan signed, furiously forming his hands in a box shape. He was getting frustrated because he didn't know the sign for whatever he was trying to tell me. I grabbed his wrist and pulled him along. All the while he yanked back like a puppy resisting a leash.

Inside, he bawled with a snotty, runny nose. "Meanie Tess!" his fingers roared.

But I wasn't playing the sympathetic sis. I left him in the storage room, tossing sponges against the supply boxes. I walked out to the counter, where Ma was scrubbing a metal topping dispenser, and told her what happened. "You gotta punish him. And get that back door fixed!" My hands were still trembling, even if it was a hundred degrees in here.

As I spoke, Jordan came running out.

"Jordan Dobson, no running off like that," Ma signed in her pidgin sign. Her *run* was so wrong, it looked like she was shooting an arrow from her chest. She turned to me. "I'll call the building manager. Between that dad-blasted door, the rusty pipes, and the broken radiator, this place is giving me hot flashes—and I'm not in menopause."

Now *my* face felt hot. "Aren't you going to let Jordan have it? At least take away his TV privileges?"

Ma looked at me calmly, like she'd just woken up. "Who's got the ID card that says parent, you or me? He got a good fright. It won't happen again."

I wanted to stomp my foot, make Ma understand this *was* a big deal. Part of the problem here was that Jordan and Ma couldn't even understand each other.

But Ma wasn't seeing it that way. Not one bit.

"This makes no sense," I mumbled. I grabbed the paints and brushes and walked away.

For the rest of the afternoon I painted in the men's room and stayed clear of my mother and my brother. Jordan kept squealing and tossing his plastic animals at the wall near the door of the men's room, but I ignored him—except for when he almost spilled the water I was using to wash my brushes. Then I had my own mini meltdown when I smudged the brown hot-fudge paint and had to sponge down the picture and start again.

Later in the afternoon I heard a whirl coming from the front counter. Then Jordan came over and handed me a milk shake with a cherry plopped on top of a dab of whipped cream.

"For you. Yummy," he signed, rubbing his belly.

I took a sip. Wow. That was *creamy* vanilla.

Ma appeared from behind the counter, her hair pulled back in a hairnet. "This place did feel empty without ice cream, so I got some from the grocery store. It's just enough to test the equipment—*our* product will be far superior, of course. You're sampling a Schenectady Snow Shake—thick with whiteout conditions, like the blizzards we get here. I added heavy cream and a teaspoon of pure vanilla extract."

I gave her a thumbs-up and kept slurping. The only improvement I'd make would be a scoop of chocolate along with the vanilla ice cream, and a handful of mini marshmallows and almonds. A Rocky Road milk shake.

Ma walked over and sat in the dining area and put her feet up. She was sipping a shake, too. "You're right about the back door being trouble. And that building manager moves slower than a beetle dipped in molasses. I'm going to install a dead bolt."

I was glad to hear it. Once in a while Ma *can* be reasonable.

"So you're going to name *every* ice cream special?" I asked, glancing at the menu board.

"You bet your jim-dandy. The *Inside Scoop* says you have to give your customers a razzle-dazzle experience. Otherwise, folks might as well head to the supermarket for whatever's on sale. We're naming specials after movie stars, Schenectady attractions, friends, and whatever else sells. Guess what ice cream magic I dreamed up this afternoon?"

"I give up."

"The 'Ain't No Mountain High Enough' Mocha-Fudge Frappe. In honor of Winnie."

"I like that!" I said, laughing.

"And how 'bout the 'Jordan Peanut Butter Party in a Cup'? Three scoops of peanut butter ice cream ladled with peanut butter sauce, whipped cream, and a cup of chopped peanuts dumped on top. Definitely not for the peanut-allergy crowd."

I couldn't help but wonder, *What about me?* I'd made the curtains. And I was deep into making ice cream art. Never mind the hundreds of hours of babysitting I'd logged in for the boss's son. *Where's my namesake?* But I didn't ask. If I did, Ma might think I had fully joined her ice cream brigade—and I hadn't.

Then I thought of Pete, and how he had spoken about his dad—happily, not at all embarrassed—and I smiled. A smile didn't cost much.

About the same moment, Jordan picked up my brushes, stuck them in his ears, and started hopping and scratching his armpits like a monkey.

A laugh popped out of my mouth. I made the Y hand, pulled it toward my face, and twisted it back and forth. "Silly."

"You should name it the 'Jordan's Driving Tess Nuts' Special," I said to Ma, taking the brushes back.

I sat down and looked around. Ma had leaned the empty chalkboard box beside the window, and Jordan was eyeing it. So I took his hand, and in that instant, I forgave him. What's that saying? "Curiosity killed the cat"? It's also what keeps Jordan going, even when he can't let us know what's on his mind.

"Follow me," I signed, leading him to the box. I cut the box in two pieces, balanced it on the floor like a tent, and placed a towel underneath it. "Cowboy Jordan's tent," I signed and spoke, deep like the western-movie voices I heard through the apartment wall last night. I gestured like I was riding a horse.

"Playing western comes natural for me," Ma said, tugging her fudge-streaked cleaning rag into her shirt like a bandanna and walking bowlegged with her thumbs tucked into her pockets like gun holsters. "I grew up on the OK Corral."

Within minutes we transformed A Cherry on Top into the Wild West, with three gun-slinging cowboys having a showdown with a pack of invisible, good-for-nothin' outlaws who were trying to make off with a Schenectady Snow Shake.

"Yee-haw! Go get 'em, Sheriff Dobson!" Ma shouted as Jordan took off in pursuit of the bandits.

Jordan rode furiously in and out between dining tables, then behind the ice cream counter before lassoing the bad guys. All the while Ma and I foot-stomp-cheered back at camp in front of the tent. "The sight of that brave cowboy makes my Texan-born-and-bred bones proud," Ma called, with her twang cranked up two hundred percent.

Minutes later Sheriff Jordan crawled back into the tent triumphantly with a six-foot grin spread under his milk-shake mustache. His fingers signed faster than a speeding bullet: "I caught the bad guys!"

Chapter 15

Select reputable suppliers who won't skimp on quality. You want folks to scream *for* ice cream—not at the taste. *—The Inside Scoop*

The cold luck of the Irish, that's what they called the nor'-easter that hit on March 17 and dumped eighteen inches of snow. Nearby, the city of Albany canceled its Saint Patrick's Day parade. School was closed, and crocuses ready to bloom got trapped under monster snow mounds.

The wintry wallop made me homesick for mild spring days back in San Antonio, especially after I got a letter from my little friend Juanita. In her purple smudgy handwriting, she wrote how she and her grandfather were already turning the soil in the garden. "Guess what? We've added a new vegetable this year: the tomatillo. It looks like a little green tomato, and my grandma says it makes a great sauce."

I didn't miss my old school, but I missed the redbud trees with their blooms bursting everywhere. I missed riding my scooter out front with Juanita and eating sopapillas on her front stoop. Come springtime, her *abuelita* always made those crispy pastry pillows and drizzled them with honey so sweet and sticky that we'd have to lick our fingers clean like cats.

But there was no time to get homesick. School here in Schenectady was copying the weather and coming at me like a blizzard. I had a Cell-ebration science lab to finish, a "*¡Vamos comer!*" restaurant poster to design for Spanish, and an English project due that involved writing ten different kinds of poems, including one called an American cinquain, which took five lines only and was created by a poet from upstate New York named Miss Crapsey. (That got the whole class giggling.) On top of all that, Mr. Win had noticed the lanyard key chain I made dangling from my jeans, and he'd asked if I would design the shirts for Peer Mediation Club. Now doing *that* kind of peer-mediation work was appealing. Only problem: he needed it soon.

Meanwhile, Ma was still charging ahead for the April 15 Grand Opening. In an effort to be part of the business neighborhood, she'd hosted a "Howdy, Partner" social at the shop and invited all the nearby retailers, including from the street's bakery, pizzeria, shoe-repair shop, dry cleaners, and insurance brokerage. "Some of these folks haven't turned a profit since before there was an Internet," she told me afterward. She'd gotten an earful about their soap-opera lives and business struggles.

Ma wasn't worried that the late-in-the-season snowfall would hurt business. "I bet this weather gets folks stir-crazy," she said. "A Cherry on Top will give 'em a good reason to pull on their boots, saddle up their horses, and head downtown."

I told her that business would do better if she toned down her Texas twang, but she had no intention of doing that.

"Yankees like us Longhorns. They know we're not quitters. Which is why I looked high and low to find a deluxe, custom-made Lone Star flag. I just ordered it, and it's going to hang proudly by the cash register. Well worth the two hundred bucks it set me back."

"Two hundred bucks?"

Ma rested her hand on her waist. "It's a collector's item," she said.

Hearing about that pricey flag got me worrying. And not just because a Lone Star flag didn't fit with a cozy café theme. What else was Ma blowing money on that I didn't know about? And did this spending spree mean that Shooting Stars was back? Ma was regularly pulling all-nighters too. "Start-up demands" was her excuse for not sleeping. Marketing ideas popped from her mouth randomly like Mexican jumping beans, and she couldn't sit still, not long enough to finish a Dr Pepper. Nobody could keep this pace up forever, and it was starting to show. When Jordan had a fit, Ma would lose patience quickly. Or when she'd drop or lose something, cusswords would fly.

I tried to get Ma to rest more and to ease up on the shopping sprees. "You'll run out of gas and *we'll* run out of money," I said. But she always quoted that annoying *Inside Scoop*— "You gotta spend money to make money."

As the Grand Opening got closer, Ma put my work gears in overdrive too. She was so pleased with how the animal parade turned out in the bathroom that she asked me to paint paw prints on the shop floor leading to the serving counter, representing the four-footed critters that lived in the nearby Adirondack Mountains. I painted moose, deer, bear, raccoon, possum, fox, woodchuck, and chipmunk tracks (that took a size 00 miniature brush). I even painted a humongous hairy print next to the trash can because I read on a Web site that Bigfoot had once been spotted in the Hudson Valley some years ago. And as a finishing touch, Ma assembled a motorized beaver riding a unicycle on a tightrope across the dining-area ceiling since that was New York State's official animal.

And as if all those bells and whistles weren't enough, Ma bought a karaoke machine to get the teens excited. And then she spotted an old Wurlitzer jukebox for sale in the newspaper. "Music makes people merry, and merry people spend money," she said, announcing we'd be buying that vintage beauty too.

The trip to get the jukebox took two hours since the owner lived in Erieville, a farm town that could easily fit right into the Texas Hill Country. Ma gave the potbellied owner four one-hundred-dollar bills for that dusty hunk of junk, which was parked in a muddy driveway next to a stinky compost pile.

We had to lug it ourselves to our car without help from the guy, who kept chewing on a toothpick and counting his money. And let me tell you, that jukebox weighed a ton.

The next morning we plugged it in and discovered it played old-fashioned records, not CDs, and it played them at warped slow speed. So Ma spent a day calling around for a jukebox repair technician. There was only one such guy in all of upstate New York. He looked older than the jukebox, and he smoked cigars the whole time he did the repair. But he got it working again—and Ma got a whopping bill for a hundred and fifty dollars. Plus we had to buy an air purifier to get the smoke stench out of the shop.

Watching Ma dole out all that money, I worried about what was left in the Ditch Fund. I even thought about knitting scarves and crocheting potholders to sell to seniors in the apartment lobby, just to bring in some cash—but what with homework, peer mediation, Operation Homebound, and watching Jordan, I didn't have enough time to *do* crafts. And when I finally got Jordan down to sleep at night, I sewed patches for Winnie's piano-bench cushion.

Operation Homebound took Chief and me longer than usual on Wednesday. The flu was going around Building One, so we had twice as many drugstore packages to deliver. And word was someone took a fall in the Assisted Living building, because EMT vehicles blocked the front and the aides wouldn't let us in right away with our cart.

But even with delays, Chief and I got the mission accomplished.

"We're a lean, mean, efficient team," he told me when we finished. Then he gave me my "chow pay" for the week: a Freihofer's marble pound cake.

"Pound cake with ice cream is a family favorite!" I called, waving goodbye as I skipped toward Building One to get my brother.

No one answered when I knocked on Winnie's door, so I took the elevator up to our apartment.

Inside, Jordan was stretched out on the futon looking pale, with Winnie standing beside him.

"What's wrong?" I asked and signed.

Winnie crossed her arms over her sweater and gestured toward Jordan. "Diagnosis: chicken pox."

"Where?" I didn't see any red spots on his face. But then he pushed his shirt up. His belly had four red button-like mounds, each with a skin blister in the middle.

"Give it twenty-four hours and your brother will be covered in polka dots," Winnie said. "About then they'll get itchy too. Our job is to keep him from scratching."

"Does my ma know?"

She nodded. "I bumped into her in the elevator this morning after she picked Jordan up from the school nurse. Poor thing was beside herself, wondering how she would care for your brother and handle her business. And it didn't help that Jordan was fussing up a storm."

I looked down at Jordan with a sad face, then drew a circle with an S hand on my chest. "Sorry."

But Winnie told me not to fret. "Us old nurses never retire, we just walk the floor for our friends. I'll care for Jordan and help out with dinners here for a while so your ma can tend to her business and you can keep up your schoolwork."

Hearing her words, I slyly reached over to the basket behind the sewing machine and covered up my quilting materials. No sense spoiling her surprise.

I glanced at Jordan. He was looking at photos of tropical fish from a photo album of Winnie's. I couldn't remember the last time he seemed so captured by anything besides cartoons.

I exaggerated sniffing and signed to Jordan, "What's that good smell?"

He grinned and pointed to Winnie.

"I heard a rumor that the Dobson kids love macaroni and cheese, so I whipped up some Winnie Mac. Along with ham, mixed veggies, and fruit cocktail."

"And I brought dessert!" I added, holding up the pound cake.

I sat beside Jordan on the futon. He was rubbing his palm against the spots on his belly.

I shook my head, snapped my fingers, and clawed at the air. "No scratching," I signed.

After dinner, Winnie stacked the plates in the sink, but I stopped her when I heard her getting flustered about the lousy sinks around here that always back up.

"Go on. I'll finish this. You must've skipped your nap today," I said, grinning.

She wiped her forehead with a napkin. "Guess I am getting a little cranky. But I'm not leaving yet. I'll park my old bones on this stool and let you do the dishes while you give me a lesson."

"A lesson on *what?*"

"Sign language. If I'm going to be caring for Jordan, we need to understand each other. I took a trip to Paris ten years ago. For the month before I left, I memorized ten French words every day. That sure helped when I had to read menus and get directions. How about you teach me ten new signs a day? Ten basic signs."

I showed Winnie *sleep, school, play, bathroom, mom, sister, happy, sad, thirsty,* and *hungry.* She got just about all of them right too—except *bathroom.* That one confused her, and I told her it gave Ma trouble too.

I shaped her hand into the letter T with her palm facing out, then shook it side to side a couple of times.

She tried again, and this time *bathroom* looked right.

Then we practiced the signs for *Tess, Ma, Delilah,* and *Jordan.* "Name signs are picked by the person they describe," I explained. "You have to capture what makes you unique. What do you want yours to be, Winnie?"

She paused. "Hmm, that's a tough one. I'm not sure."

She asked me to show her *nurse, singer,* and *super senior,* but none satisfied her. Then I signed *piano player* and *gourmet cook,* but she passed on those too.

"It's tough to capture my plus-sized personality in a word or two," she said, laughing.

It was Jordan who finally gave Winnie an idea. As he ate his pound cake and ice cream, he pointed his fork to Winnie's left hand and giggled.

"Snake!" he signed, waving a bent V hand from his mouth, still giggling as he touched the ring on her pinkie. It was silver, shaped like a snake with gold-studded eyes and a sparkly red tongue.

Winnie looked down at her ring and smiled. "Elston gave me this for my birthday when he was in the second grade. Hard to believe it was forty years ago," she said, dreamy-eyed. "It might've come from a gumball machine for all I know, but it sure made me feel special. No other mom in the neighborhood had one." Then she paused and turned to Jordan and spoke very slowly. "Show me *snake* again," she said, and he read her lips.

When he did, she asked me to sign the letter W.

Then she finger-spelled W and signed *snake*, and that became *Winnie*.

Chapter 16

Man does not live on ice cream alone. Stock the shelves with cookies, candy, and other sweet-tooth satisfiers. Secondary products are first-rate for your bottom line. —*The Inside Scoop*

Sweet surprises blew in the late March wind. I got a perfect score on my Cell-ebration lab and an A on my poetry project! The teacher even scribbled "Very moving!" near the cinquain I called "Standing on the Shoulders of Giants." (And Pete was flattered when he discovered I wrote a poem about our outing.)

One afternoon I showed up at Winnie's apartment after school to pick up Jordan and discovered a side of my brother that I'd never seen.

Winnie was belting out her Motown tunes at the piano, and Catherine was sitting in her wheelchair choreographing a dancer—*Jordan*! He was standing on the coffee table, wearing sunglasses and a black felt hat and shaking his body like a dog coming out of a pond. A CD player blasted music from underneath the coffee table.

"Don't you just love the Four Tops?" Catherine said, smiling. Rudy the cat was stretched out on the rug, all whiskers and grins, as if he was a true Motown fan too.

"Next one goes out to Tess," Winnie shouted and signed as a new song began.

"Ooooh, Sugar Pie, Honey Bunch. You know that I love you," Winnie sang along with the Four Tops, and Jordan signed with his head bobbing.

Meanwhile, Catherine stuck her arm up to demonstrate the next move, and Jordan twirled around.

"Legs. Use legs!" Catherine signed, and I was impressed that she finger-spelled *legs* properly.

Jordan's timing was good. *Really* good. He shook his leg like a tambourine with each *ooooh*. He clapped his hands to the beat. And every time Winnie sang the chorus, he tipped his hat and jiggled his shoulders. Even his tongue wagged to the rhythm.

I couldn't believe it. How could Jordan be dancing? He couldn't hear!

But he was dancing. And then it hit me fast, like the drumbeat. Jordan *felt* the music from his sneakers, through the wooden table. That was why Winnie put the CD player underneath. Just like how I thump the floor hard to get his attention when he's not facing me.

"Bravo!" I clapped. And I laughed. But I also felt guilty. All these years we could have cut loose together dancing, had I given Jordan the chance. I'd gotten on Ma for not signing enough, but I hadn't even thought about finding another way to help him enjoy music.

Jordan had come through the chicken pox without one scar thanks to Winnie, so Ma asked her to stay on as his regular afternoon babysitter, five days a week. I worried that Ma didn't have enough money to pay for babysitting, but when I asked, Winnie just said she was compensated more than adequately, thank you. And Winnie found out about a playgroup nearby for deaf kids. I got the feeling that she liked the company as much as Ma liked not having to run back and forth between the shop and the apartment so much.

Something was different about Jordan lately. Maybe it was the friends he was making at playgroup and all the new signs he was learning at school. Or maybe it was because life at the Mohawk Valley Village was improving. Chief had posted a DEAF CHILD PLAY AREA sign in the parking lot so Jordan could ride his bike, and he'd gotten a telecommunications device for the deaf installed in our apartment. The TDD looked like a tiny laptop computer, and it allowed Jordan to phone Ma at the shop whenever he wanted by typing messages across its screen and reading Ma's messages. Thanks to a relay service, the TDD helped him communicate with others too. Jordan even learned how to order takeout. One week we had pizza four times!

Whatever it was, FrankenJordan wasn't rearing his ugly head as much. And that was fine by me.

Another surprise waited for me at A Cherry on Top one cloudy, drizzly afternoon. I'd just come from my last "observational" peer-mediation session. This one involved Ellie (my meet-and-greeter) and another player from the girls' basketball team. They'd gotten into a shoving match on the basketball court. Kim and Gavin did the mediating, and it turned out the hidden agenda was a doozie. Way back in kindergarten Ellie had been a bed wetter, and the other girl had blabbed to the whole team about it in the locker room, embarrassing and infuriating Ellie. (Basic need: to be treated with respect.) Kim and Gavin looked like they'd been running sprints themselves by the time the mediation ended. Listening to that verbal dueling made my neck break out with blotches again. And I was scheduled to mediate at the next session.

When I walked into A Cherry on Top, Ma was leaning over the counter, pouring goopy chocolate on a marble slate with a big copper kettle beside her. "Howgozit with peer mediation?" she called.

"Intense. There sure are lots of people getting mad at each other." I poured lemonade from the mini fridge Ma had just bought and took a long sip. "What are you making?"

"Homemade fudge, aka a revenue booster that's gonna bring in gobs of money. Tourists always splurge on fudge."

"What tourists?" I asked. I doubted rusty old Schenectady was listed in a travel guide as a vacation destination.

"Tourists from NYC or across the Canadian border. 'If we make it, they will come.' That is, if we make it taste good."

"I don't get it," I said. "This is an ice cream shop. Shouldn't we stick with ice cream?"

"Customers want all sorts of treats, and that's not just me talking," she said as she banged the wooden spoon inside the kettle. "The *Inside Scoop* says so."

The problem with selling homemade fudge is that it has to be *homemade*. Both of the trial batches Ma made that afternoon came out terrible. One tasted sickly sweet, and the other, like stale oatmeal.

For hours on end she made batch after batch, adding more corn syrup, then less corn syrup, boiling it five minutes longer, then boiling it five minutes less, but it all looked like a gloppy mud cake—tasted that way too.

Eventually Ma started to *melt* down. First she let out a loud "Hell's bells!" and then she flung the spoon toward the sink but missed, splashing chocolate across the counter and against the wall.

"I feel like a chocolate train wreck. This is terrible, terrible, terrible! I can't afford to mess this fudge up—or this business," she moaned, slinking down against the counter and putting her head between her knees.

Her crying, and acting like this was a life-or-death matter, got me worried again. Was this the start of a crash?

I rinsed off the spatula. "Rome wasn't built in a day, right?

We'll figure this out with some time and practice. I'm taking over as official fudge maker."

Turned out that fudge making is kind of like doing a science lab. The secret is following the recipe directions *precisely*—Ma's style of guesstimating when she measured out ingredients didn't work. Using the very best unsweetened chocolate helps too, and the right tools. When our dollar-store candy thermometer cracked in the boiling mixture, I went out and bought an upgraded model that gave a more accurate reading.

Not that I mastered fudge making all by myself. My first batch didn't set, so I called the best troubleshooter I knew: Winnie. "Fudge isn't my expertise, but I'll refer you to a specialist," she said.

Talk about a coincidence. Catherine was born on Mackinac Island, Michigan—also known as the fudge capital of the United States—and she gave me *The Authentic Mackinac Island Fudge Cookbook*. After reading it, I realized my problem: the mixture needed to be spread more smoothly, and I had to allow more cooling time. And Catherine gave me a tip that explained our first day's disaster: "Make fudge when the sun shines. It doesn't set well when it's humid."

I have to admit I got caught up in fudge mania. I should've been spending every waking moment on homework, preparing for peer mediation, and sewing patchworks for Winnie's bench cushion. Instead, I was at A Cherry on Top, listening to Elvis on the jukebox and whipping up dozens of exotic varieties of fudge. White chocolate, peanut butter, cherry rippled, coffee and ginger, macadamia nut, Kahlúa—and my favorite, of course: Rocky Road. Ma was thrilled with all of them, giddy like a little kid as she watched me mix and pour each new creation. And every night I'd bring back samples for Jordan to taste. He always gave the peanut butter fudge five stars.

Then, after I'd created more fudge flavors than you could count in a minute, Ma reconsidered and decided to stick with three classics: chocolate, caramel, and peanut butter. "No sense in overwhelming customers," she said, biting into a freshly made piece. "Better to save the variety for the real stars of the show: the ice cream."

Ma made me wear an apron, plastic gloves, and a hairnet while I cooked.

The hairnet itched something awful, but she was a stickler about sanitation. "The Schenectady Health Department will be checking on us," she said. "And besides, right is right. Who wants hairy fudge? Good grief!"

On the first Friday afternoon in April, I was delirious from a marathon candy-making session. There I stood in my apron and hairnet, stirring the chocolate-butter-cream mixture over the heat to make yet another batch of fudge. Only I wasn't feeling like a cheery Food Channel chef. My clothes smelled like fudge, my fingernails were rimmed in fudge, and I had a callus on my thumb from gripping the wooden spoon. The last thing I wanted was to make *more* of this stuff. And to make things worse, the old radiator was running on overdrive again. The shop felt hot and steamy like a rain forest.

"One more batch and you get time off for good behavior," Ma said, rubbing my shoulder as I smoothed the mixture.

Then she pulled red dress heels from behind the counter, stuck them on her feet, and dabbed matching lipstick on.

"Where are you going?" I asked.

"Out to dinner," she said, slinging a purse over her shoulder.

"Without me? No fair."

"This is strictly business, Tess. The monthly meeting of the Schenectady Chamber of Commerce. Winnie's having Jordan for his first sleepover at her apartment, and I'll be back here for you by ten."

But I didn't want to stay at the shop alone at night. It was almost dark outside—and creepy. "That's too late. I'm tired. And it's so hot in here."

"I know, honey. That sorry excuse for a landlord says he can't fix the radiator until tomorrow. In the meantime, I'll crack a window open."

I looked around. The shelving unit behind the ice cream counter had to be assembled, the menu board still wasn't complete, and the windows needed washing. Plus we hadn't designed a flyer to circulate yet for the Grand Opening.

"There's so much to do, Ma, and we've got less than two weeks. Why waste time at some boring dinner?"

"You gotta schmooze to make a buck in Schenectady, Tess. If I give these folks some attention, they'll spread the word about A Cherry on Top. And Mayor Legato will be there. I'm going to ask him to do the honor of cutting the ribbon at our Grand Opening."

I frowned. "Why would he want to help us after what happened to his car?"

She nodded as she buttoned her jacket. "One hand washes the other in local politics. This shop is going to brighten Schenectady's business horizon. Believe you me, every politician's mouth drools for sweets *and* publicity."

Ma handed me a five-dollar bill and a check made out to the ice cream wholesaler. "After you finish this batch of fudge, get yourself supper next door at Bianco's Pizzeria. I was over earlier helping Mrs. Bianco wash her blinds, and I said you'd be by. But hurry back. The ice cream delivery is coming later and it's a costly frozen bundle. We have to make a killing when we open."

Ma started for the door, but then stopped, looked back, and smiled.

"What?" I asked, wiping fudge from my elbow.

"You, working so hard. This business. It's all good. We're out of the storm. Once that cash register starts ringing, it'll be sunny skies."

"Don't jinx yourself," I said, pointing the drippy spoon at her.

"That reminds me," Ma said as she plugged in the dipping cabinet's electric cord. "I better get this chilling before the ice cream arrives. And be sure you lock the door behind you later!"

Chapter 17

For optimal flavor, store ice cream at 0 to −25 degrees
Fahrenheit. —*The Inside Scoop*

An hour later I was back in A Cherry on Top, nibbling on pizza
crust, reading through the peer-mediation training folder, and
rehearsing lines like "Please explain what's been going on" and
"What would you like to see happen now?" in my best take-charge
voice when someone tapped on the door. It was a UPS guy with
a package. The deluxe Lone Star flag Ma ordered. Three
cheers for Texas.

A few minutes later, the ice cream wholesaler arrived with a full load of five-gallon tubs. I showed him the dipping cabinet, and he started filling it with the ice cream.

"Phew. Is this working?" he called, banging his hand inside the case. Sweat glistened on his ruddy face.

"Think so," I said. "It just got turned on."

He swiped his forehead. "Well, it's not cold yet. And it feels like the Sahara Desert in here."

He went back to his truck for two more loads, and I gave him Ma's check.

"How much ice cream is this altogether?" I asked, looking at the jam-packed dipping cabinet.

"Twenty-eight tubs: twenty-one ice cream, four frozen yogurt, and three sherbet. Don't you have an extra freezer in the back?"

I shook my head. Ma had bought plenty of overpriced gizmos, gadgets, supplies, and decorations, but not an extra freezer.

After he left, I stuck my hand in the dipping cabinet. Yikes. It wasn't cool at all. The thermometer hanging in the corner read sixty-six degrees. I touched the side of the mint chocolate chip. Rock hard—good.

I shut the glass top quickly to keep the heat out. Then I put my peer-mediation folder away. I started embroidering another patch for Winnie's bench cushion, a tribute to her favorite Motown music group, Gladys Knight and the Pips. Cross-stitching four singers on a six-inch square was hard enough, but fitting three Afros was *really* tricky. I planned on presenting Winnie with the cushion for her birthday in June. Summer might seem like a long time away to most people, but not quilters. I had sixteen customized patches to go, and each took a long time to make.

Embroidering in a steamy room made me sleepy. I took a break, stretched my legs, and then started writing the ice cream flavor label cards using my nice calligraphy pen. Twenty minutes later I opened the dipping cabinet to put the label cards in place, but the temperature hadn't dropped; it went *up* another degree! The shop *did* feel like the desert. How long would the ice cream stay frozen before the freezer kicked in? I opened the top of the mint chocolate chip tub. It wasn't rock hard anymore.

An hour later, Ma still wasn't back. I touched the strawberry tub, afraid to open it and discover a pink puddle. Luckily, it was still cool—but not cold. And instead of having a thin layer of ice on the outside, it had tiny water beads.

I thought about carrying the ice cream outside. The April night air was downright cold, but then I remembered Ma warning me to keep the place locked up. Troublemakers walked the streets at night, and I didn't want them messing with our product.

Ice. I'll get ice.

I locked the shop and ran to Bianco's Pizzeria. They'd help.

Uh-oh. A CLOSED sign hung in the window. I walked two blocks in the creepy dark to a gas station with an ice machine. But I only had $1.75 change left from dinner, which bought just one bag of ice. I rushed back and dumped it over the ice cream.

Darn, it barely covered two tubs!

I found an old fan in the storage room. I dragged it out and propped it on a chair so it would blow right at the dipping cabinet.

But thirty minutes later the ice was melted and I felt a panic attack coming on. All the ice cream we'd just bought with the last of our money would be ruined. I had to do *something*. If only Ma had gotten around to getting a cell phone and I could call her.

I picked up the phone. "Chief, it's Tess. I need help."

Chief came limping into the shop with a husky old man wearing a Yankees cap. "Mr. Murray here is Albany's best retired refrigeration technician with a union card," he said, unzipping his parka. "We play poker together, and he's got a cool hand there too."

The best retired refrigeration technician with a union card wasn't into small talk. He didn't say hello, but he mumbled that he needed the freezer on its side. So Chief and I unloaded the ice cream quickly, like nurses preparing a patient for emergency surgery.

Working on his knees, Mr. Murray tightened and loosened bolts, pulled apart coils, and blew dust off the metal underbelly. But half an hour later, he dropped his wrench and stood up, shaking his head. "Looks like your mother needs a new freezer. The compressor's dead as a turkey on Thanksgiving."

"Do they cost a lot?" I asked.

"Sure do, but you got no choice." He grabbed a napkin and scribbled down the name of a secondhand-restaurant-equipment supplier.

Chief glanced at the wall clock. Nine-thirty-five. "Where's your mother?"

"At a meeting. She'll be back soon."

He pointed at the ice cream tubs on the floor, already sitting in puddles. "Being so hot in here, this stuff's melting fast. You can't wait. How about we load the ice cream into my truck and drive over to Thrifty King? They'll probably let you store it in their walk-in freezer until your mother figures something out."

But Ma didn't like Thrifty King. Jordan had accidentally dropped a plastic animal into the lobster tank, and the seafood-department manager had yelled at him, even after Ma explained that he was deaf. Ma had told the guy off and stormed out of the store, vowing never to return.

I remembered Ma's words. She'd be back by ten. "Thanks, Chief, but my ma's due back any minute."

"Well, don't wait too long. This ice cream won't last," Chief said, and he and Mr. Murray left.

Ten o'clock and no Ma.

Ten-thirty and no Ma.

Eleven o'clock. Still alone. *It's dark out with no one around. I'm sleepy, scared, and sweaty, babysitting lots of mushy ice cream.*

At eleven-thirty Ma skipped in the door. "Delilah did it again—the mayor said yes to the ribbon cutting!" she shouted, jingling the car keys in her hand proudly like she'd won Olympic gold.

I glared at Ma with a sour taste in my mouth and my eyes cold as the dipping cabinet should've been.

"Delilah did it, all right. And here's the twenty-eight tubs of melted ice cream to prove it."

Chapter 18

Expect setbacks.

—*The Inside Scoop*

When the sour taste finally went away, I felt sorry for Ma. Sure, she should've checked to make sure the freezer worked ahead of time, but you can't foresee every single thing that can go wrong.

The saddest sound that night was the *click-click* of her red heels on the blacktop alley as we carried all that soupy ice cream out and tossed it in the Dumpster. Ma used to be a heavy smoker, two packs a day. She told me she started as a teen, alongside the ranch hands who worked for her parents, and she didn't stop until ten years later, when she got pregnant with me. Quitting was the hardest thing she ever did. "I'd have taken a root canal over going without a cigarette any day of the week," she said.

Years back, on the night Pop stormed out for good with all his stuff, I remember Ma sitting on the front stoop holding a toothpick between her lips. Puffing hard, like it was a cigarette.

After midnight, when we'd tossed the last of the ice cream, Ma started pretend smoking again—only this time, on a straw.

"Are we buying a new dipping cabinet today?" I asked at breakfast the next morning.

"Can't," Ma said as she scooped grits and corned-beef hash on my plate. Mascara clumped under her eyelids.

Jordan was still at Winnie's sleepover. I'd slept in, though I'd woken during the night and noticed the kitchen light on. Ma's calculator and working papers were scattered beside me on the counter.

I sprinkled Tapatío sauce on my hash. "Why not?"

"We're broke," she said, slamming the refrigerator door shut.

Broke? A told-you-so chorus played in my head. And flashbacks to those pricey banana-split ceramic napkin holders that Ma bought for each dining table. The jukebox. The speakers, menu board, and silk-screened aprons, not to mention the customized sundae dishes. How could she have blown all that cash and not saved for important stuff?

Something came to me then, something I'd read in the peer-mediation training manual: "Avoid accusing you-statements when you're having a disagreement. That approach makes people feel threatened."

"We *have* to get a dipping cabinet, Ma. An ice cream shop sells ice cream, and ice cream must be frozen!" I pleaded.

My stomach tightened. I pictured vultures swooping over A Cherry on Top, clutching eviction notices in their talons.

"I know, I know," Ma answered with despair clipped to her words. "But you gotta *have* money to *make* money, and we plumb ran out."

"What about the *Inside Scoop*? What's it say to do when you run out of money?"

"Can't find that section. Look, we've had more expenses than I expected. Who knew that the jukebox was broken, or that business insurance would be so expensive in New York State? And now we have to buy more ice cream *and* a dipping cabinet. Dawgonnit, I still gotta pay this month's store lease—never mind the apartment rent." Ma banged her fist down on the calculator.

Why had I let her draw me into her fool's plan? After all our work, the only thing opening would be the door, to force us out—make that two doors, one on State Street, the other here at Mohawk Valley Village.

I pushed my plate away, my breakfast barely touched. My face felt warm, even though the wind blew cold through the drafty window.

Tart words started flying out like thumbtacks.

"So I guess it's time to pack up again, huh, Ma? Same old, same old?"

"Aw, stop your picking. I'll figure something out." Ma glanced down at the frayed copy of the *Inside Scoop* on the counter, her messy gray-and-black hair flopping forward.

I went out to the living room, sat on the futon, and picked up my cushion patch and embroidery. My fingers trembled as I cross-stitched a microphone in Gladys Knight's hand. Everything felt wrong.

Ma began washing pots in the kitchen. The scratch-scratching of steel wool was all I could hear for a while. But then the scrubbing stopped and she started *singing*.

First it was a country tune. Then one of Winnie's Motown hits. Then on to that Elvis song about blue suede shoes. Ma kept singing and raising her off-key voice.

I tried to stay focused on my needlework, even though I suspected that singing meant *something*.

Sure enough, she marched into the living room, wearing a big grin and a dishtowel tucked in at her waist.

"I got a simple solution to a simple problem. Banks give money out, right? I'm going to visit a bank and get me a loan."

That didn't sound like much of a solution to me. I knew Ma's credit report read like the *Titanic*, especially after the last two years of Shooting Stars spending sprees. Any bank would find out about her evictions, bounced checks, and canceled credit cards.

"What about all our money problems in San Antonio?"

"Like you keep telling me, this ain't Texas. And we only need a small bundle to hold us over until the shop opens. Then we'll have enough cash to burn a wet elephant."

●●●●●

I got another hundred on a math test on Monday, and my teacher said he was going to recommend that I move up to advanced math. I wanted to tell Ma, but our money dilemma was weighing heavy on my mind.

I took the school bus downtown, got off at Lafayette and State streets, and walked into the ice cream shop, only to hear sobbing from the storage room. I stopped before reaching the back so Ma wouldn't see me.

She was leaning over the sink, dabbing a tissue to her nose and talking out loud to herself. "How come every time I lower my bucket into life's well—*snap!*—the dawgone rope breaks! My own daughter must think I'm the sorriest person alive. I'm not fit to mother the rats I see out back in the alley."

I froze. How bad were things now? And *what* rats?

Ma kept sniffling and rambling. "I wish I could crawl under a rock and sleep this off. Why does my life *always* feel harder than yesterday's cornbread?"

Not now, Ma, I thought. *Don't lose it. I can't handle carrying you and caring for Jordan again. This isn't fair. Why can't I be the moody middle schooler having hissy fits and meltdowns?*

A tiny voice in my head told me what to do next. *Run, Tess. Slip away. You need to chill.* This was too much to take after school and practice for peer mediation.

I tiptoed back to the shop entrance and left.

I walked down State Street over to Broadway, bought myself a Dr Pepper at the deli, and kept going, past the hardware store. The cool spring air cleared my head, and the sweet soda moistened my dry throat. I glanced over at the trailers where Pete lived, and wondered which one was his. Maybe he was nearby, riding his tandem bike and taking pictures. Or maybe he was over at the dump with his dad, sorting through a fresh delivery, as he called it. Yuck—not my idea of entertainment. But at least they were together.

That made me think of Pop.

It was nearly five o'clock, close to quitting time. I imagined him punching his card and unstrapping his tool belt. "Later, Jake," one of his big buddies in work boots would call, and Pop would touch his index finger to his ear and motion toward the guy. Then he'd jump into the Dodge Ram and head home.

With no wife or whining kids to pester him and nothing to stand in his way, he'd probably shower, splash on his Aqua Velva, and gun the truck on over to whatever watering hole he spent his nights in near Galveston.

I kicked an empty water bottle on the sidewalk. *Who cares?* He was missing out on seeing Jordan and me grow up. That *was* a big loss. *For sure, Ma makes plenty of mistakes, but Pop's the one who makes no sense. Beer always tastes the same, but with Jordan, well, every day has a new flavor.*

I turned around. Time to go back.

Ma was standing on a chair behind the counter, writing on the mounted menu board. The jukebox was playing "Hey, Good Lookin'," that whiny Hank Williams song Ma likes.

"Hiya, sweetie," she called. I could tell she'd washed her face, though her eyes were still red.

"Hey, Ma. What happened at the bank?"

Ma shook her head. "Mr. Moneybags turned me down. So much for that CUSTOMERS ALWAYS COME FIRST sign hanging over his desk. That fellow is so stingy he wouldn't pay the ransom even if his own mother was hog-tied."

Ma turned back to the menu board, and I let out a sigh. She heard me and whipped her head around.

"Aw, quit looking like a frog in a frying pan. I got a Plan B." She pointed to the menu board. "How do you like my ice cream specials so far?"

I glanced at Ma's scribbling.

A Cherry on Top Mucho Delishous Specials

"Mohawk River Runs Through It" Carmel Swirl
SmAlbany Strawbery Shake
"Troy's Gone Nutty" Taffy Sundae
Steel Magnolia Float

"They're making my stomach growl. Better check the spellings. And what's in a Steel Magnolia Float?"

"I dunno yet, but you know that's my favorite chick flick. I just love Dolly Parton. . . ."

I pointed to two large unopened boxes behind the counter. "What's in there?" We were sitting on the brink of bankruptcy and Ma had done *more* shopping?

"The cash register and the waffle-cone griddle finally shipped. But don't bat your eyelashes. I prepaid for them."

"What are we going to do about money, Ma—and the dipping cabinet? We're supposed to open next week!"

She hopped off the chair. "Stall, that's what. Delay the Grand Opening for a little while till I make some quick cash."

"How?" I asked, unable to hide my doubts.

"I'll only tell if you quit your worrywarting."

I crossed my arms. "Tell me."

Ma took a straw from the straw dispenser and tucked it between her lips. "I'm going to be a barmaid at Little Miss Muffet's on Eastern Parkway."

"What's a *barmaid?*"

"A waitress who serves booze. After being married to your father, I've got plenty of job experience."

"Doesn't that mean working late at night?"

"Probably from suppertime until one a.m., but only for a little while. Little Miss Muffet's is a hole-in-the-wall, mostly for the Union College students. Tips are good and the owner says he'll pay me off the books."

"For how long?"

"As long as it takes to make two thousand dollars."

Two thousand dollars is *a lot* of money. It made me think about doing well on my math test and how the teacher recommended me for the advanced class.

But I didn't tell Ma about that.

●●●●●

Dobson insomnia struck again that night. I got out of bed without stirring much so I wouldn't wake Jordan beside me, and I pulled a spiral notebook from my backpack.

With the night-light softly illuminating the page, I sat cross-legged on the floor and started writing Pop a letter. Didn't matter that I had no stamps or envelopes handy. I had something to say.

I formatted the letter like the script that peer mediators use in a session. I began with a greeting and told him a little about what was happening in my life. Then I got to what was (and wasn't) going on between him and me since we hadn't heard from him in two years. It's hard to conduct a peer mediation when you're both mediator and disputant—not to mention the other disputant not being present—but I tried my best to state the facts and my feelings using those empathetic I-statements. How at times I was doing his job. (Basic need: to play.) How Jordan and I missed being with him. (Basic need: to be loved.) Lastly, I closed with a few open-ended questions that gave him the chance to respond.

I tore the page out, placed it on the night table, and crawled back into bed. I was about to close my eyes and fade off to sleep when it hit me: Ma didn't even have Pop's address. After all that, I couldn't even mail the letter.

So what? I was glad I did it.

I wrote that letter for myself.

Chapter 19

The R in *retail* also stands for *resilience*.
—*The Inside Scoop*

I found a yellow slip of paper in our mailbox after school a week later.

RENT LATE. PAY IMMEDIATELY WITH $50 PENALTY OR BE SUBJECT TO EVICTION.

There was also a bill from Ma's car insurance stamped OVERDUE! and one from Sears, the only credit card Ma still had.

I knew that the Mohawk Valley Village wasn't going to be patient about missing rent. Rental managers smile and offer treats from their candy jars before you sign the lease, but afterward, all they care about is getting their money on time. This meant trouble. A few nights of work as a barmaid wouldn't be enough to cover both the rent and store lease, never mind the dipping cabinet and ice cream.

My head felt like it was balancing a sack full of marbles. And on top of this, Mr. Win had stopped me after homeroom to remind me that my first peer mediation was scheduled for Wednesday. Only two days away and I still hadn't memorized all the steps in the process. Even worse, last night I had a nightmare that my first mediation turned into a slugfest with disputants throwing punches and me crying like a baby.

I left the mailroom and saw an OUT OF ORDER sign taped to the elevator again.

"Psssst, Tess—over here!"

Winnie and Jordan had just stepped through the automatic lobby doors. Jordan was carrying a bulky brown box. Winnie carried a grocery bag and held her finger to her lips.

I relaxed both of my Five hands in front of me, hunched my shoulders, and jutted my head forward a little. "What?"

Jordan let out a squeal, then tapped his A hand against his mouth. "Secret."

My brother looked ready to burst with excitement. But if he kept making those dolphin-screeching sounds, I wasn't so sure that whatever was in that box would *stay* a secret.

I touched the cardboard top. "Show me," I sign-pleaded, and Winnie laughed. A blue headband was wrapped around her bouncy curls like a Hula-Hoop.

Jordan gently rested the box on the floor and lifted one flap, revealing a rectangular glass tank and a turtle about eight inches long. It looked like a red-eared slider, with a speckled shell and a red patch behind each eye. Just like Bandito back home.

No sooner had I looked in than Jordan covered the box and signed furiously, "Hide! No turtles allowed!"

Now, that was impressive. Not only did Jordan understand that turtles were unwelcome so he needed to be discreet, but he knew that *hide* combines *secret* and *under*. Lately Winnie carried a compact ASL dictionary in her purse everywhere, and she frequently whipped it out to look at the pictures and show Jordan.

"There's a spring fashion show going on in Assisted Living," Winnie said. "We're taking advantage of that distraction to smuggle this in."

I glanced out the window at the parking lot. There were more cars than usual parked by Building Three. But a maintenance worker carrying a toolbox was headed this way. I tapped Jordan's shoulder to get his attention, then pointed toward the stairs. "Hurry," I signed. "The elevator's broken again and someone is coming to fix it."

Quickly we climbed the stairs. Winnie stopped to catch her breath after we passed the second floor.

I turned and looked at her. "Winnie, will they make us leave if they find the turtle?"

"Oh, they'd squawk for a bit because reptiles carry germs, but they'd get over it," she said. "No worries. We'll keep this little fella undercover. Just like we would expensive jewelry, if we had any."

I took the grocery bag from her arms before we continued. Her forehead already had tiny sweat beads.

Up we climbed the last two flights, slowly now—Jordan feared we were scaring the turtle. The whole time I kept thinking about our late rent. When we reached the fourth floor, I asked Winnie another question. "Have you ever known anyone who got kicked out of this place?"

"There was that retired roofer two years ago in Building Two. If you ask me, he'd baked in the sun too long, because he showed up in the laundry room buck naked on a Sunday morning. I couldn't blame them for sending him packing. Who wants to see that sorry sight in between wash and rinse cycles?"

I giggled. "Anyone else?"

"Can't think of any. But I'm sure they'll make folks leave if they don't pay rent," she said as we reached our apartment.

In the living room Jordan pulled the tank from the box. He rested the turtle on the floor while he filled the tank with gravel and moss, and he added a tiny plastic frog from his animal collection. Then he plugged in the sunlamp and pointed it overhead.

"Turtle likes sunshine," he signed.

Lastly he pulled a handful of twigs from the box and scattered them in the tank, using a wider one to form a bridge across the tank.

"What about food? He can't eat mostly peanut butter like

you," I signed, and Jordan reached into the box and pulled out a bag of live crickets.

Yikes, a snack with legs.

Winnie gave Jordan an old margarine tub for a water bowl, and after he filled it, he put the turtle back into the tank. We all stood there ready to watch that red-eared slider run for its supper.

But it didn't move. Its head was tucked in, and it stayed still like a stone, even when Jordan gave it a gentle nudge.

Jordan's face cringed with panic. "Dead! Dead!" he signed. Then he fell backward on the carpet, kicking his legs up and shrieking à la FrankenJordan.

But Winnie reached for the ASL dictionary in her purse, thumbed through it, and signed and spoke the same words over and over: "Scared turtle, *not* dead turtle. Be patient, Jordan. Be patient."

So Jordan got up and composed himself. And after a few long minutes, the turtle pulled its head out of its shell and crept toward the water.

"*Not* dead. Happy turtle!" my brother signed, beaming.

"The man at the pet store said you can tell if a turtle's healthy by the brightness of its eyes. Looks to me like this fella's fit as a fiddle," Winnie said. "All my years nursing would've been a breeze if a diagnosis was that simple."

I nodded, but I wasn't really listening. I was back mulling over our money troubles. If only we could find a solution as easily as this turtle found food.

Winnie looked up from the tank to me. "Wouldn't it be

nice if we could stick our heads down our shirts when life gets rough like this creature can?" Then she took my hand and led me into the kitchen. "Is the turtle what's got you looking glum? I promised Jordan I'd get it for him if he didn't scratch his pox marks, and your mother seemed to think it was okay. But if it upsets you, I'll keep it at my place."

I shook my head. "The turtle's fine. Everything else is a mess."

Winnie looked around. "This apartment sure isn't a mess. You've done a fine job sprucing it up with your painting and crafts."

I shrugged, not ready to talk.

"Sounds like something inside of you needs pulling out. But first I'm making a cookie run. I give better advice when I'm nibbling on a cookie," she said as she walked out the door.

Minutes later she returned with a plate of cookies and a thermos full of Chocolate Heaven. She called the cookies snickerdoodles, and I wolfed down three big ones at the kitchen counter with her. They were left over from the Salty Old Dogs jam session, and they sure tasted buttery sweet and full of cinnamon.

There was no getting Jordan to sit still. He stuffed a whole cookie in his mouth, picked up his turtle, and charged to the bathroom. "Turtle swim!" he signed.

A few sips of Chocolate Heaven later, I was pouring my troubles out to Winnie again. Everything from the melted ice cream to Ma's overspending and how I was afraid we'd get kicked out of the apartment. I even admitted that I was picked to be a peer mediator, but I was afraid that I'd be awful at it. I swear Winnie could make a tree talk about why it was mad at the wind.

"Kids scream and fuss in peer mediation, and it's my job to keep things calm and under control. I'm not sure if I can handle it," I said.

But Winnie said I had the perfect disposition for the job—steadfast and patient, and nonjudgmental. "It makes sense that you'd feel nervous about this, Tess; you've never done it before. Sometimes nervous energy is good. Kind of like a runner who's trembling before the race starts, and then it turns to adrenaline when the gun goes off. I think you'll help those kids, and you'll help your ma."

"But I don't know *how* to help Ma. And even if I did, she wouldn't listen!"

Winnie nodded. "Maybe you can apply some of that peer-mediation training at home. Think carefully about what you say to your ma and the way you say it. Maybe you can help her make good choices for herself."

I looked over at Winnie's hand wrapped around her mug and noticed the snake ring. She'd said her son gave it to her. "Did Elston listen to you?" I asked.

Winnie chuckled and fiddled with her ring. "He listened about one out of every five times I spoke—and that was on a good day. Right now he's stationed in the Middle East on combat duty—Marine Corps. He didn't listen to what I thought about that, even if I am proud of him." Her eyes got glassy, and I felt bad for bringing it up.

But just as quickly she smiled again and reached over and touched my hand. "You know what I see when I look at you, Tess?"

I shook my head.

"I see a smart, strong young lady who's sitting up taller than she did on that cold winter day I first met her. Your ma, too, even if she's hit a few bumps in the road."

"But they might kick us out of here. Then we'll be homeless!"

She shook her head. "People move slowly in Schenectady in the spring. They need to thaw out, just like the ground. And those folks in the rental office—well, they put their pants on one leg at a time like the rest of us. They can be reasonable if they're treated that way."

With that, Winnie stood, saying she had to get going. "Melvin's taking me to dinner. And after all the cookies I just ate, I better wear control-top panty hose—extra heavy on the control," she said, grinning and patting her blouse.

As she was leaving, Jordan ran over and wrapped himself around her leg.

"I love turtle—and Winnie!" he signed.

Winnie's eyes lit up as she hugged him back. She didn't even attempt to sign something.

She didn't have to.

Chapter 20

Invest in your operation. Don't cut corners, don't scrimp on quality ingredients, and don't use cheap equipment. —*The Inside Scoop*

Jordan named his turtle Lucky, and wouldn't you know, we got lucky shortly after he arrived. Not only did I survive my first session as a peer mediator, but I earned high praise! When it ended, the disputants, two eighth-grade boys, agreed to stop scribbling nasty stuff about each other on the bathroom stalls and then came over and thanked me, saying *I* made them feel comfortable enough to actually talk to each other! Ritchie, my co-mediator, shouted, "Way to go, Texan!" like I was Sam Houston himself.

"Fine work," Mr. Win said, high-fiving me afterward. "That could've easily turned into a shouting match, but you got them listening and considering each other's feelings." I thanked Mr. Win and told him Ritchie deserved plenty of the credit too.

Not only did the session go smoothly, but afterward, Peer Mediation Club voted unanimously to make the team shirts I designed, and that decision required no mediation. I'd proposed an off-white collared shirt with "Ottawa Creek MS Peer Mediators" stenciled on the front in sparkly red and yellow paint (the school colors), and "Peace in Progress" on the back, encircled in all our handprints. Gabby offered to host the shirt-making session at her house, providing that Mr. Win brought cookies and I showed everybody what to do.

After peer mediation, I stopped in the Mohawk Valley Village rental office to speak with the manager. I was ready to apply the same conflict-resolution principles that had just served me well. And so while the manager finished talking on the phone, I reviewed the peer-mediation checklist in my head:

1. Present opening statement of facts.
2. Tell your story clearly and without anger or judgment.
3. Identify the problem.
4. Brainstorm for a win-win solution.
5. Build an agreement together.

When the manager got off the phone, I took a deep breath and introduced myself, making sure my body language was clear and nonthreatening.

"Tess Dobson, as in the Dobsons in Building One, apartment 418?" he asked in a deep voice, his fingers rubbing a mustard stain on his tie.

I nodded and started in with my opening statement about a "matter involving monies owed." So far so good. He listened as I explained how my family was having difficulty coming up with this month's rent on time because my mother was launching a new business. Onetime business costs had led to a family budget deficit, I explained, which led to late rent.

Having defined the problem, I assured him that we intended to be trustworthy tenants, if we could have a slight extension to the due date. "My ma's taken a second job, so the money is coming. It should be no more than two weeks."

Then, in case that wasn't convincing enough, I upped the ante, appealing to his side of the win-win solution.

"I happen to be a nice sewer and decorator, and no offense, sir, but residents in Building One can't stand the lobby's dull decor. If you give my family extra time to pay, I'll make cheery curtains and slipcovers to spruce things up. No charge."

The manager nodded, then spoke in a deep, intent voice. "I appreciate your honesty, Tess. We don't like to see a pattern of late rent, but we understand circumstances arise. Okay, we'll give your family an extension for this month only. I'll expect to see full payment in this office in fourteen days." Then he grinned. "As for your additional offer, I can't contract work with minors. But let me say that if some new pillows just so happen to show up on the love seat, I certainly wouldn't throw them out."

"You've got a deal, sir," I said, shaking his hand and making direct eye contact. "And a favorite color?"

"Dark blue. Like the Mohawk River," he said.

That same week Ma started at Little Miss Muffet's. The bad news was that she worked seven nights straight, and she hardly ever made it back to the apartment before two a.m.

On Friday night, she didn't show up until three-thirty.

I was up, battling my insomnia, plus I was worried that some drunk might bother her. The good news was she had made *a lot* of tip money.

"One hundred fifty bucks of liquor loot. Yahoo!" she shouted as she pulled a wad of cash from her bra and threw it on the counter.

"You smell like beer," I said, yawning as I stared at the stains on her white button-down blouse. I wanted to tell her all about my good grades and my first peer-mediation session.

But Ma didn't ask about me. She just kept counting cash and humming a country song. And when I told her how Winnie took Jordan and his deaf buddy Russell to Central Park to feed the ducks, she didn't say a word. She was too excited about tallying up her liquor loot and figuring how much she still needed to buy a dipping cabinet.

That got me mad. Important events were happening in my life and Jordan's, too. The whole world didn't revolve around ice cream!

Ma made up the money she owed the Mohawk Valley Village like I promised. And she set May 5 as the new Grand

Opening—she even had fancy flyers printed. Her late-night work as a barmaid didn't seem to squash her business drive. She'd leave the bar at closing time and go straight to A Cherry on Top and work into the wee hours. She was soaring high again, racing too fast.

One night she didn't return at all. She showed up as I was pouring cereal for Jordan at breakfast.

Calmly as I could, I looked right at her and stated that being out on State Street all night was dangerous.

Her face was pale, the circles under her eyes so dark that she looked like a vampire.

"For starters, working too many hours will get you burned-out and sick. And you've said it yourself: that part of Schenectady has more than its share of troublemakers. A mother with two children shouldn't be putting herself in harm's way."

Ma told me not to worry so much. Hard work and late hours ran in her genes, thanks to those early years on the ranch. "I grew up roughhousing with horse wranglers; I can handle myself," she said.

Attempt number one at Ma mediation didn't produce the best resolution. She didn't quit working long hours late at night. But from then on she did leave a note taped to the fridge with what time she'd be home. And mostly she stuck to it.

One Saturday morning, Ma got me up early to go to the secondhand-restaurant-equipment dealer with her while Jordan went with Winnie to a Salty Old Dogs jam session. We found a used dipping cabinet in like-new condition that was bigger than the old one and came with an extended warranty.

Ma bought a couple of fire extinguishers too. "I learned my lesson with that broken dipping cabinet. We're turning over a safety-conscious leaf. Starting tomorrow, I'm reviewing safety procedures and conducting fire drills at the shop. We gotta be ready for the good, the bad, and the ugly," she said as she handed the cashier a big wad of bills.

I told Ma to hurry up because today was the Peer Mediation Club shirt-making session at Gabby's house, but she just kept talking to the cashier as usual. She wanted to avoid paying a hefty delivery fee, so she asked if they could hold the dipping cabinet until we could figure out a way to pick it up.

Then Lady Luck visited again, or so I thought. We bumped into Chief in the mailroom after we got back. Chief told Ma that he'd just bought himself a gently used Ford truck. Navy blue, fittingly, with new brakes and less than fifty thousand miles. One thing led to another, and Ma explained about the dipping cabinet, and he offered to pick it up with the truck later.

"Mmm. Something smells chin-lickin' good!" Ma called when we returned to our apartment around lunchtime. The Temptations were blasting "The Way You Do the Things You Do" from under the coffee table, and Jordan and his friend Russell greeted us wearing aprons with WAITER signs taped to them.

Winnie had made chicken cutlets with scalloped potatoes and fresh asparagus, and Jordan and Russell had set the counter with five place mats. So what that they forgot forks; it looked nice. I couldn't wait to dig in.

The phone rang just as we sat down to eat. It was Gabby. "Can you come a little early today, Tess? I need help setting up all the paints and brushes. This will be a blast!"

"Let me check," I said, and I asked Ma if she could take me after lunch.

"Take you *where*?"

"To Gabby's house. We're making the Peer Mediation Club shirts today, remember?"

But Ma didn't remember. And worse. She flat said no. "The restaurant-equipment store is closed on Sunday, so we gotta get the freezer today. Chief's kind enough to let us use his truck, but he can't do heavy lifting."

"*Please*, Ma. Everyone in Peer Mediation Club is going. They need me to show them how to make the team shirts."

"I need you more. The Grand Opening is riding on us getting the dipping cabinet."

"Could I take Tess's place?" Winnie asked.

"That's awful sweet of you, Winnie, but freezers weigh a ton. I need her young muscles."

I felt my face redden. And then in an instant, *poof*, I turned into FrankenJordan's witchy older sis.

"Well, *I* need to go to Gabby's!" I roared. Jordan's and Russell's eyes got all big. No need to sign to them that I was angry.

Ma put her napkin down. "Can't you do that another day? The family business has to come first. Decorating some pretty shirt isn't a good enough reason to abandon your duties."

The family business? Abandon my duties? Ma had hit my detonation button, and I blew up.

"I haven't abandoned my duties. I've got fudge calluses and varicose veins from working at that shop!"

My eyes burned through Ma's like lasers. Winnie stared at me, her fork frozen. I wouldn't look back at her. I knew she was thinking, *Where's all that peer-mediation training gone?*

"This is so unfair! It's *your* business, not mine. I never wanted anything to do with A Cherry on Top!"

Caught up in the moment, I hadn't been signing like I usually do around Jordan. He and Russell looked at me like I had four heads.

My appetite was gone. I picked up my full plate and brought it over to the sink. "Excuse me," I signed and spoke.

Then I stormed out of the apartment, down the elevator, and into the woods behind the building, where I cried until my eyes puffed up like pink balloons.

Chapter 21

Offer a wide range of ice cream flavors. There's a shoe for every foot and a flavor for every personality. —*The Inside Scoop*

The only reason I climbed into Chief's truck to get the dipping cabinet later was because I knew I'd have to fetch Ma from the ER after she threw her back out moving it without me.

What a crummy way to spend a Saturday. As darkness blanketed State Street, Ma, Chief, and I grunted as we lugged the dipping cabinet through the alley. The darn thing felt like a tractor-trailer without wheels.

Despite Ma's pleas, Chief refused to sit this one out.

He carried the dipping cabinet right beside me, wearing steel-toed boots and camouflage pants like he was the moving crew foreman. I tried not to stare, but his right boot was so loose, it made his prosthesis look like a pole in a bucket.

I hadn't uttered one word to Ma since lunch. I kept remembering the opening page of the peer-mediation training manual, which explained how conflict can be productive if people express their feelings in a positive way to reduce anxiety and reach a resolution. I hadn't done that earlier with Ma. But then again, she wasn't an easy disputant to deal with.

"Steady as she goes, Tess!" Chief barked.

Ugh. My hands were barely holding on, much less able to steer.

I thought about Gabby. She'd sounded so disappointed when I called and said I couldn't come to her house. I hadn't explained everything—I was too upset to go into the whole bit about picking up the dipping cabinet. Right now the Peer Mediation Club was probably sponge-painting their handprints on the back of the shirts. I sure hoped they understood the directions I'd given Gabby, especially the part about making sure the peace-sign decal was smooth before ironing.

Meanwhile, here on the chain gang, Ma was bragging to Chief how A Cherry on Top would be offering thirty-four fabulous flavors. Three more than Baskin-Robbins, she said, thanks to this deluxe, extra-deep dipping cabinet.

"Big whoop," I muttered to myself, adjusting my grip.

"Variety matters to customers," Ma said. "You agree, Chief?"

"Don't go by me, Delilah. All my life I've been a one-flavor guy. Used to be this great ice cream stand by the Norfolk Navy Station. Every time our ship came off deployment, I'd grab my best girl and head over there for some butter pecan."

I tried to imagine Chief as a young sailor with a girl on his arm. He must have looked so different then, before he lost his leg.

Ma started quoting that silly *Inside Scoop* again—research about the "flavorology of ice cream," or how the flavor you pick reveals your personality.

"So what does butter pecan reveal about me?" Chief asked, between grunts.

"As I recall, it says you're orderly, careful, ethical, and fiscally conservative," Ma said.

"Yes to all of that," Chief replied proudly, like he'd been showered with compliments.

"As for me, I'm a coffee ice cream lover, and you can't keep our kind down," Ma said. "We're lively and dramatic, and we thrive on the passion of the moment. And we go by our hunches when we make decisions."

I could say a thing or two about Ma's hunches, but I kept quiet. Like they say in peer mediation, why use words to wound? I was too weary to talk anyway. This dipping cabinet had to weight ten thousand pounds.

"One other point," Ma added, all smiles. "Coffee fans are romantically compatible with strawberry fans. I'm putting that out there in case you notice a good-lookin' bachelor eating a strawberry ice cream cone."

Chief paused for a minute, his eyes gazing off like he was

thinking. "I know a bachelor who eats strawberry ice cream, but frankly, he's not your type. Cal is at least thirty years older than you, Delilah, and he's addicted to Match.com."

Ma let loose a loud laugh.

Chief looked over at me. "What's *your* favorite flavor, young lady?"

"I'm not wild about ice cream anymore," I said coolly.

"Bite your tongue, devil!" Ma cackled.

I was fibbing. Of course it was Rocky Road. Every other flavor is second banana compared to that heavenly mishmash of marshmallow, chocolate, and nuts. And I wouldn't admit it to Ma, but I was curious to know what that said about my personality.

Just when I thought she'd tell me, we reached the back door of the shop, and Ma suggested we rest the dipping cabinet on the ground.

A few minutes later we picked it up again and attempted to push it through, but it was too wide to clear the jamb.

"Dad-gummit, what bad luck!" Ma groaned, shoving it with all her strength.

Chief shook his head. "It's not going to fit, Delilah. The doorjamb's too thick. And State Street is blocked due to a water-line break."

That meant we couldn't load it back into the truck and drive it to the front. We'd have to lug it all the way around the building.

Chief's face was red now. The veins on his forehead were bulging like tree roots.

"Time out," said Ma, noticing his weary look. "Let's take a breather."

"That you, Tess?" a voice called from the alley.

It was Pete, riding that tandem bike. His camera was strapped around his neck again.

"Hey, Pete!" I called.

"Where are you-all moving that?" he asked as he got closer.

"Around front, to my ma's shop."

He parked his bike. "So *that's* where your ice cream shop is, huh? Cool! Let me help. I've got a six-pack of muscle under this ripped T-shirt." He smiled at Chief and greeted Ma. "How ya been, Miz D.?"

"Doing fine, Pete. And we'd appreciate the help. Fancy camera you got there."

"Got a great shot earlier of the fading sun splashing shadows on the sidewalk. I call it 'Good Night, Schenectady.' "

So Pete took Chief's place carrying the dipping cabinet, and Chief led the way, holding a flashlight. Slowly, the three of us shuffled our way around the building, all the while listening to Pete ramble on about how he'd just watched *The Alamo* on TV for the fifth time.

"That Santa Anna sure was one mean dude. Good thing Jim Bowie knew how to handle a knife. Hey, Miz D., did you know that some of those rebels weren't even *from* Texas?"

"Sure did, but we forgave 'em for that," Ma said as we turned the corner of the building.

A chorus of relieved sighs broke out when we finally brought the dipping cabinet inside the shop.

Ma plugged it in right away. It worked. "Purring like a kitty cat," she said, smiling.

The front door jingled, and Gabby walked in.

"What are you doing here?" I asked, surprised. I didn't even think she knew where the shop was.

"I came to help, but I guess I'm too late. I called your apartment, and your friend Winnie explained what happened." She put her hand on my shoulder. "You should've told me about what was going on, Tess."

Ma walked over and extended her hand. "Hello, Gabby. I'm Miz Dobson. Pleased to meetcha. Welcome to A Cherry on Top."

"Thanks. Gosh, this place is adorable!" Gabby squealed, looking around.

Pete rubbed the chrome on the shake machine, then started clicking away with his camera. "Yeah, it feels like we stepped back in time to the golden-oldie days," he said.

Ma said she was aiming for a post–World War II look, since back then the soda fountain was the town's social hub. "And the soda jerk was *the* showman. Young men destined for greatness competed intensely for that job."

"Nice work if you can get it," Pete said, taking a picture of Chief sitting on a stool at the counter.

Ma was pleased with Pete's interest. "Bet you didn't know that some distinguished Americans got their start as soda jerks."

"Like who?" he asked.

"Harry Truman, Duke Ellington, Jerry Lewis, Malcolm X, and that pointy-eared guy from the old *Star Trek* show," she said.

"Mr. Spock? Whoa. Now we're talking famous!" Pete said.

Gabby tapped my shoulder. "We didn't make the team shirts," she whispered.

"Why not?"

"It wouldn't be fun without your crafty know-how, and we'd probably mess it up. Mr. Win said we only have one mediation scheduled for next Wednesday, so we'll have time then."

Wow. They'd waited for me. I thought of Kaylee and the other girls at my old school who had poked fun at my homemade vest. Here they actually liked my crafty know-how.

A lump formed in my throat. "Great" was all I could get out.

Suddenly Ma clapped her hands. "¡Bueno! I'm treating my hardworking field hands to supper. Make yourselves comfortable while I run over to Bianco's and grab some pizza and buffalo wings."

Pete charged the dining area, followed by Chief, who said he was so famished he would chow down more than all us young whippersnappers together. Gabby kept walking around the dining area, gazing down at the floor paw prints and up at the beaver cycling across the ceiling. "Who did all this?" she asked.

"Ma's the brains. I helped with the decorating," I said.

I showed Gabby the artwork in the bathrooms. (She especially liked the tiger holding a cone.) When we came out, I told her and Pete about Ma's test-market session at Mohawk Valley Village and the jukebox-buying adventure. Talking about it made me realize something. In the last few months Ma *had* done a lot.

Gabby put her hand to her chest and smiled. "I *love* the name A Cherry on Top. It makes me think of the movie *It's a Wonderful Life*. Remember when George makes a chocolate sundae for Mary? She whispers in his bad ear, 'George Bailey, I'll love you till the day I die.' Ice cream shops offer endless possibilities for romance."

I pointed toward the counter, piled with paper supplies needing unpacking. "This one offers endless work. My ma hasn't heard about child-labor laws."

"My father exploited me when he opened his law firm too," Gabby said. "I set up files, answered phones, dusted leather chairs, and watered plants for my whole summer vacation."

"At least the law is interesting. You use your brain instead of your scooping muscles."

Gabby's eyes twinkled behind her red glasses. "Guess what, Tess? My Zen archery instructor just had a baby. That means that except for peer mediation on Wednesdays, I have afternoons free. I could help here too! Think of what a team we'd be, the ox and the tiger. You know how to decorate, and I can use feng shui to add harmony."

I thought of my ugly exchange with Ma earlier. "Harmony is good," I agreed.

Fifteen minutes later, Ma returned, her arms piled high with pizza, wings, and pop bottles. I grabbed paper plates and brought them to a dining table. Pete pulled the chair out for Gabby to sit down.

"Thanks," she said.

"My pleasure," he replied, his voice deeper. "I'm trying my best to behave like a soda jerk."

Maybe it started because we were tired and punchy. Or maybe it was because the veil of darkness outside made it feel cozy inside. Whatever it was, one thing led to another, and before you knew it, Pete, Gabby, Chief, Ma, and I were going around the table telling jokes and having a good ol' time.

Those were some corny jokes, especially Pete's: "How do you make a dinosaur float? Duh, by adding ice cream!"

The lamer they were, the louder we laughed. I guess after we'd carried a heavy dipping cabinet for so long, anything seemed funny.

Chapter 22

The key to Grand Openings is to do 'em up big. Ring bells, wave flags, and pull out all the stops. You know the saying: nice, quiet businesses finish last. —*The Inside Scoop*

The next Tuesday, Gabby and I went straight to A Cherry on Top after school. We were the only ones there since, at Winnie's nudging, Ma had taken Jordan and Russell to playgroup. But before she left, Ma gave us flyers to pass out to city shopkeepers.

Gabby gazed down, reading the flyer on top of the stack. "I wonder why your mother picked May fifth for the Grand Opening. Is five her lucky number?"

"Doubt it," I said. But then it hit me. Maybe she *had* picked this date on purpose. "Come to think of it, that's Cinco de Mayo."

"What's Cinco de Mayo?"

"A Mexican holiday. It's huge in San Antonio. Lots of parades, dancing, and whoop-de-doing. People think it's Mexico's Independence Day, but actually, it marks the date when the Mexicans clobbered the French in a battle."

Talking about Cinco de Mayo made me think of Juanita. Her letters had stopped coming. I hadn't written in a while either.

We started passing flyers out to nearby State Street businesses first. Bianco's Pizzeria, Polaski's Dry Cleaners, Knickerbocker Shoe Repair, and Civitello's Italian Pastries agreed to post one in their stores. But a few doors down from us, Mr. Harley at Adirondack Jewelers refused to take one, saying he didn't like "tacky advertisements."

Right about then, Gabby took a page out of the peer-mediation playbook, all the while relying on her tiger charm. "Mr. Harley, did you hear that Miz Dobson is naming ice cream treats after Schenectady sites? Plenty of merchants want in on that free publicity."

Whoever said you gotta give to get sure knew retail. Faster than you could say *Grand Opening,* our flyer was posted on the wall behind the bracelet display, and Mr. Harley was shouting out all sorts of goofy names like Adirondack Sapphire Sundae and Harley's Gem of a Milk Shake.

Gabby and I covered three blocks west on State, handing flyers out to merchants, shoppers, cops, trash collectors, and folks waiting for buses, until we reached Proctor's Theater, where we left a stack in the box office with the ticket agent. As we walked through the theater lobby, I couldn't stop staring at the majestic decorations: velvet draperies with tasseled cords, ornately patterned gold wallpaper, and marble staircases suitable for women in ball gowns.

We headed up Broadway and crossed over to Franklin Street and walked into Barley's Convenience Store. The manager was a big man with soft eyes and a crinkly mustache. He didn't seem enthused when we told him about my ma's new ice cream shop. Not one little bit.

"I've heard about this new business, and I've got a question," he said, raising an eyebrow as he loaded hot dogs into the cooker. "Will your ma be serving lunch fare?"

"No, sir," I answered. "She's sticking with ice cream."

"But we'll gladly direct customers your way if they're craving something heartier," Gabby added with a sweetheart smile.

Relieved, the manager not only agreed to post a flyer by the beverage station but offered us a free hot dog. Gabby politely said no thanks, being a vegan, but I took mine to go with two packets of hot sauce.

"My name's Mac Kelsh. Come again!" he shouted as we said goodbye.

A few streets later we reached the northwesternmost part of the city, the Stockade District. Historical row houses with tidy lawns lined the streets. "My dad says this is one of the oldest neighborhoods in the country," Gabby explained. "It's been around since 1661, only then it had a sturdy barricade to protect the

Dutch settlers from warring Indians. George Washington actually slept in one of these old houses."

I noticed the well-kept wrought-iron entrances. Many homes had American flags flying and flowerpots already filled with pansies. The sidewalks were clean. No empty chip bags or dog poop. And no smudged windows or MAKE MONEY FAST advertisements nailed to telephone poles like on State Street. I liked this look. Farther in we came to a village square with a giant statue of Lawrence the Indian. The marker explained how he helped the Dutch rebuild after the massacre.

Turning back, Gabby stopped on the corner before Erie Boulevard, by a professional building with old-fashioned charm. The ground floor had a small shop with a sign: VICTORIA'S CLASSIC INTERIOR DESIGN.

"Fancy Vicky decorated my father's law office last year," Gabby said as we passed the door, sticking her finger in her mouth.

"That bad?"

"Actually it won a citywide decorating award, and my dad and his partners love it, but I think it's gloomy and doomy like a funeral parlor. But you know me. I'd slap smiley-face stickers all over the world if I could."

I stared at the antique sleigh bench in the window. The cushion was upholstered in a silver taffeta with silk-cord edging. Gorgeous.

"Wanna skip this one?" Gabby asked.

Skip it? I couldn't *wait* to get inside. "Let's go in. They might have a lot of clients."

Inside, an apple-potpourri scent greeted us. Bolts of upholstery fabric in dozens of textures, colors, and prints lined the shelves against the back wall.

A middle-aged woman with glasses dangling from a chain around her neck looked up at us. Her snow-white cashmere sweater matched her French-manicured fingernails perfectly. "Welcome, girls. I'm Victoria. May I help you?"

"Hello. We're passing out flyers for a great new ice creamery on State Street. Would you be willing to post one?" I asked.

"You mean Jerry's shop, Van Curler Creamery?" she asked, less than enthusiastically.

I nodded. "It's called A Cherry on Top now. Delilah Dobson, my ma, is the new owner, and it's had a total makeover."

Victoria shook her head. "Sorry, girls. I cater to a different clientele than that part of State Street."

"Don't worry, rich people love ice cream too," Gabby said, grinning.

Victoria rested her hands on the table, revealing a ring with a sparkly pear-shaped diamond. "My customers like ice cream, but they don't like shopping surrounded by stray trash, vacant buildings, unswept cracked sidewalks, and faces that don't seem bothered by it all. And they don't feel safe there in the evening."

The door jingled as a lady with short black boots strutted in. "Excuse me," Victoria said, and she walked over to greet her.

Gabby whispered in my ear. "Fancy Vicky is such a snoot! You want me to name-drop—you know, bring up my dear ol' dad's law firm? We'll guilt her into hanging a flyer!"

I did feel ticked off at Fancy Vicky. A Cherry on Top met every spic-and-span standard in the *Inside Scoop*. It wasn't Ma's fault that businesses had closed, or that the police didn't patrol that area much. Yet something about being around this lady with design expertise made me want to prove myself on my own merits.

Victoria was giving the customer her undivided attention. "I've come up with some fantastic ideas for your sunroom, Diana," she said, reaching for a folder on the table. "Knowing you like southwestern style, I think this poncho weave would make a lovely sofa upholstery," she said, holding up a fabric swatch.

The lady touched the fabric, then wrinkled her nose. "Too itchy."

Victoria pulled another fabric swatch from the folder. "Well then, how about chenille in a soft pastel?"

The lady shook her head. *Uh-uh.*

"This cotton blend would give the room a soft feel, and the fading-sunset pattern is soothing," Victoria suggested.

"It clashes with my wrought-iron furniture," the lady said. "I prefer a more natural look."

Listening to Victoria offer ideas reminded me of the time Juanita's grandparents asked me to spruce up their den. I had to do a sell job there too, especially since their budget was under fifty dollars. I found a tin-framed mirror tucked away in their basement that hung nicely next to their old chair, which I reupholstered in a cheery floral chenille. Then I tossed some Native American–inspired pillows on the daybed and rearranged some of Juanita's *abuelita*'s pottery on the coffee table. Pardon the bragging, but that den ended up looking like it belonged in a homes and gardens show (Tex-Mex edition, of course).

I turned toward the lady in boots. "Excuse me, ma'am. I couldn't help overhearing. I'm from San Antonio, and I decorate for friends and family. These samples here—well, they really capture the look you're after."

"Really?" The lady looked intrigued.

I nodded. "When you choose a southwestern style, you have all kinds of images to play with in your fabrics and accessories. Stuff like cactus, horses, sunsets, and cowboy hats. And don't shy away from daring colors like oranges, yellows, and reds."

"But I've got lots of dark-toned furniture in that room," the lady said.

"Woods and metal accessories mix in beautifully. For example, you might consider espresso leather for the couch—accented with fiesta-patterned red cotton throw pillows. And a Pueblo-weave tapestry would work nicely behind the couch, along with some metal wall art."

"Espresso leather does have that rustic look I like. I ride horses myself," the lady said. "And I bought some metal sconces at a swap meet in Tucson last year." She turned to Victoria. "Show me what you have in espresso leathers."

"Gladly," Victoria said, turning toward the fabrics.

"Good luck!" I called to the lady as Gabby and I started to leave.

But before we reached the sidewalk, Victoria was out the door after us.

"Wait. Tell me your name again, young lady," she said, looking at me, and I told her.

"Thank you, Tess. I'm *very* impressed. You have a real flair for design. Did you help your mother decorate her ice cream shop?"

Gabby answered for me. "You bet. And that place is cute as a button."

Victoria smiled and extended her hand. "That woman is not easy to please. Your ideas really helped. On second thought, I will take a flyer. I'll let clients know about A Cherry on Top—as long as you pass on my suggestion for improving that part of State Street."

"You've got a deal," I said, handing her the flyer.

For the first time since she took the barmaid job, Ma had a night off. She'd heard about a diner in Schenectady's Goose Hill section where kids eat free, so we went there for supper. While we waited for our food to be served, I told her all about the Stockade District with its stately buildings and manicured lawns. "It's been a settlement since 1661, and there's an awesome statue of an Indian named Lawrence who helped out the settlers after a massacre."

Ma seemed interested. "Jordan would like to see that. Me too."

Then I told her what Victoria said about State Street being sloppy and unsafe. When I finished, I leaned back against the creaky booth, expecting her to let loose about snooty rich dames looking down on straw-hat folks.

But—surprise, surprise!—she agreed with Victoria.

"State Street does need to clean up its act. Who wants to stroll down dirty sidewalks and visit shopkeepers with mopey, glum faces? But you can't saddle all the blame on the shopkeepers. Seems to me that Mayor Legato buddies up with the Schenectady neighborhoods that make him look good. And from what I've seen, State Street hasn't been doing that for years. Plenty of its businesses suffer from low self-esteem caused by folks flat leavin' them for more appealing shopping elsewhere."

The waitress put a plate of chicken fingers in front of Jordan. He dropped the plastic animals in his hands and reached for the hot sauce.

"How is A Cherry on Top going to make money if customers don't like coming to State Street?" I asked.

"Oh, they'll come if we give 'em a reason to come. *Una razón especial*," Ma said, hiding a yawn.

I bit into my pulled-pork sandwich. The meat wasn't quite as tender as back home, but the tangy sauce swooshed and tingled in my mouth. "And what would that reason be?"

"Not sure yet, but I'm working on it." Ma looked across at Jordan, then back to me. "Tess, what's the sign for *good day* again?"

When I showed her, she signed to Jordan, asking about his day.

He flashed a bubbly smile, then started signing quickly. "Teacher read book. Mouse with big ears and many mean—"

He paused then, narrowing his eyes, trying to come up with the right sign. Then he brushed his nose twice with his R hand. *Rat*.

"What's the name of the book?" I signed.

But he couldn't sign the name, just more about the mouse with big ears and mean rats. "Mouse loves princess!" he added.

"Oh, I know," I signed and spoke, finger-spelling *The Tale of Despereaux*. I loved that book too.

"Despereaux, now that's a great name," Ma said, with a salty smile. "It's got character, and who hasn't felt desperate? After this past year, my fingers should be able to sign *desperate* by themselves." She looked away, toward a couple with a baby in a high chair, her eyes suddenly teary.

I snuck a look at Ma. She hadn't had a color rinse in months, and her silver-streaked hair reached past her waist, scruffy like frayed rope. Her eyes were underlined with dark shadows, but her skin was still pillow soft. She wore no blush or lipstick, just a dab of mascara. Ma loves the bluebonnets that grow wild along the roadside in Texas, and something about her accidental beauty reminds me of them.

Ma yawned, then explained how she'd worked even later than usual last night—at a private bachelor's party—and that she almost hadn't heard the phone ring early this morning.

"Wouldn't ya know, it was Jordan's teacher," she said, biting into her sandwich.

"Uh-oh. Did you get in trouble?" I signed, facing him.

He smiled with a French fry sticking out of his mouth, then pointed to a gold-star sticker on his shirt pocket.

"Jordan got picked as Second-Grade Superstar. That means he's been paying attention, doing all his work, *and* behaving himself. Imagine that, teachers calling when kids are acting good!" Ma said, grinning.

"Yeah, Jordan!" I signed. I looked across at Ma. "Have you noticed how much more he signs now? Yesterday he called Lucky a brilliant reptile. I didn't even know the sign for *brilliant* or *reptile*."

Ma smiled at Jordan. "Yessirree, he's coming along nicely. I owe a world of thanks to Winnie."

Thump! Jordan's elbow hit the ketchup bottle and knocked it into the napkin holder. The noise startled both Ma and me, but not Jordan. Even after all these years, it still saddened me that he couldn't hear sounds around him. I wondered if he imagined what a rocket ship sounded like. Or a dog barking, or a whistle blowing. I wondered if he even thought about sound. Once, I shared this with Winnie, but she told me to stop thinking that way. "That child is perfect just the way he is. Who says hearing is better than not hearing?"

Ma wiped hot sauce from Jordan's mouth. Watching her made me realize that she too had been helping Jordan adjust. The school here in New York *was* good for him.

Maybe Ma buying the shop wasn't messing everything up. Maybe she was proving me wrong. Maybe she could hold her own *and* her business if she got a little help. Something to keep *her* on track.

I had an idea. Now I needed to present it in a way that respected her feelings.

"Ma, you know how I helped you move the dipping cabinet, even though I had something else planned?"

She nodded.

"Sorry for having a bad attitude about it. Making that delivery was important. I'm glad I helped."

"That makes two of us," she said, winking.

"Well, I need you to do something that's important too." I kept up the eye contact with a sincere but nonthreatening facial expression.

"What?"

"Go to the doctor. Opening this ice cream shop is really demanding. I don't want you to get sick."

Or crash, I thought. *I don't want you to crash.*

Ma started singing her old tune about doctors being good-for-nothin' time wasters. "What does some pill wrangler with a stethoscope swinging from his neck know about my inner workings? I've been holding my own for thirty-five years without those quacks. I'm not about to let them tinker with my brain now."

Time to redirect this nonproductive talk, but how? I thought about how Winnie repeats her favorite sayings. She calls them mantras, and they do have a way of driving home a message.

"A retailer must be healthy, Ma. A retailer must be healthy."

"Who says I'm not healthy?" she asked accusingly. "I was just over at Knickerbocker Shoe Repair helping Flora repair a giant shoe rack that got loose from the wall and came undone. The day before, I kept Mr. Harley from losing it when his alarm system tripped and wailed for three hours straight. If that didn't require bucketloads of sanity, what would?"

"I know you're sane, Ma. I'm just saying the pace you keep could make you sick, and then what would happen to A Cherry on Top? A retailer must be healthy."

Finally, she agreed—just so I'd stop with the mantra, I think. "Enough. Quit badgering me. I'll look around for a doc when I have time."

Once again, peer-mediation training played in my head. *An agreement needs a specific action plan.* "Tomorrow," I insisted, swallowing the last of my pulled pork. "Winnie knows a clinic where you can walk in without an appointment."

"Okay then, tomorrow," Ma said, reaching for the dessert menu that the waitress dropped off. "Can we change the subject now? I'm more interested in discussing what kind of pie they got."

That should've had me yahooing like I'd made a breakthrough. Ma just agreed to go to a doctor. Progress! I should've been doing a belly-bursting, high-fiving cheer inside. But instead I sat there quietly, poking my pickle.

Why? Because I watch the Weather Channel. The eye of the hurricane is where everything feels calm and secure—right before the worst winds blow. Even here in Schenectady, with our new friends and the promise that Ma might get help, the same fears swirled in my head like a soft-serve twist. What if Shooting Stars came back and ruined everything?

Chapter 23

Nothing beats a themed promotion for driving
traffic to your shop. —*The Inside Scoop*

It took two hours to make the Peer Mediation Club shirts on Wednesday, but everyone loved how they came out. Gabby called them "bold and daring, even if we are a peace-seeking group." Malika liked the chain of handprints on the back. And Ritchie said the turned-up collar gave him the slick look he was hoping for to impress the ladies.

Afterward, I caught the bus to downtown Schenectady.

"Hey, Ma!" I shouted as I walked into A Cherry on Top.

"Be right out!" she called from the back storage room. Giant bags of M&Ms, Oreos, chocolate chips, nuts, cookies, sprinkles, and gummi bears were lying near the open glass jars on the counter. I washed my hands and started filling them.

"Get a load of me!" Ma shouted as she strutted out wearing shiny red lipstick, a puffy blouse, hoop earrings, and high heels.

"Wow. Why are you dressed like that?" A sparkly orange bow dangled from her hair, and a blue ruffled skirt flowed past her ankles.

"I got these clothes at a thrift shop. I couldn't resist their fun fiesta flair. As president of the newly formed RSSA, I figure I should make a splash at our first meeting."

"What's RSSA?" I asked.

"The Resuscitate State Street Association. It's my idea for getting local merchants to join forces," she said, reaching behind the counter for her jacket.

"Join forces for what?"

"To wipe the cobwebs off their marketing plans and blow life back into their profit margins. We need change around here. I just passed Polaski's Dry Cleaners. The sign in the window said CLOSED FOR THE DAY DUE TO INDIGESTION. For crying out loud!"

Ma listed all the improvements she was going to pitch to the RSSA, like starting a neighborhood crime watch, sprucing up storefronts, and group advertising on TV and radio to draw more customers to the area. "The way I see it, we've got to stick together and give folks a reason to return to State Street. That's what I plan on telling them."

It sounded good to me, but Ma sighed as she reached for her

pocketbook. Even with those festive clothes and her go-get-'em attitude, she looked blue like her skirt. Blue with black circles under her eyes.

I walked over and adjusted the bow in her hair. "I bet all of State Street's businesses will want in on the RSSA. So why aren't you excited?"

" 'Cause I'm feeling overwhelmed. Who knows? Maybe the shopkeepers might think all this Grand Opening hullabaloo is only going to help my business, not theirs."

"They won't think that way. Don't *you* think like that." I looked her square in the eye. "Did you go to the doctor today like you promised?"

She batted the air with her hand. "As a matter of fact, yes. I wasted two hours in a stuffy doctor's office, sitting next to a slob of a fella who never learned to cover his mouth when he sneezes."

"What did the doctor say?"

Ma wouldn't look up at me. "A whole lot of gobbledygook medical jargon. Ten-dollar words like *bipolar*, *manic*, and *rapid cycling*. As if I'm a looney-tune with two poles sticking out of my brain. How would she know? It's not like there's a blood test that proves anything."

"I'm glad you went," I said sincerely. "I've heard of bipolar disorder, but what does that mean, exactly?"

She shook her head and started to look angry. "Nothing, that's what. Look, I promised I'd go to the doc, and I did. Now let it go. There's too much going on right now that needs my attention."

"But there's got to be things we can try. Medicine you can take—"

"I said it before and I'll say it again. I'm *not* letting a total stranger tinker with the chemicals in my brain!" Ma yelled, swinging her pocketbook over her shoulder. "Put a fork in it, Tess. This conversation is done!"

And it was. Even peer-mediation training didn't give me a rebuttal to that.

As soon as Ma left for the RSSA meeting, I started crushing Oreos in a bowl and pouring them into a candy jar. I thought about how badly Ma needed a big crowd for the Grand Opening. It made me think of Cinco de Mayo back in San Antonio. Ma always took the day off from Albertsons, and we went to Market Square. The air was filled with sweet, spicy smells from the vendors selling Mexican food, with visitors from all over Texas and beyond. We'd stroll around for hours, listening to mariachis strumming, and looking at the craft booths. Ma always bought Jordan a balloon.

The crowd . . . the food . . . the music . . . Ma's fiesta clothes . . . That's it!

I charged out the door and ran two blocks. "Wait up, Ma!" I shouted when I saw her flashy outfit up ahead.

She turned around, surprised.

"I've got an idea for the RSSA. Tell them that we'll host a *streetwide* Cinco de Mayo celebration—outside, up and down our part of State Street. The Grand Opening *is* on May fifth, after all. And you said yourself that themed promotions bring in customers, right? Everybody will get in on the money-making!"

Ma's eyes brightened like her hair bow. "Catch your breath, honey, and then keep talking. I like the way those wheels are turning inside your head."

"We'll decorate the shops with southwestern flair, and we'll have sidewalk sales just like the booths back home in Market Square. A parade too!"

"Yee-haw! That sure would fill customers with a slaphappy spending spirit. I could talk to Winnie about having the Salty Old Dogs perform. And I'll open a concession stand on the sidewalk selling delicious homemade tamales."

We always eat tamales on Christmas Eve. Everyone in San Antonio does. Ma cooks them the authentic way, which takes a *long* time, but they sure taste delicious. Mexicans say tamales bring good luck.

"And I'll paint a sign for the concession stand!" I added.

"That's my girl!"

We walked another block down Jay Street. Ma stopped in front of the Open Door Bookstore, right in front of a cheery display window full of gardening books. "The RSSA is meeting here," she said. "Wish me luck. Thanks to you, I'm armed with a strong case for Cinco de Mayo."

Ma skipped into the shop an hour later holding two Dr Peppers. The RSSA had voted unanimously to support the streetwide Cinco de Mayo celebration.

"Being from New York, they hardly knew how to *say* Cinco

de Mayo, never mind what it's all about," Ma said, pausing to drink her pop. "But I told the shopkeepers we were chock-full of fun fiesta ideas. They're interested in using your free-of-charge decorating services to add some south-of-the-border flair to their shops."

Ma's energy level had zoomed past the rooftop. She was zipping around the shop, her skirt ballooning, rattling on about the RSSA's "decisions" and "resolutions" like it was the Supreme Court. She kept tossing out ideas to make Cinco de Mayo bigger and bolder. Chili-pepper party lights strung up and down the telephone poles. An inflatable cactus beside every shop entrance. Face painting, cowboy hats, guess-your-weight booths, even pony rides if we could find a pony. "I'll make sangria to sell with the tamales too if they let me. And we'll dress up State Street with balloons, festive flags, and streamers. State Street is going to rock, Tex-Mex-style!"

I looked over at the dipping cabinet and suddenly felt nervous. Opening an ice cream shop seemed hard enough, never mind running a streetwide celebration.

"What about *our* business, Ma? You said yourself we have to make a killing. Would the *Inside Scoop* say all this outside attention might draw customers away from our shop?"

"Cinco de Mayo will bring families to State Street, and families love ice cream. Plus another idea hit me when I stopped at Barley's Convenience Store earlier. We'll get clowns in our shop to entertain the kiddies!"

"I'm *not* wearing a clown costume," I said firmly, anticipating her next request.

She laughed. "Not you. A man was waiting in line next to me, impersonating a chipmunk singing opera. He had me howling. Turns out he and his son own a clown business, no joke. He gave me a dirt-cheap price for Silly Billy & Son to appear at our Grand Opening."

Little kids do like clowns, I thought, *even though they give me the heebie-jeebies.* Mostly I was pleased it wouldn't be *me* under a big red nose and wig.

All afternoon, Ma kept shouting out more Cinco de Mayo ideas fast and furious, including hanging a ten-foot ice cream cone piñata outside the shop and sponsoring a raffle.

"What's the prize?" I asked.

"So far all I can come up with is a gift certificate to Little Miss Muffet's, but I'll keep thinking," she said.

I thought about Victoria's Classic Interior Design with its upscale image. What would Fancy Vicky say about Ma raffling off a bar gift certificate, peddling sangria, and inviting kids to swing a bat, right near our front window?

As exciting as all this was, Ma and I agreed on one thing. The shop wasn't ready for the Grand Opening. Menus needed to be made, the three top-selling ice cream flavors were still on back order, and we hadn't figured out how to work the waffle-cone griddle without making the cones look like fat pencils.

On the drive back to the apartment, Ma asked me to get the word out at school about Cinco de Mayo and A Cherry on Top's Grand Opening.

"Tell all your teachers, your friends, and your peer

mediators. Heck, tell the kids who need mediating! Ice cream warms the heart, no matter what you're fighting about," she said as we turned into the Mohawk Valley Village parking lot.

Imagining the kids from school recognizing me behind the ice cream counter made me think about my wardrobe. What would I wear? Ice cream called for a whimsical style. I could sure use a pair of capri pants with a smocked top, preferably in a bright, spring pattern. Silver bangle bracelets would be swell too since customers would notice my wrists as I scooped.

"Any chance I could get a new outfit for Saturday—and a haircut too?" I asked, touching my big ears.

"Not now. We've got to concentrate all our efforts on making the product look good."

"But we can't host a Cinco de Mayo celebration with sloppy clothes and messy hair. I bet the *Inside Scoop* has a whole section on dressing for success."

"Clothes don't make the retailer. Besides, you're a beauty as is," Ma said.

"Well, I think you need to review that section on employee attire," I growled.

Ma saying no again made me cranky like a tired toddler. For months I'd met every one of her paint-it, sew-it, and clean-it requests. I'd never asked for so much as a tube of lip gloss. But *I* was the one who'd hatched the whole Cinco de Mayo plan. Wasn't that worth something?

Even if I didn't get new clothes, I wasn't going to be her ice cream slave laborer without having some demands met.

"Now that you've appointed yourself grand marshal of

Cinco de Mayo, who's going to help behind the counter? If we get the kind of crowds you expect, Gabby and I won't be able to handle it alone. Customers don't like long waits."

"You're right. I've got to hire someone special. Special *and* hardworking."

"Not Chief," I said. "I can just see him barking at customers to lick their drippy cones ASAP."

"Chief will be our guest, not a hired hand. And not Winnie either—she's done enough babysitting for Jordan, plus her band will be playing. No, I need someone young and peppy with a good work ethic *and* charm. Someone who's not afraid to get silly. And in keeping with tradition, it should be a male."

"All that just to scoop ice cream?"

"The job I'm filling is soda jerk. Problem is, I don't know any young men in Schenectady who fit the description, and I sure don't want to ask that brainless twenty-something bartender at Little Miss Muffet's. Last night, he got distracted making drinks and grabbed the wrong bottles. Customers got tomato juice in their piña coladas and pineapple juice in their Bloody Marys!"

"Can't think of anybody," I said. But then, as Ma turned into the Mohawk Valley Village, a face came to mind. A face surrounded by red hair, on a kid riding a tandem bike.

Pete was hardworking, plus he was the only one I knew who seemed as interested as Ma in all this soda jerk business.

"I've got just the right person for the job," I said. "Mr. Alamo himself."

Chapter 24

In the final week before the Grand Opening, Gabby and I turned into lean, mean cleaning machines. We scrubbed the cracked, dirty sidewalks up and down State Street. Automobile-oil and cigarette-butt stains were the toughest to remove, and they were everywhere. So was nasty old chewing gum, but Mr. Bianco gave us a secret weapon that got it off: WD-40.

We washed the windows and awnings at A Cherry on Top and Civitello's Italian Pastries too. (Ms. Civitello had bad knees from forty years of standing and making pastry. Ma insisted we help her, and she insisted on rewarding us with a tasty cannoli each.) Gabby hosed down all the nearby city trash cans and re-arranged them in a gentle curved pattern along the sidewalk. Curves, she said, allowed chi energy to flow better than sharp angles.

Oh, we made fudge too. Tray after tray. I trained Gabby, and within a few days she was turning out fudge that met our high standards. Ma and I both agreed that it was a little strange how she closed her eyes and hummed as she stirred, but Gabby called it Zen fudge, and who were we to argue?

If Gabby and I were busy, Ma was busier. She borrowed benches from Daly Funeral Home and placed them up and down the sidewalk for watching the parade. She went door to door, offering shopkeepers an extra hand fixing this or dressing up that so their businesses would shine during Cinco de Mayo. She spent afternoons rehearsing customer greetings, posting pricing, hauling in more glasses and takeout containers, fixing wobbly chairs and tables, and practicing how to operate the shake machine. She wanted Gabby and me to get used to handling the cash register, but I said it looked as easy to use as a calculator. Our creative juices were put to better use elsewhere.

"Keep on prettying up this place," Ma kept shouting, and did we ever. We hung colorful streamers across the ice cream counter, arranged potpourri baskets by the entrance, and set yellow silk flowers in porcelain ice cream cone vases on each table. (Ma bought the vases during a shopping spree at a cutesy boutique for twenty-five dollars each.) "Yellow's a yang color that promotes warmth and happiness. Warm, happy people splurge for ice cream," Gabby said. I agreed. Besides, yellow matched my curtains.

On top of all the shop prep, Ma was still working at Little Miss Muffet's at night. I wished she would quit. "You need sleep!" I pleaded, but she said we needed money more. I kept bugging her to eat too because she looked like she was getting skinnier by the minute. I hardly saw her eating, just drinking Dr Pepper.

I stayed home from school the day before the Grand Opening. There were a million and one things to do, and meanwhile Ma had scheduled a meeting of the RSSA, this time at A Cherry on Top, and she needed help. I could tell that Grand Opening jitters were rattling inside her, because she was running around the shop with a straw pressed between her lips.

But, thankfully, there was no sign of her crashing. She was bright-eyed and on her game. She greeted the RSSA members as they arrived for the meeting in her *hace grande* style, dressed up in her fiesta clothes again and blasting "La Bamba" from the jukebox. Talk about a fired-up bunch of storekeepers! They wore cactus-print vests and custom "State Street Cinco de Mayo" baseball caps, shouting "*¡Arriba! ¡Arriba!*" as they piled in. Ms. Civitello gave a groundskeeping update, beaming from beneath her thick glasses when she announced that her niece had planted the pansies up and down the nearby State Street sidewalks. Mr. Harley from Adirondack Jewelers had a total change of heart. He kept calling Ma the Can-Do Cancan Lady because of her cheery outfit and way of offering everybody marketing ideas. He even held up a sparkling emerald bracelet and donated it for the raffle, as long as the proceeds went toward a Safe State Street neighborhood watch. And Mr. Bianco ran through the parade lineup since he would be leading the way. Even Mac Kelsh, the Barley's Convenience Store manager, showed up and announced that he'd provide free coffee and donuts to the parade marchers. He didn't say much besides that, but I caught him smiling at Ma.

After the meeting ended, Ma treated everybody to free sundaes plus a sample slice of fudge, and they sure liked that. Moose Tracks was to be our featured ice cream flavor for the Grand Opening, and they all agreed this was the perfect pick to "cause a buzz." Being around Ma seemed like it got all the RSSA members talking in retail lingo.

Then Chief arrived with a toolbox, ready to mount a fiesta flag in front of each shop. Ma had already dashed off to the bank and to run last-minute errands, but before she left, she gave strict orders *not* to let him do the installing. She'd said, "Chief's been around since Paul Bunyan was swinging an ax. Climbing ladders is too dangerous, especially with one leg." I told her I'd do it. With all my experience installing curtains, handling the power drill was a piece of cake.

Sounded good until I told Chief. You would've thought I'd tossed a pie in his face, with how he huffed and puffed and stormed out of the shop. Then he grabbed the ten-foot ladder off his truck and dragged it along the sidewalk, fully intent on installing those flags himself, no matter what I said. Smoke was coming from his ears, and lugging that ladder made his prosthesis limp even more apparent.

"Nothing personal, Chief. We just don't want you to get hurt!" I pleaded.

"*Me* get hurt?" he growled. "Young lady, I'll have you know I was running up and down gun-turret ladders aboard battleships before you were even born!"

I shrugged. Reasoning with him was like trying to pull an aircraft carrier across the ocean on a string.

"If I held steady on two legs during a North Atlantic storm, by God I can handle a landlubber job with my one leg," he barked, setting the ladder down in front of Bianco's Pizzeria.

I gave up. You can't beat the U.S. Navy. I handed him the flags and hardware, but I insisted on being his "assistant."

What a painful job *that* was. Chief kept dropping the screws from the top of the ladder, misjudging where to drill the holes, and complaining that the materials he was working with were to blame. "They don't make parts like they used to," he said. After nearly two hours we'd only managed to get one flag flying. We'd just crossed the street to install one by Polaski's Dry Cleaners when the sun disappeared behind a cloud. Wind picked up and thunder rattled, and before you knew it, rain was slapping at us sideways.

"Shouldn't we finish this later?" I called up to Chief, holding the bottom of the ladder steady. Water dribbled off my forehead.

"This job has to get done ASAP," he said, just as lightning crackled near the fire hydrant.

Suddenly Mrs. Bianco came shuffling toward us, wearing her hairnet and sauce-stained apron and holding a rolling pin in her hands. "You old fool!" she roared at Chief. "Get yourself and poor Tess out of the rain before you both get electrocuted!"

Well, you would have thought she was Admiral Bianco, what with how fast Chief flew down that ladder, grabbed my arm, and hobbled back to the ice cream shop.

Inside, Ma gave Chief and me towels to dry off. Winnie and Jordan had stopped by on their way to playgroup, and Ma fixed us all a Schenectady Snow Shake. We laughed as Winnie described the fancy vests that the guys in the band would be wearing for Cinco de Mayo and the bombshell gown that would be her costume.

"Melvin says my sparkly dress reminds him of Diana Ross," she said. "And who cares if one of my thighs weighs more than both of hers?"

The Salty Old Dogs had been rehearsing some hot little Tejano numbers for five days straight. "None of us speak Spanish, so we don't know *what* we're singing, but it sure sounds good. Even Melvin's warming up to it, and he's strictly an Ella Fitzgerald type."

I turned and smiled at Jordan as he slurped his shake. He was carrying Lucky in his "travel case," a hatbox that Catherine had given him, smiling ear to ear. "Russell is bringing his hamster to the park. New friend for Lucky!" he signed excitedly.

After Winnie and Jordan left, Chief walked around the shop, taking in all Ma's decorations.

"This place passes muster, Delilah. It looks, what's that word—Cinc-aay de Mayo-ish," he said, as if he was describing mayonnaise.

"That's a true compliment coming from you, Chief," she said, curtsying, and then she whispered in his ear.

Minutes later, Mr. Bianco walked in wearing a toolbelt instead of his pizza apron. Chief got up and they left.

"Thanks, fellas. Y'all do good work while we're gone, ya hear?" Ma called before grabbing her pocketbook and car keys.

I turned to Ma, confused. "What's going on?"

She wouldn't answer me.

"Did Chief fire me as his assistant?" I asked, getting suspicious.

"He replaced you," she answered, motioning toward the door. "And now we've got to bolt like bullets with feet."

Uh-oh. Trouble was back. What happened? Money problems again? Ma had just come from the bank. What did they say? Were we evicted from the shop or the apartment—or worse, both?

"Tell me what's wrong," I said as Ma grabbed my sleeve and pulled me along.

Whatever it is, don't let it cancel Cinco de Mayo. Please. . . .

"Later, Tess. Let's go."

I dug my heels into the floor. "I'm not moving until you tell me *where* we're going."

Ma sighed. "There's no pulling the wool over your eyes.

You were right. The *Inside Scoop* does say employees should doll up some. I've already called Gabby and Pete to make sure they dress their best tomorrow. As for us, we both have appointments at that fufu hair salon on Union Street for one o'clock. You've been wanting a cut and highlights, and my messy mop needs trimming. And if we got enough time, we'll find a cute outfit for you. Lord knows you deserve it."

It felt like Christmas and my birthday had come all in one day. "Wow, Ma. Is this for *real?*"

"Sure is, unless our Toyota turns back into a pumpkin," Ma said, all grins.

"Can we afford it?"

"As long as we outrun the creditors," Ma said, winking.

"Thank you, thank you, thank you!" I shouted, hugging Ma and holding on long after I should've let go.

Chapter 25

Expect the unexpected once your sign says OPEN.
—*The Inside Scoop*

May 5. Cinco de Mayo. I woke early and checked in the bathroom mirror. The neck and shoulder forecast showed scattered red blotches. Right away I spritzed my hair with gel spray. Yes. I liked my new haircut, especially the blond highlights.

By the smell of tamales floating through the apartment, I could tell Ma had put in a late night cooking for the concession stand. She calls making tamales a labor of love because it takes eight hours to cook and shred the pork roast, soak the corn husks, and prepare the masa dough, and that's before you start rolling and steaming them.

Jordan was sound asleep as I left the bedroom and walked into the kitchen, where two gigantic foil-covered boxes sat on the counter. I peeked in. Just as I thought. Warm, wonderful tamales. Yum. Even early in the morning that smell made my stomach growl.

"Ma?" I called, but no answer.

I looked back in the living room and bathroom, but no Ma. Where was she? Her pocketbook and keys were still on the counter, so she hadn't driven anywhere. She wouldn't have left for State Street without Jordan and me. I went downstairs to look around.

The lobby was empty. So were the mailroom and laundry room, so I walked outside. The sun was just starting to cut through the morning mist, and the world was hushed. No one in the parking lot except for a deliveryman unloading supplies over at Building Three. I turned to walk back inside, and that's when I spotted Ma.

She was leaning against the apartment building holding a cigarette, sitting between two yellow forsythia bushes.

Holding a *lit* cigarette.

I scrambled between the bushes to reach her. "*What* are you doing, Ma?" I shouted, pointing to the cigarette and shivering in the damp morning air.

She took a drag without looking at me, almost as if I hadn't spoken. And with that I knew, sure as the sun creeping up in the sky beyond the apartment building. Shooting Stars was back.

I could tell by her glazed eyes and empty expression. By the way the cigarette trembled in her hand. By the mascara streaked down her cheeks.

"You didn't go to bed last night, did you?" I asked, noticing she was wearing the same outfit from yesterday. Only now her shirt was wrinkled and covered with food stains.

White smoke rings coiled from her mouth like an old-fashioned telephone cord, but still she said nothing. She turned her back slightly and looked away, toward the daffodils planted beside the parking lot.

Twelve years Ma had fought off the urge to light up again. Twelve years—my whole life—and here she was smoking again. I wanted to grab that dumb cigarette from her mouth, break it in half, and grind both pieces in the dirt.

But I couldn't.

I couldn't because Ma was sick.

"What is it, Ma? Tell me what's wrong!"

She kept looking over at the parking lot, and then she mumbled softly, "The corn husks. I didn't soak 'em long enough. I should've known better. The tamales won't be perfect."

"Nobody from Schenectady is a tamale expert," I said. "Pour some hot sauce on 'em and they'll be great!"

But Ma kept shaking her head, repeating the same thing. "I should've known better."

I thought about how Ma had been working double shifts,

at the bar and at A Cherry on Top. Day *and* night. How she'd planned hundreds of details for Cinco de Mayo—not only for us, but to revive all the businesses that were hurting on State Street. Mr. Harley wasn't the only one who considered her the Can-Do Cancan Lady; everybody did.

Now, on the biggest day of her retail life, she was slumped in the dirt, gloomy and doomy like the sky was falling down, all because of how long she soaked the corn husks.

I squeezed closer and touched her shoulder, trying to mix words together in a healing potion to get her up on her feet. "No wonder you're wiped out from all you did, Ma, especially staying up late making tamales. But they'll sell big today—I know it. Go take a shower and you'll feel better. I'll make you coffee with the socks on and get Jordan up before we leave."

Ma shook her head and exhaled. "I'm not going, Tess. My rocket's run outta fuel. I've hit bottom again. What a loser I am. . . ."

My hands shook. "You're *not* a loser! It's Shooting Stars! No, it's got a real name. Bipolar disorder. We've got to get you back to that doctor to get medicine."

"Medicine won't change a thing," she said, wiping her wet cheeks. "We're all stuck with whatever life dishes out. My paw saw all sorts of doctors, and he killed himself anyway."

A chill went up my back. My grandfather died long before I was born, but Ma never mentioned suicide. Why hadn't she told me?

Tears streamed from Ma's eyes like she was chopping onion. "You were right when you said I was crazy to start a business again. I tried my darnedest, but I can't handle all this pressure. I just want to hole up and sleep. For a long, long time. With no noise, no troubles, no nothing."

"I was *wrong*!" I yelled. "State Street is going to be bursting with customers today, and it's all because of you." I told her that the *Inside Scoop* said you had to be willing to be flexible and revise your plan, and we would. Gabby, Pete, and I would scoop ice cream so she'd be off her feet. The RSSA shopkeepers could take over the parade and Cinco de Mayo activities, once they knew she was sick. And her tamales—well, they'd practically sell themselves. "But you've got to be there. You're the *owner*. You hear me?"

Ma didn't answer. She crushed the cigarette butt with her shoe and walked back inside.

Maybe this was a good sign. Maybe she was snapping out of it. I followed.

"You're going to get dressed now, right, Ma?" I asked as we stepped out of the elevator to the fourth floor.

But Ma didn't utter another sound. And when we got into the apartment, she wrapped herself in a blanket, sank into the futon, and started weeping again.

I sat dazed at the kitchen counter, staring at the "Saratoga, Top of the Stretch" poster and smelling the tamales. Jordan was still sleeping in the bedroom, and I could hear her weeping in the living room, her voice muffled by the blanket. I wanted to cry too. If Ma couldn't work, there would be no Grand Opening, and the shop would close. We'd go belly-up and get kicked out of Mohawk Valley Village. They'd given us a one-time-only rent extension. No matter how well I mediated, the manager wouldn't let us stay here for nothing. That meant another move and another new school for Jordan—just when he was finally settling in.

Same old, same old. Nothing had changed.

Or had it?

What Winnie had said was true: both Ma and I had become stronger since we moved here. Shooting Stars was awful, but maybe it didn't have to destroy everything we'd worked so hard to start in Schenectady. Maybe I'd changed, 'cause like Pete with that camera, I saw things differently now. There was our family to fight for and others that Ma had helped too. State Street would still look dumpy and neglected if it hadn't been for the Resuscitate State Street Association—and that was all Delilah Dobson's doing.

Resuscitate. The word pumped oxygen down my dry throat. No way would I watch our lives get ruined like the melted ice cream.

As Gabby might say, the hardworking, dependable ox would take charge.

But how? I hadn't read the *Inside Scoop* cover to cover like Ma. And I sure didn't have her howdy-doody welcoming way. Plus I didn't know how to work the cash register.

Could I pull it off?

Chapter 26

Repeat after me. The customer is always right, even
when he's wrong. —*The Inside Scoop*

Twenty minutes later, Chief drove Jordan and me to A
Cherry on Top. I explained as best I could about Ma crashing
and that I'd be running the business today. I asked him to stick
around all day, in case someone official came looking for an
adult in charge. Then I braced myself for a long string of his
bossy orders, but it didn't happen. Instead, he nodded, put his
bony hand on my shoulder, and softly said, "Sure, Tess. I'll do
whatever you need."

It took several trips to unload our supplies from Chief's

parked truck, including the tamales and the giant concession-stand sign I'd painted. Jordan carried Lucky's travel case and heat lamp with the cord dragging behind him looking like a tail. He'd fussed when I explained that Ma wasn't coming. Letting him bring his turtle was the only way I could get him out the door.

Once Ma and I watched a movie about a guy who had to crash-land a jet plane, even though he wasn't a pilot and, worse, he was afraid to fly. Standing there behind the ice cream counter and knowing I was in charge—well, I had that same in-over-my-head feeling. My throat was dry. My knees shook—so much that my new capri pants made a scuffing sound. And my shoulders felt heavy like I'd been lifting dumbbells.

First thing I did was read Ma's start-up checklist, which told me to turn on the waffle-cone griddle, the shake machine, the soft-serve machine, and the hot-fudge dispenser, just like I'd seen Ma do. I checked the freezer temperature—five degrees below zero, where it should be. Then I turned my attention to the cash register. Sure wished I'd listened when Ma told me to practice on it. No matter how many buttons I pushed, I couldn't get the dumb drawer to open.

After the tenth try it was still stuck. "Darn!" I shouted, whacking it with my fist.

Chief looked up from loading napkins into the dispenser. "Let me have a look," he said. "I operated sonar in a navy CIC for thirty years. A cash register can't be more complicated than that."

So Chief pulled out the operating manual that was stowed

under the counter, and I turned my attention to mixing waffle batter. Then Jordan came out from the storage room, plopped Lucky's travel case on the dining-area floor, opened the top, and started pouring crickets into the food bowl.

"No. Lucky stays in the storage room," I signed firmly. "Turtles don't go with ice cream."

"No! No! Lucky wants to crawl," he signed, puffing his lower lip.

I couldn't bend on this rule. I remember Ma saying that a health-code citation is the fastest way to shut down a food business. Time for a win-win solution. "Turtles can't be near food," I signed again, pointing toward the back. "Lucky can crawl in the storage room. That's okay."

So, reluctantly, Jordan carried away the travel case and the sunlamp with the dragging cord just as the front door opened.

"*¡Olé!*" Gabby shouted, clicking castanets and wearing strappy heels and a sparkly gold skirt. A rose was tucked behind her ear, and her pretty dark cheeks were dusted with glitter.

"*¡Qué bonita!*" I called, remembering Juanita's *abuelita's* favorite saying.

Chief whistled. "Fine sight like that makes me wish I was a young sailor again," he called.

Gabby pulled me from behind the counter and twirled me around. "Cute outfit, Tess! Love those highlights, too. Fiesta chic!"

I thought of how Ma and I had spent the perfect mom-daughter afternoon yesterday, getting our hair done and shopping. I must have tried on twenty pairs of pants, with Ma at my side in the dressing room all along, sipping a Dr Pepper and saying I looked as pretty as a polished pearl. My heart sank to the midseam of my smocked top. Yesterday felt like a year ago.

"Something's happened," I told Gabby. "My mother won't be here today. She's sick."

Gabby's pink-lip-glossed smile faded. "What's wrong with her?"

"It's called bipolar disorder, and it's kind of like this roller coaster she rides of happy and sad spells. Right now she's sad. Really sad. Can't-get-out-of-bed sad."

Gabby's eyes watered up. "Poor Miz Dobson. I'm so sorry. Doesn't seem fair—she's always cheering everybody else up." She glanced over at Chief at the cash register and asked, "Who's in charge?"

I rested my hands against the bowl of waffle batter. "Me."

Gabby paused, then took the rose from her hair and gently tucked it behind my ear. "Then this place is in good hands. And you're not alone. We're in this together. Right, Chief?"

"Right as rain, Gabby," Chief called. "And speaking of right, this cash register is squared away now. So as you young folks say, 'Show me the money.'"

I found Ma's clipboard and reviewed the schedule. The Cinco de Mayo parade and sidewalk sales would start an hour after A Cherry on Top opened. The raffle would be held at lunchtime. And Mayor Legato and the TV reporter would arrive later in the afternoon for the ribbon cutting, with the piñata to follow. The clowns would be here all day.

As I finished reading the schedule, Gabby got the jukebox cranking, and the door jingled open. "Thought you all might enjoy some bagels to kick off your Grand Opening. Compliments of Barley's," Mac Kelsh called, smiling as he dropped a brown bag on the counter. For a big guy, he sure had a soft voice.

I walked over to him. "Thanks a lot, Mr. Kel—"

"Call me Mac," he said, gazing around the shop. He wore a sage-green collared shirt that matched his khaki pants nicely. His STORE MANAGER KELSH, HERE TO SERVE YOU name tag was centered neatly above his shirt pocket.

Gabby reached for a poppy-seed bagel, and I started slicing a plain one for Jordan.

"Is Delilah around?" Mac asked.

I shook my head, reluctant to say much.

He looked surprised. "When do you expect her?"

"Not sure. She appointed me acting shop manager. You need something?"

"I wanted to compliment Delilah on her presentation and merchandising," he said, looking over at the fudge display and topping jars and up at the beaver cycling overhead. "Engaged customers make more impulse purchases, and this place is a real attention grabber."

I smiled. "I'll pass on your kind words."

After he left, a familiar voice called from the storage room. "Soda jerk reporting for duty!"

Pete walked out and Gabby, Chief, and I all spoke at the same time. "Whoa!"

He was dressed like he'd time-traveled back seventy years, with a spiffy white tuxedo jacket with tails, a bow tie, and a paper hat covering his slicked red hair.

"Look at you!" I blurted out.

Pete grinned proudly. "Miz Dobson expects us soda jerks to serve with distinction. In the old days we were the superstars. Knowing that, well, I did some serious picking to upgrade my wardrobe."

"Through trash?" I whispered, grimacing.

"Naah." He straightened his bow tie. "The Salvation Army just got a new shipment." Then he whistled at Gabby and me. "Never mind me. Get a load of *you* ladies. Not one, but two eighty-seven and a halves!"

"Huh?" we both said at once.

"That's soda-jerk slang for *pretty ladies*," he explained, pulling an index card from his back pocket.

I motioned for him to come behind the counter and wash his hands. "Gabby and I could use a refresher lesson on sundae making. My ma won't be here today, and everything has to operate on schedule, just the way she planned."

Pete raised his eyebrows, then nodded without asking any questions. "Good thing I memorized the recipes for all forty of the sundae specials. Miz Dobson trains her soda jerks well, plus I took notes from the last S&P session."

"S&P session?" Gabby asked.

"Scoop and pack. The top two essential skills for a soda jerk," he said matter-of-factly.

Gabby gazed at Pete with amorous eyes as he scrubbed his hands. "I can see why soda jerks were considered superstars."

I couldn't take any more of this employee flirting. I spread peanut butter on a bagel for Jordan and walked back to the storage room.

The smell of smoke struck me before I even got there.

"Oh no!" I shrieked, my heart racing.

Flames shot out from the corner of the storage room. Lucky's sunlamp had fallen into Lucky's travel case. The box was melting and browning, with a giant hole through the center getting bigger and bigger.

"Jordan!" I yelled. He was on the opposite side of the room, his back to the fire, kneeling over Lucky, unaware of what was happening.

Ring! Ring! The smoke alarm went off.

I rushed over and grabbed the fire extinguisher from under the sink. Ma's fire-safety training flashed through my mind, and I quickly pulled the pin off the extinguisher. Aiming at the base of the fire, *not* the flames, like she told me, I squeezed the trigger and swept side to side.

"Should I call 911?" Gabby shouted, rushing in.

"No, definitely not!" I said, worried that firefighters would discover the owner wasn't here and shut us down.

Back and forth I swept the foam for a good five minutes

until the flames subsided. A gray smoke cloud hovered above the sink, but the danger was gone.

I waited a few minutes and then picked up the charred remains of the box, only to realize the ash and extinguisher foam had ruined the tamale sign beside it too. I gathered it all and a giant ruined box of plastic spoons and tossed them out back in the Dumpster.

When I returned, Jordan was clutching Lucky to his chest, crying. "Stuffy nose. Smell nothing," he signed.

I rubbed his head and wiped his wet cheek. "It's okay. Don't be scared," I signed.

Pete, Chief, Mr. and Mrs. Bianco, and Mr. Harley were all huddled in the storage room. Chief grabbed paper towels and started wiping up the mess. I pulled the box of tamales away. Luckily they hadn't been destroyed.

"Everything's under control," I said, reaching for a broom to clear the soot on the floor. Pete gave Jordan a big bowl to hold Lucky temporarily.

"And I'll get more spoons," Pete said.

"Where's your mother?" Mr. Harley asked me, his face worried.

"Home. She's in bed, sick," I explained yet again. "But Cinco de Mayo goes on as scheduled. It must."

Mr. Bianco's mouth dropped open. "But you're a kid. No one can expect a—"

"Please, Mr. Bianco," I said. "I've *got* to do this. For my ma's sake. I can't let her down."

He nodded and then, along with Mr. Harley, picked up

more ashy debris as Mrs. Bianco took the broom from my hands. "Delilah Dobson reaches out every time she sees someone needing a hand on State Street. You don't have to do this alone," she said.

Mrs. Bianco put her hand on my shoulder. "We won't *let* you do it alone."

Chapter 27

Forewarned is forearmed. Study your local competition
like a general preparing for battle. —*The Inside Scoop*

"Here you go, ma'am, two twist cones with rainbow sprinkles," I said to the lady with a stroller. "Enjoy!" I added, using Ma's closing salutation.

Quickly I started mixing the next customer's SmAlbany Strawberry Shake. No time to idle. The line was out the door and snaking down the sidewalk. Pete had just dashed off to Barley's for more spoons, and we were already missing him behind the counter.

"If only I'd memorized the sundae specials like our soda

jerk did," Gabby whispered as she ladled blueberry syrup on a Yankee Doodle Dandy.

"Yeah, I'm getting whiplash from turning around to read the menu board. And we're running out of spoons. Sure hope Pete gets back soon," I said.

"I hope Peter hurries, because he's soooo funny," Gabby gushed as she placed three pieces of caramel fudge in a box with tissue.

"*Peter?*" I asked.

She nodded, handing the box to a customer. "*Peter* sounds more fitting for a soda jerk."

A Cherry on Top was wall-to-wall customers. People were laughing, talking, digging into sundaes, and licking away at cones. Silly Billy & Son had just arrived, and little kids were crowded around them as they set up their show. The clown son looked about my age, though it was hard to tell with that bushy red wig and white-painted face.

Then, with a shockingly loud honk from a bazooka, the clowns got busy, shouting out jokes, squirting water guns, and twisting balloons into animal shapes.

I'd never seen so many kids giggle at once. "Me! Me!" they squealed when Silly Billy asked for an assistant for a hat trick. Nearby, two older girls in softball uniforms pressed their faces against the jukebox, studying the song selections.

Not that you could hear the music very well. The door was propped open, and the Salty Old Dogs were drawing crowds on the sidewalk with their upbeat Tejano tunes. Winnie and Melvin stood in front singing, and three gray-haired men sat behind them playing drums, a trumpet, and a fiddle. (I recognized Sam on trumpet from Ma's test-market session.) Every so often Melvin picked up a harmonica and started playing that too, just like I told him the mariachis do back home. They all wore matching wide-brimmed hats and silver-studded *charro* jackets.

"Next customer, please!" Gabby called.

I thought of Ma. If she was here, she'd say the line of customers was growing faster than a weed after a month's rain. People were getting antsy with the wait. A short lady with big hair and an even bigger mouth started complaining. Feeling pressured, I rushed to pack a double scoop of pistachio and crushed the cone in my hand.

"This long a wait, they must be milking the cows out back!" the lady whined to the man in front of her.

I felt my stomach knot. Then Ma's voice channeling the *Inside Scoop* played in my head. *No matter what, the customer is always right.*

But before I could say a word, someone with a cultured voice spoke. "I've heard this ice cream is certainly worth the wait."

I looked up to see a lady with a pinstripe blazer and a Louis Vuitton bag on her shoulder. Victoria! I waved at her, and she returned a glamorous smile.

"We'll be with you as soon as possible, ma'am," I said to the Complainer with my best soothing smile. The truth was I felt like spraying whipped cream in her beehive.

We needed another scooper fast. But who? Jordan was

playing with Lucky in the storage room (and he wouldn't hear customers anyway), Winnie was singing with the band, and Chief was in the street manning the concession stand, as he called it, with his own long line of customers to deal with.

I glanced across the dining area, where kids' eyes were glued to Silly Billy pulling handkerchiefs from a hat. Son of Clown was standing off to the side with his arms folded, watching. Hmm . . . maybe he could take a break from clowning?

I tapped him on his polka-dotted shoulder. "Excuse me. I'm desperate. Could you pitch in behind the counter until Pete gets back? We can't keep up."

He smiled and adjusted his red nose. "Sure thing, Desperate."

Pronto, Son of Clown tied an apron over his jumpsuit and started S&P'ing alongside us. He caught on quickly. Watching him, customers seemed to forget they were miserable waiting. Especially the little kids.

"Look, Mommy. The clown's making ice cream!" squealed a little girl holding a balloon. Soon lots of kids were telling their parents, "I want the clown to make *my* ice cream!"

Five minutes later Pete returned. "Spoons R Us!" he shouted as he worked his way behind the counter with a bag and put his paper server's hat back on.

"Are we glad to see you! We were so panicky, we recruited a clown," I whispered, wiping splattered cream from my face with the sleeve of my smocked top. Looking down at my fudge-stained apron, I wondered why I'd worn my new clothes.

"Sounds like the crowd's getting testy. Miz D. warned me

this might happen. Time to dig deep into my soda-jerk training and bring out the shtick."

With that, Pete ran over to the karaoke machine and grabbed the microphone. "Greetings, ladies, gents, and wee widdle ones. I'm Pete Chutkin, official soda jerk at A Cherry on Top. No, not *jerk* like the guy who cut you off in traffic, or the boy who stuck a KICK ME sign on your back. Once upon a time, I was the coolest cat in the ice cream biz. The master of the milk shake. The prince of the phosphate. And speaking of cool, get set for the Soda-Jerk Swing!"

Then, without one ounce of humiliation or the tiniest trace of reserve, Pete adjusted his bow tie and started tapping his shoes, rocking back and forth, and rapping.

> *"Hippity-hop*
> *to A Cherry on Top!*
> *Miz D. will make a shake*
> *that you know ain't no fake.*
> *And ya say ya want fudge?*
> *Tessy's tastes nothin' like sludge. . . ."*

Just when it couldn't get lamer, Pete busted out the moves, break-dancing, spinning on his heels, and even adding a cartwheel that looked good until he crashed into the jukebox. And then Son of Clown charged from behind the counter and joined in as Pete's backup dancer, shaking his wig, swinging his arms, and kicking his legs Charleston-style.

For the closing stance Pete blasted out the lyrics even louder:

> *"So grab those dollars*
> *and all your dimes,*
> *and march yo' feet*
> *to the beat*
> *of this soda jerk's rhymes!"*

The middle-school me was so embarrassed, I was tempted to dive into the dipping cabinet and die of brain freeze. But as shop manager, I *liked* all this razzle-dazzle. The cash register was ringing, and customers kept smiling cheek to cheek like the wait was fine and dandy. Two little girls started copying Pete's dance moves in front of the jukebox, shaking their hearts out along with all the braids on their heads. And even the Complainer flashed a teeny smile when the Soda-Jerk Swingers took their final bow.

Chapter 28

The proper way to scoop and pack a cone: (1) temper the ice cream so the dipper slides in easily; (2) move your hand in an arc to form a scoop the size of a tennis ball; (3) now easy does it as you pack it onto the cone. —*The Inside Scoop*

The Cinco de Mayo parade got under way at eleven. Mr. Bianco led the way down State Street, holding a baton and strutting in a skin-tight velvet blazer that Mrs. Bianco said fit him back in Sicily, thirty years and forty pounds ago. The Save Their Tails Animal Protective Society followed, with rows of dogs yapping and sniffing and lifting their legs at fire hydrants along the way.

The Rotary Club came next, wearing their own pit-bull scowls suggesting they thought the parade order had gone to the dogs. Next up were the Schenectady Light Opera Company, the Boy Scouts, preschool ballerinas pliéing along, and World War II veterans propped high in convertibles and waving tiny flags.

General Electric's Young Inventors Club drew the most cheers. A bunch of brainy-looking kids in shirts and ties waved lightbulbs, cameras, and pictures of telegraphs. I overheard a lady explaining to her daughter the story of how Thomas Edison founded his company here and helped the city prosper. *Back in those days the streets of Schenectady were paved with gold*, I thought, remembering Pete's words.

Ma had designed the parade route to travel west on State Street past Proctor's Theater, turn right on Broadway, cross Erie Boulevard, and down to Union Street before looping back. Initially the RSSA wanted it to lap around Jay Street to please the mayor inside city hall, but Ma convinced them to have it pass through more struggling neighborhoods instead. "They need the extra TLC," she said.

If this parade was a train, then the Salty Old Dogs were the caboose, walking in the rear as they sang and rattled tambourines. Only Winnie's parade appearance came to an abrupt halt. The brisk pace got to her before she'd gone five hundred yards. From the window I saw her huffing and puffing as she clomped along in her heels. Worried that she'd faint, Pete and I ran outside with a water bottle.

"You okay?" I asked, gently pulling her out of the parade formation to a bench on the sidewalk.

"Never been crankier," she said, guzzling the water and

squeezing my hand as if to say thanks. "I love all this whoop-de-doing, but me and exercise never have gotten along."

I smiled back. I hadn't told Winnie about Ma being sick yet. Now wasn't the time; she needed to catch her breath. She'd been on her feet performing for hours.

"People are raving about the Salty Old Dogs, Winnie. A kid from my school grabbed your flyer and asked his dad to book you for his bar mitzvah."

"That so?" Winnie said, looking pleased.

"Yup! Diana Ross, eat your heart out—and gain some weight!" I shouted.

Now *that* brought a smile to her chestnut cheeks.

Honk-honk. Chief's truck pulled up beside us. "Here to pick up the diva!" he shouted, flashing a parade-float permit. "Hop in and we'll catch up with the rest of the Salty Old Dogs. They might want a ride by now too. I've got special authorization to chauffeur the senior talent."

"God bless the U.S. Navy!" Winnie shouted, standing up.

Chief piled blankets into the back of his truck to make it more comfortable for Winnie. That way they'd be visible to parade watchers. But just before she got in, she rested her tambourine on the grass. "Wait just a minute," she told Chief, and she turned back to A Cherry on Top.

"I've got to get my little James Brown," she said, inside the shop. "I know Jordan would love being in the parade and shaking his groove thing to the beat."

We went back for Jordan. His eyes lit up when he heard the news. But then he signed, "Lucky come?"

Winnie shook her head. "Too loud. Lucky will be scared."

"Jordan no go. Stay with Lucky," he signed, looking like he'd burst into tears.

The line for ice cream was growing long again. Gabby and Pete were struggling to keep up. I had to get back to work. "Go, Jordan," I signed quickly. "I'll watch Lucky." I pointed toward the counter. "Bring him to me, covered, so customers don't see."

"Promise you take care of my turtle?"

I pressed my index finger to my mouth and then placed my palm down against my other fist. "Promise."

So Jordan brought me the bowl, discreetly covered with a towel, and I tucked it under the counter on a shelf near the extra cups. Then he and Winnie left to catch up with the parade.

The crowd inside the shop thinned out after another hour, especially when Mr. Harley announced that the grand raffle would be drawn at the jewelry store shortly. So Gabby, Pete, and I used the downtime to clean tables, restock topping jars, and replace empty ice cream tubs. Then Pete made a sandwich run to Barley's, and we sat down to eat with the clowns.

Noticing a Lego toy left on a chair, Son of Clown told us he was crazy about Legos. "I just built the *Star Wars Millennium Falcon*, and *that* used five thousand pieces. Took me six months," he said, and I thought about how long I'd been working on the piano-bench cushion for Winnie.

I tried to avoid making eye contact with Son of Clown, knowing how he must've been dying a thousand deaths wearing that wig. But the funny thing was, he didn't seem embarrassed. He was boasting about how his dad graduated at the top of clown school. And they both beamed when they talked about "the family business."

With only half my sandwich finished, I glanced up at the clock. The mayor would be arriving in thirty minutes for the ribbon-cutting ceremony. I had to get this place set up pronto—a TV reporter was coming too. And I had to think about what to say. I needed to sound informed and squared away, as Chief would call it.

So as the others continued talking, I started arranging rows of chairs for the audience and a makeshift podium with a microphone for Mayor Legato to use for his speech. Worry must've been smeared across my face like fudge sauce, because Gabby, Pete, and the clowns cut their lunch short and came over to help.

I pointed to the *Inside Scoop* lying on the counter beside the napkin dispenser and turned to Pete. "Did you study that training manual like my ma did?"

"You bet your egg cream I did. All two hundred fifty-six pages, including the yawner part on milk pasteurization and homogenization."

"Can you summarize all that in five minutes or less? I need to sound like an expert around the reporter."

Pete rubbed his forehead. "Where should I begin?"

"Give me a brief history, then explain what's in quality ice cream, and end with why this shop is good for Schenectady."

Pete took a deep breath and began spewing like a tour guide on his fourth cup of coffee. Legends about Marco Polo bringing the recipe back from China and how a Roman emperor killed his slaves if they didn't fetch his dessert ice fast enough. How George Washington spent two hundred dollars on ice cream one summer, how FDR always picked chocolate, and how Ronald Reagan liked all flavors, so much that he designated July as National Ice Cream Month.

"And back in 2009, one of President Obama's inauguration balls served up BaRocky Road," Pete explained, and I smiled.

I felt like I had brain freeze from ice cream trivia overload, so I thanked Pete and we finished arranging chairs. Then Clown Dad started setting up a coin trick as a Little League team charged toward his table. I grabbed the piñata and went outside to hang it, but I couldn't reach the awning. I turned to go back inside and nearly ran into Son of Clown holding a stepping stool.

"I can do that. I'm used to hanging model airplanes," he said, setting the stool down. He hopped up, and before I could say *Clown to the rescue*, that giant papier-mâché ice cream cone was swinging in the wind.

"Thanks," I said, sneaking a closer peek at him. He had warm, easygoing eyes—light green, like mint chocolate chip ice cream minus the chips.

Son of Clown shrugged under his polka-dotted jumpsuit. "Glad to help, especially since I heard the owner didn't bother showing up."

"Delilah Dobson made this business what it is. Don't go blaming her if she's sick!" I yelled.

He jerked back a step. "I'm sorry. I didn't know. . . ."

I didn't stick around to hear more. I couldn't. I went inside to string the ribbon.

Shake-shake. Jordan and the Salty Old Dogs burst through the door, rattling maracas.

"Attention: Mariachi bandits have entered the building. Turn over the ice cream and nobody gets hurt!" Winnie shouted. Melvin and the other men wore their sombreros. Winnie's was on Jordan's head now—cocked sideways. All their hair looked windblown.

Pete cleared his throat and raised his ice cream scooper to his mouth like a microphone. "As A Cherry on Top's official soda jerk, I declare ice cream is on the house for all mariachis!"

"I'll drink to that," Melvin shouted, bowing ceremoniously before ordering a Schenectady Snow Shake.

Now, this was good timing. I worked my way over to tell Winnie what happened to Ma. But just as I got near, Catherine was wheeled into the shop by Jack. Winnie bent down to hug her, and they started talking.

I walked behind the counter again, put some fudge slices onto a plate, and returned to Winnie and Catherine. "Care for a sample, ladies? We serve the world's best fudge. Thanks to an exclusive recipe from Mackinac Island, this stuff is flying off the shelves!"

Catherine smiled her elegant dancer smile as her trembling hand reached for a piece. After one bite she paused, then nodded. "Creamy, rich, and chewy. Extra scrumptious, just like when I was a young girl!" Then Jack wheeled her over to the dining area, and Winnie followed.

Minutes later Chief came inside from the concession stand with the empty tamale boxes. He stepped up to the counter arm in arm with Adelaine Heisey.

"I'm here to report four hundred and twenty dollars of sales. Those tamales sold like hot tamales!" Chief said, grinning. Then, gently touching Adelaine's shoulder, he added, "Mee-lady here prefers sugar-free ice cream. Got any?"

"We have sugar-free chocolate chip, sugar-free black cherry, and sugar-free *and* fat-free caramel swirl," Gabby said.

Adelaine picked black cherry. "I never order fat-free ice cream. What's the point?" she said. "I don't even trust the people who eat it."

"Then give me two scoops of butter pecan, extra fat please!" Chief said, and Gabby and I giggled.

As Gabby scooped their cones, Chief leaned over and whispered in my ear, "You holding up, kiddo?"

I nodded and walked back behind the counter. I'd lost my chance to talk to Winnie; the line was growing again.

Ten minutes later, I was making an "I Loved Him Tender" Banana Royal for a woman police officer when I felt a tug on my shirt.

Jordan.

"Where's Lucky?" he signed, pointing below the counter.

My eyes darted down. *Uh-oh.* The bowl was flipped over. I must've knocked it when I was reaching for more cups. Lucky had escaped!

I searched through every nook and cranny behind the counter—on the shelves, under the sink, and near the garbage pail—just as some kids shouted my name at the same time.

It was Ritchie, Kim, Devin, Malika, and the others—Mr. Win too—all wearing their Peer Mediation Club shirts.

"We heard conflict is reduced when people eat ice cream, so we're here to test the theory," Mr. Win said.

"And if you make my cone really big, I promise there'll be no disputants," Ritchie added.

"You got it," I said, smiling. Meanwhile, my heart was racing and my eyes were scanning every square foot under the counter. Where was Lucky?

The door jingled open again, and a lady with thick makeup, a power suit, and high heels walked in with a guy carrying a video camera. That was no ordinary lady. That was the Channel 13 news anchor! She'd come looking for a story, and yikes, was there one to be found!

I turned to Jordan. He was crawling under the counter, yanking cabinets open and making a mess ripping through boxes. His face looked two tears short of a meltdown.

My mind flashed to the day that Jordan slipped out the back door and I'd blamed Ma. Here I'd promised I'd take good care of Lucky and I'd been the world's worst turtle sitter.

I bent down and tapped his shoulder, my fingers nervously pleading. "I'm *really* sorry, Jordan. I'll find Lucky. But it *must* wait. Very busy. Please be good."

Then I braced myself, fully expecting FrankenJordan to unleash his angry shrieks and kick the counter—or worse, toss glass jars.

But instead, he wiped his glassy eyes with his shirtsleeve and stood up.

"Okay, Tess. I find Lucky myself," he signed.

Chapter 29

When it comes to food retail, cleanliness is next
to godliness. —*The Inside Scoop*

"Trouble alert: Lucky's on the loose and a newshound is sniffing for a story," I whispered to Gabby.

Gabby's eyes bulged. "Uh-oh. You handle Lois Lane, and I'll stay here and help your brother search," she said.

I walked out from behind the counter and greeted the reporter.

"I'm Christine Perkins. News anchor at Channel Thirteen," she replied, clutching a clipboard. "We're doing a story on Schenectady's business revitalization, and I'd like to interview Delilah Dobson."

Ma's moment to shine had arrived, yet she wasn't here. I could feel tears pooling just thinking about it, but no—I wouldn't let that happen. *Cleansing breath, Tess.*

So, as Ma would say, I stayed calm as a platter of spit. "I'm Tess Dobson, acting shop manager. Delilah is tending to other affairs, but I can help."

Ms. Perkins looked slightly suspicious. "You sure you're old enough?"

"This is a family operation, and I'm the Dobson family spokesperson," I said firmly, pointing quickly toward Winnie and Catherine, who were sitting eating their ice cream with the Salty Old Dogs, as if they were my aunts.

Without leaving room for further questions, I jumped right into my shop spiel and tour. "A Cherry on Top is for all kinds of ice cream lovers." I paused and gestured toward Chief and Adelaine in the corner, licking their cones and making lovey-dovey eyes at each other. "As you can see, we welcome the young and the young at heart."

Ms. Perkins nodded but didn't say a word, so I kept going.

"Our ice cream is made with only the purest, freshest ingredients, starting with milk from black-and-white Holstein cows," I said, recalling everything Pete had told me about manufacturing ice cream.

Just as I continued describing ingredients, Elvis's "All Shook Up" blasted from the speakers, and Jordan dashed toward the dining area. Scooting from one table to the next, he lifted tablecloths, squatted down, and looked between customers' ankles, searching furiously.

Fortunately, Ms. Perkins didn't notice. She was distracted, telling the camera guy to film customers walking in—people of all ages, shapes, and looks. Some wore designer clothes as if they shopped at Victoria's Classic Interior Design, while others had frayed jackets and unshaven faces.

Pointing the microphone at me, she said, "So tell us about this Resuscitate State Street Association. And why did your family choose to launch a business on State Street, of all places? Most retailers would stay clear of this no-growth area."

What a rude statement! But this was no different from peer mediation. I had to state the facts without getting defensive. I recalled what Pete had told me during our ride to Central Park, about Schenectady's glory days and later hardships, as well as Ma's plan to make State Street more welcoming.

"Sure, this city has some wear and tear, but so does a scruffy old teddy bear and that's lovable," I said. "From the Erie Canal to the first railroad built in New York State, Schenectady has been the cradle of innovation. Sure, maybe jobs have left for the Sun Belt since then, but resuscitating State Street is going to bring the sparkle back."

Then I cut to the chase, rattling off reasons why ice cream and State Street went hand in hand. "And it's only a short stroll from the renovated Proctor's Theater, where people have been enjoying live entertainment since 1926. Now folks will have scrumptious ice cream to enjoy after the show!"

Ms. Perkins said she'd heard we came from Texas. "So what brought you all the way to Schenectady?"

Tough question. Tougher than my worst batch of fudge.

I couldn't tell her about Jimbo's wife's cousin's stepsister, who convinced Ma to come here and then bailed out to sell lottery tickets in Buffalo. That wouldn't give us points for credibility.

Desperate, I pulled out two of my favorite words.

"Was it destiny or serendipity? You be the judge," I said with a voice smooth like a circus announcer's. "All I know for sure is we were drawn to this city and its lovers of frozen treats."

I kept loading Ms. Perkins up with local trivia. I explained how the upstate New York town of Ithaca claims to be the birthplace of the first ice cream sundae, back in 1891. "But as far as I know, nobody offers a Schenectady Snow Shake but us."

Ms. Perkins didn't look impressed. Or like she believed me. She *had* to become a believer. What could I do? *Mr. Win says be an advocate for resolution, and always speak the truth*, I remembered.

"There is *another* reason why we opened A Cherry on Top here," I said, lowering my voice. "A reason that's more confidential and juicy, if you must know."

Ms. Perkins's waxed eyebrows jumped up an inch. "What?"

I touched her suit sleeve. "Have you had a bad day lately, Ms. Perkins—and I mean so bad that if it was a fish, you'd throw it back?"

She shrugged. "Who hasn't? Yesterday I woke up with an allergy attack, and that construction traffic on Erie Boulevard made me late for work."

"Delilah Dobson created A Cherry on Top as a welcoming watering hole for when life leaves you roughed up. Trust me, she's got her share of bumps and bruises, and she's met plenty of Schenectady folks who've also struggled through heartbreak. Down but not out, that's what Delilah says."

I pointed to Pete, who was serving up a smile along with a Rotterdam Root Beer Float. "Our soda jerk doesn't exactly live in a penthouse, but he's a budding photographer who always pictures the good in the world. And Gabby, our curly-topped scooper—well, she's an enlightened tiger-vegan who's always willing to lend a hand. That's the kind of people A Cherry on Top attracts. Sweets for the folks who need a little sweet in their lives."

Ms. Perkins jotted that down on her clipboard. I almost detected a smile under all that makeup.

I gently suggested that her cameraman switch from filming the cracked sidewalks and graffiti-covered buildings outside and instead home in on the happy families licking cones and enjoying themselves on State Street, thanks to the RSSA's cleanup and neighborhood watch.

And then I *had* to pass on Ma's famous one-liner. Only now it was starting to feel like it belonged to everybody at A Cherry on Top. Walking Ms. Perkins toward the front counter, I spoke clearly into the mic. "We like to say, 'Ice cream warms the heart, no matter what the weather.' "

She scribbled that down too, and then started checking out all the flavors in the dipping cabinet.

I could almost hear Ma's twang. *Attagirl, Tess. You got her two-stepping.*

"How about a cone, Ms. Perkins? I bet we've got your favorite flavor!"

She grinned. "It's peanut butter, and it's hard to find."

"We've got it, all right. My brother's a huge peanut butter fan."

I walked behind the counter, washed my hands, and grabbed the scooper. I was about to reach for a cone when I heard a scream from the dining area.

"What's moving over there?" a woman yelled.

"Tell me it's not a mouse!" a second woman said, her hand covering her sundae.

All eyes were fixed on the front display window. My heart felt like it would skip a beat. I knew exactly what was going on, what was moving under that blinking banana-split sign.

Just then, Jordan charged the window, shrieking his bat shrieks. He jumped up on the ledge, knocking down a collection of ceramic smiley-face cones and reaching his hand under the light until he pulled out Lucky.

The camera guy filmed it all—like he was collecting evidence—as the crowd in the dining area looked on. Kids abandoned the clowns to watch Jordan. Most of them were giggling, though some of the adults looked bothered.

"Turtles carry diseases, don't they?" Ms. Perkins asked, her words dredged in disgust. She didn't look like she was willing to let this red-eared slider slide.

My voice locked, sensing danger, dreading that Channel 13 would have a breaking news story later: "Ice Cream Shop Shut Down After Serving Up Salmonella and Sickening Hundreds."

Suddenly a clown stepped in front of the microphone—make that Son of Clown. "Aha, there's my stage assistant. Hard to get good help these days."

"You brought that reptile into this food establishment?" Ms. Perkins asked, frowning.

He nodded, shaking his wig. "He's a special turtle—show sanitized. You see, I promised the kids I'd bring an empty sundae bowl to life. Guess I should've warned them it wouldn't sit still."

Boys and girls holding twisty animal balloons rushed toward Jordan, who was holding Lucky, and shouted, "Ooooo!"

Ms. Perkins said nothing. Son of Clown had made a gracious cover-up attempt, but I knew she wouldn't buy it. She just kept staring over at Lucky in Jordan's arms with the camera guy standing beside her, filming away. I had this sinking feeling he was filming the rise and fall of our business.

But on closer look, it was *Jordan* she was watching now. Then she turned to me and asked, "Who is that boy?"

Speak the truth, I told myself. No more holding back. I opened my mouth. "My brother Jordan. And that's his turtle. He went missing."

After another moment she walked over to him and signed, "I'm Christine. Cute turtle."

Jordan squealed like he always does when someone unexpectedly signs. "His name is Lucky. Okay to pet his shell. But careful. Lucky shy."

Ms. Perkins turned back to me. "My cousin is deaf," she spoke, then signed, facing Jordan so he'd see.

Quickly I took Lucky from Jordan, put him in the big bowl, and whisked him back to the storage room, letting out a Texas-sized sigh. I thought Jordan would follow, but he didn't. He stuck around signing more to Ms. Perkins, something about seeing her on TV and could he get on TV too?

At that point I washed my hands again and began S&P'ing two perfectly shaped cones with peanut butter ice cream, feeling relieved that Channel 13 wasn't going to ruin our big day. At least not on account of turtle trouble.

Winnie called me to the storage room just as the crowd gathered for the ribbon cutting. "Where's your ma?" she asked. "I haven't seen her all day."

I swallowed a lump. "At the apartment. Shooting Stars is back."

Winnie's eyes widened like her sombrero. "Why didn't you tell me?"

"I wanted to, but things got so busy."

She listened to the whirl of talking and motion up front. "You mean you've managed all this by *yourself*?"

"Everyone's helped. Pete, Gabby, Chief—and you too."

Right away Winnie arranged for Melvin to go back to Mohawk Valley Village and check on Ma. "Bring her a sandwich and sit with her," she told him. Then she hugged me so tight, I felt the sequins on her gown. "I'm so proud of what you've done," she said.

"Tess? Mayor Legato's here!" Gabby shouted.

Uh-oh. I turned to Winnie. "The mayor could cause problems if he finds out that Ma's not here. What'll I say?"

"Act like a politician and say as little as possible," she said, rubbing my back as we walked out front. "Don't you worry, girl. When the mayor gets a look at the crowd whipping out their credit cards on State Street and the TV crew covering it, he won't have any questions."

Sure enough, the mayor arrived in a perky mood, shaking hands, name-dropping, and taking credit for Cinco de Mayo like he'd dreamed up the whole idea. And as soon as the camera was running, he delivered his speech, smiling while he used punchy power words like *urban renewal* and *economic development*. He credited Delilah Dobson and the RSSA for "revitalizing State Street and choosing to invest in the future of Schenectady." I couldn't help but feel proud hearing him go on about Ma. A part of me wanted to giggle, especially when he described her "natural flair for business." I kept thinking about the flares the cops set up on the road when Ma ripped his car door off.

After the ribbon cutting, all the kids ran outside for the piñata ceremony. The clowns went too, and Pete and Son of Clown took turns covering kids' eyes with a bandanna and spinning them before they took a whack. Wouldn't you know it was a teensy, tiny Asian girl named Theresa who finally broke it open and sent candy flying on the sidewalk and kids scampering to grab it.

For the first time all day, Gabby and I were the only ones in the shop. She scooped herself a cup of lemon sorbet ("nondairy and vegan friendly"), and I had a double scoop of Rocky Road. Then we sat in the dining area with our feet up.

You'd think that ice cream wouldn't be appealing after the billion cones we scooped today, but it was. Rocky Road always tastes like ice-cold heaven in my mouth.

"Ooh, my tired tootsies," Gabby groaned, pulling her feet out from her heels. "I don't have what it takes to make it in retail."

I grinned. "If it means chapped hands and achy shoulders, I don't *want* what it takes."

"But look at all this," Gabby said, pointing outside. "People are strolling and smiling when they used to rush to get past State Street. Lots of kids from our school came too. And did you hear Mr. Win? He said we're going to have our end-of-the-year Peer Mediation Club party here!"

I smiled. "My ma deserves most of the credit. You, too, Gabby. You're a true friend."

"This tiger is lucky to call you my friend," she said, playfully punching my shoulder. "And speaking of special friends, I was right about ice cream shops offering romantic possibilities, wasn't I?"

I bit into a chunk of marshmallow. "I know. Our superstar soda jerk stole your heart."

"Peter *is* really nice. And guess what? He wants to come to my Zen archery class later in the summer and take photos. But I'm not talking about him. Someone else has been watching *you*—a cute male someone."

I stopped licking my cone. "Who?"

"Son of Clown."

Son of Clown? With highlights in my hair and a brand-new outfit, I got noticed by Son of Clown?

"No matter what, I am *not* dating a clown!" I shouted. After I said it, I felt a little guilty. He had tried to save the day with that smooth line about a show-sanitized turtle.

"C'mon, Tess. Embrace life's adventure. Romance with a clown could be thrilling," Gabby teased.

Thinking about that, a silly volcano erupted from deep inside my stomach, and I couldn't stop giggling. It must've been contagious, too, because Gabby joined in, laughing so hard she practically tipped her chair over.

Chapter 30

The wise retailer will heed Aristotle's words: "We are what we repeatedly do. Excellence, then, is not an act, but a habit." —*The Inside Scoop*

The sign on the door said A Cherry on Top closed at ten p.m., but a chartered bus pulled up at nine-forty-five. It was a church group from way north in the Adirondacks, packed with chirpy people singing show tunes, and we didn't have the heart to turn them away. We scooped the last cone about forty-five minutes later, and then quickly flipped the sign to CLOSED and got to work cleaning the shop.

It was just Gabby, Pete, and me left. Winnie had taken

Jordan home earlier, and Chief was outside helping RSSA members sweep the street and stack the benches on loan from the funeral home.

"Yikes, this floor looks like somebody's been finger-painting with fudge," Gabby said as she swooshed the mop in the dining area.

"Can't say us hired help have been much tidier," Pete said as he scrubbed the prep counter, which was covered with sauces, nuts, and melted ice cream.

I emptied the trash, restocked the freezer, and pulled apart the hot-fudge dispenser like I'd seen Ma do. Sanitation was a top priority for her, and even though I felt like I could stretch out on the counter and fall asleep in five seconds flat, I wouldn't dare stop until all the equipment looked shiny new again.

Thirty minutes later, Pete and Gabby were yawning and looking like they'd just run a marathon. Gabby's feet were so blistered, she'd taken off her heels. Pete had raccoon eyes, and his tuxedo tails had strawberry syrup stains like he'd done battle.

I took money from the cash register, sorted it into two piles, and then added an extra ten dollars to each.

"Here you go. A day's wages plus a bonus for outstanding service," I said, giving them the money. "Now go home. Get some rest."

After they left, I reorganized the topping jars and filled out the inventory chit for reordering. Mac Kelsh had been nice enough to offer to open the store tomorrow so I could take care of Ma, and I made sure to leave the store-opening checklist on the counter. Then I counted the money. I'd heard Ma say breaking even on Opening Day meant pulling in eight hundred dollars. We'd brought in double that amount!

I wiped down the dining-area tables, and then Chief and I locked up. We walked slowly to the truck, drinking in the refreshing night air. Mr. Bianco was standing in front of the pizzeria with Mr. Harley, his arm resting on a broom.

"Super job, Tess. You made State Street proud!" Mr. Bianco called.

Mr. Harley whistled. Then he said, "You go home and tell the Can-Do Cancan Lady we're all thinking about her."

I checked on Ma as soon as I got into the apartment. She was sleeping deeply on the futon, snoring. I wished I could wake her and tell her all about the day. But she wasn't up for that talk, and I could barely hold my head up. Instead, I tossed my filthy clothes into the hamper, put on my pj's, and jumped into bed.

The soft pillow under my head had never felt so good.

I woke the next morning to the smell of fried eggs and onions. Someone was in the kitchen whipping up a Tex-Mex breakfast to die for. But who? It couldn't be Ma. Not after Shooting Stars.

But it *was* Ma in the kitchen, leaning over a frying pan on the stove.

"What are you doing up?" I asked as she turned around.

"Making huevos rancheros. Lord knows you deserve this and a whole lot more," she said, her voice faint but sincere.

Ma looked awful—pasty pale and scrawny like a desert

lizard. Her hair was tangled and matted, and her whole body trembled as she held the spatula.

"You're sick. Let me do that," I said, reaching for the spatula.

But she wouldn't let go. Tears streamed down her pale cheeks as she slumped over the stove weakly. "Winnie told me all you did yesterday," she said. "I feel so proud to be your mama. Ashamed too, for what I put you through. Not right that my young daughter has grown-up headaches on account of crazy me."

"It's okay, Ma. Really. And you're *not* crazy," I said, hugging her. I begged her to let me finish up, and she finally did, once the eggs were cooked. I scooped them onto the tortillas she had resting on two plates. Then I ladled them with chili sauce, topping it with Tapatío sauce and a handful of cheese.

I set the plates on the counter and poured some juice, and Ma and I ate. I ate, anyway; Ma picked.

Then I described the sights and sounds of the Cinco de Mayo parade, full of marchers and floats and smiling spectators. I told her about Pete's flashy soda-jerk dance and the line out the door for ice cream, and how Son of Clown saved the day after Lucky got loose. I explained how I got the Channel 13 reporter on our side by telling her about our philosophy that ice cream warms the heart, so much on our side that she'd be doing a special report on the shop next week.

"We struck gold, Ma. Sixteen hundred dollars. Like you would say, that's not chump change!" My mouth was full of spicy eggs and my heart with gratitude. Because I might have been acting shop manager yesterday, but Ma made this all happen.

Ma took in all I said, her sunken eyes pleased, but she said very little. It seemed like she was caught in a net of sadness, without the strength to untangle herself.

"The *Inside Scoop* was right, Ma. Secondary products do affect the bottom line. We sold out of fudge! And you should've seen customers going wild for all your sundae specials," I added, sipping my juice.

When I finished my eggs, I pushed my plate away and folded my hands on the table. If Ma was going to change, I had to change too. No more avoiding the elephant in the room. Time to speak up.

"Guess what? Mac Kelsh is running things at the shop for us today so I can be with you. Isn't that nice?"

She nodded. "Mighty decent."

"Everyone's pitching in, Ma, because of *you*. You helped so many people, and they believe in you. Now it's your turn to help yourself. To do something different, even if it's hard."

Her eyes grew moist again. "I know where you're going with this, and it's a dead end. I'm not tougher than this ugly monster. He just keeps coming back and beating me down."

This time I wouldn't let her throw in the towel. I wouldn't blame her either. I touched the top of her bony shoulder. "It's not a monster, Ma. It's a medical condition. But it doesn't have to rule your life. Doctors have medicine that can help. I mean, it's probably not like strep throat that gets fixed fast with antibiotics, but if you stick with a plan—just like you did with A Cherry on Top—well, you *will* get it under control."

I expected to hear the usual excuses and down-with-no-good-doctor lines, but that didn't happen. The only sound in the kitchen was the refrigerator humming.

Then I spoke the hardest words I ever did say.

"I'm scared, Ma. Scared that unless something changes, you'll end up like your paw. You've got to fight it because Jordan and me—well, we couldn't take that."

With that, Ma's eyes turned into sprinklers, tears shooting down her cheeks so fast, one plopped on her plate. Without a word, she stood up and walked into the bathroom. The faucet water ran for a while—a long while—and then the door opened.

Ma's hair was combed and her face washed when she came back into the kitchen and looked at me.

"The way you took charge yesterday was amazing, Tess. You made me prouder than a goat with four horns. You're my inspiration, you hear me? I promise you this: I'm down now, really down, but you and Jordan *won't* lose me. I'm going back to the doc. I'll do whatever it takes."

"I love you, Ma," I said, and now my eyes were sprinklers too.

She reached for her car keys, her hands still shaking.

"Can I come to the doctor with you?" I asked. "Winnie says family can sometimes help describe symptoms even better than the person who's sick. And I know Chief wouldn't mind driving us. He loves cruising in his truck."

Ma paused for a minute, her face hollow like an empty bowl, her hands still shaking. Then slowly her mouth opened. "That'd be swell. I'd like your company."

Chapter 31

Turns out the formula for a successful business requires three attributes: hard work, a willing heart, and a stubborn-as-a-mule, no-quit spirit. —*The Inside Scoop*

Ma's first visit back to the doctor turned into repeated visits, as many as two or three a week. And like she said, sticking with a medicine routine was no walk in the park. The first drug the doctor started her on made her a zombie. The second made her sick as a dog. Plenty of the ice cream shop's profits went into paying for all her medical bills, and at times she looked even worse than before she'd gotten help.

But she'd meant what she said: she'd do whatever it took,

even if that meant trying new drugs and treatments. And she kept that chin-up attitude much better than I could have if it'd been me getting poked and swallowing all those horse pills.

"Way I see it, there's good news and bad news with this bipolar business," Ma told me one day at the pharmacy while we waited for a prescription that was supposed to minimize the side effects of the other drug she was taking. "The good news is I'm not necessarily headed for the last roundup in the sky. The bad news is this here's an alligator I gotta wrestle my whole life. Like it or not, I'll be taking medicine and making docs rich for years to come. And I have to make lifestyle changes too."

"Like what?"

"Being more aware of what makes my moods seesaw up and down. Having a regular sleep routine. Using relaxation techniques and exercising. And I gotta start psychotherapy. That means talking to a trouble expert and coming up with ways to better handle life's whammies."

"That *is* a lot, but you can do it," I told Ma, and I said I would help track her mood swings. "I see them coming, Ma, especially when you're under the gun, stressed."

She smiled. "RSSA members tell me you've got a good head on your shoulders. Makes sense for me to listen to you."

Even with her born-again mental outlook, Ma wasn't up to running the ice cream shop yet. Chief had taken over as acting shop manager because I had school, and he and Mac Kelsh organized work shifts with the help of RSSA members. Pitching in, Mac said, was what respectable retailers in the same business region did for each other, but Gabby and I thought he went above and beyond when it came to Ma. He visited her at our apartment after his work shift ended every single day, even when she was stuck in bed and acting grouchy. He brought her flowers, coffee, and donuts (Barley's, of course). And he told her jokes only retailers would find funny.

State Street merchants feared that business would die again after Cinco de Mayo, but they were wrong. The RSSA continued with clever promotions and advertising, and State Street kept hopping with customers. Especially at A Cherry on Top. Not only did the warm weather get Schenectadites in the mood for ice cream, but Channel 13's special business report brought in peanut butter fans wanting to try the Jordan Peanut Butter Party in a Cup. (Wisely, we made peanut butter the featured flavor for June.)

For me, the most satisfying news came when the *Daily Gazette* ranked our fudge number one in the Capital District. Reading that review brought tears to my eyes, as if my own child had won a beauty contest.

After a few weeks of filling in at the shop, the other RSSA members had their own flourishing businesses to tend to, and we needed more counter help, so Ma hired two waitresses from Little Miss Muffet's, Franny and Jillian.

Ma's progress had setbacks. Sometimes she seemed like she was on the mend, full of energy like her old sassy self. But then she'd fall deep into a valley, and that hollow look would return to her face. But eventually the doctor found a drug that balanced her mood swings most of the time. And then one morning in late

June she tucked the *Inside Scoop* inside her pocketbook and headed back to A Cherry on Top full-time.

As summer marched on, Ma kept coming home late on Wednesday nights. She had her shop-closing routine down now, so I knew that wasn't it. I wondered what was going on.

After making me swear silence on a stack of peanut brittle, Winnie let me in on the secret. Ma and Mac Kelsh had dates on Wednesday nights! That was Mac's night off from Barley's, and the two of them got a bite to eat and took walks in Central Park. One week they even attended a sign-language class, Winnie said.

"Why doesn't Ma just tell me she's going out with Mac?" I asked Winnie.

"She will when she's ready, and when she feels sure *you're* ready," she said. "For now she's taking life one day at a time and trying hard to stay healthy. Be happy for her. Mac's a good influence."

I finished sewing the last patch for the piano-bench quilt just in time for Winnie's birthday. Ma and I decided to throw a little party for her at A Cherry on Top.

When she walked in the door, Ma, Franny, Jillian, and I sang "Happy Birthday." Then Ma fixed up a round of "Ain't No Mountain High Enough" Mocha-Fudge Frappes, and we all sat together in the dining area.

As Winnie sipped her frappe, I gave her my present.

"Precious, this is precious," she said, gazing at the cushion, her fingertips touching each patch.

The nurse cap made her sigh. The yawning Winnie Bear

made her giggle. The Gladys Knight and the Pips patch made her break out in song. And the "Down with Exercise" frowny face made her smile and declare, "My sentiments exactly!"

A tear rolled down her cheek when she saw the last patch: Colonel Elston Lincoln, with "Semper Fi" embroidered on his pocket.

Winnie rubbed the embroidered letters with her shiny purple fingernail. "Six more months until Elston comes back to the States on leave. This will be the first thing I show him," she said.

Just as we all started getting watery eyes too, Mac arrived, smelling like mouthwash and wearing his STORE MANAGER KELSH, HERE TO SERVE YOU name tag smartly above his shirt pocket. He made a big fuss about Ma's hair looking nice, and it did. (I'd run a rinse through it last night to get rid of the gray.) And he gave Ma a box of nicotine gum to help her quit smoking again since she was back up to a pack a day of Winstons.

Right when Ma was paying attention, I walked straight up to Mac and gave him a high five. "Glad you could make it!" I said.

"I couldn't miss the birthday of my favorite mariachi," he said, winking at Winnie.

Then Ma tapped a spoon against a glass. "Attention, please. We're celebrating the birthday of a true friend and one terrific lady. And while we're all gathered, there's another lass present who also deserves special recognition."

I looked up, and Ma was smiling back at me. Then she

pointed over to the menu board behind the counter, which was covered with a sheet.

"As you know, Tess, we've got sundaes named in tribute to all kinds of movers and shakers. Today, A Cherry on Top announces a new special, named after the smartest, sweetest gal I know."

With that, Ma charged the counter, yanked off the sheet, and shouted, "Voilà!"

Tess's Rocky Road Treat

Rocky Road ice cream was created to give folks something to smile about during the Great Depression, but this version's gone upscale: two whopping scoops of luscious chocolate and vanilla ice cream blended with walnuts and more marshmallows than you can shake a stick at.

Dedicated to a young lady who's ridden the rocky road with class.

"That captures you, all right," Winnie said, squeezing my hand.

"Wow. Thanks," I said, feeling like I was onstage holding an Oscar at the Academy Awards. Who knew an ice cream special could make a person feel so special?

"Well deserved," Ma said, glowing as she stood beside Mac. "I'm predicting this treat draws more attention than my Lone Star flag!"

"Let's hope it pumps up the incremental volume!" Mac added, serious like a true retailer.

I rolled my eyes and everybody laughed.

Jingle-jingle. A customer came through the door. "I'll handle it," I said, walking back behind the counter.

"Hey, Desperate. Remember me?"

A boy with an easy grin and a fine sense of style was looking at me. He wore a collared shirt, khaki shorts, and a dog-tag necklace.

I smiled awkwardly. He looked familiar, but from where? With those high cheekbones and that classic look, I *should've* remembered.

"I brought you something so you'll never forget my family business," he said, placing a tiny plastic dog on the counter. "Go on. Press the button on his tail."

So I did—and his back leg lifted like he was peeing and squirted water in my eye!

"You're Son of Clown!" I blurted out, laughing. What a difference an unpainted face and no wig made; he was undeniably cute!

"Actually I go by Kevin when I'm off duty."

"Yeah, Kevin. The kids loved you on Opening Day, and—well, thanks for trying to help when Jordan's turtle got loose. About the Grand Opening . . . I'm sorry for snapping at you."

He shrugged. "Don't sweat it. Besides, we clowns are tougher than we look."

I pointed at the dipping cabinet. "You want a cone? No charge."

"Sure. I'll take cookies and cream," he said, and *poof!* He pulled plastic flowers from his sleeve. Goes to show that, even off duty, you can't take the clown out of the kid.

I introduced Kevin to everybody and made cones for the two of us. Then we went for a walk outside in the sunshine. We squeezed past couples who were enjoying lunch in the newly opened alfresco dining area of Bianco's Pizzeria. I peeked at my reflection in the window—making sure my hair was smartly covering my ears. The air felt thick with fresh summer heat and the clicking of cicadas. A ruby-red sun lingered above us.

We crossed Barrett Street, right where Ma's Toyota was parked. A giant A CHERRY ON TOP banner was draped across its rear window.

"Is that your mother's car?" he asked.

"Unfortunately, yes."

"Sure is green," he said, grinning.

"And it's equipped with air-conditioning, all year long," I added.

Kevin licked away at his melting cone, telling me about the latest *Star Wars* model he was working on and asking what I liked to do when I wasn't scooping ice cream.

"I'm into arts and crafts—and peer mediation," I said proudly.

I snuck a sideways peek at him when I said it. He nodded approvingly, and my heart started pitter-pattering like rain on the roof. Now it was Gabby's voice that played in my head: *Ice cream shops offer endless possibilities.*

As we crossed Franklin, for a second I thought of Pop and the letter I'd written him, still on my night table. I couldn't call him or write him now, but who knows. That might change one day; so much had changed in my new home.

Home. Was I actually thinking of rusty old Schenectady as home? It practically made me laugh. But it *was* home, apartment 418, even with that rickety elevator that was always breaking down and the guy next door blasting war movies.

Kevin looked over and caught me daydreaming. "Back at the shop I noticed the special of the month has your name, Tess. What's up with you and rocky roads?"

I smiled. *Oh, if he only knew.*

A Smattering of Ice Cream Recipes
from A Cherry on Top

Schenectady Snow Shake

"Thick with whiteout conditions, like the blizzards we get here."

2 cups of the tastiest vanilla ice cream you can find
1 cup heavy cream
½ teaspoon vanilla extract
½ cup ice

In a blender, combine ice cream, heavy cream, and vanilla extract. Add ice and blend for 2 minutes. Pour into fancy-schmancy glasses and serve with a straw. Mmm, delish! Serves 2.

Yankee Doodle Dandy

"Sells big with upstate conservatives—and liberals love it too!"

⅓ cup sugar
1 teaspoon cornstarch
1 cup water
juice of ½ lemon
½ cup red currant jelly
2 cups rinsed blueberries

2 scoops strawberry ice cream
whipped cream
red, white, and blue sprinkles

Make the blueberry sauce first: In a saucepan, combine sugar and cornstarch. Stir in water and lemon juice and bring to a boil over medium heat. Reduce heat to medium-low and add jelly, then simmer for 5 minutes. Gently add blueberries and simmer over medium-low heat for 20 minutes until thick and syrupy.

Scoop ice cream into a cheery red bowl, then ladle blueberry sauce over it. Now get your patriotic groove on by dressing up this creation with whipped cream and sprinkles. Store leftover sauce in the fridge.

Made in the USA—marvelous!

"Ain't No Mountain High Enough" Mocha-Fudge Frappe

"In honor of Winnie: a nurse, an entertainer, and a soulful fairy godmother wrapped in one."

4 cups chilled coffee
½ cup crushed ice
4 tablespoons instant chocolate milk powder
1½ cups milk
½ cup whipped cream (plus more for garnish)
4 scoops vanilla ice cream

Pour coffee, ice, instant chocolate milk powder, and milk into a blender and mix. Add whipped cream and ice cream and blend at FRAPPE setting. Pour into a mug and garnish with additional whipped cream. Serves 2.

Note: Taste is enhanced by listening to Motown on your iPod.

Tess's Rocky Road Treat

"Hands down, the finest sundae ever created, according to Tess Dobson."

1 whopping scoop each of luscious chocolate and vanilla ice cream
½ cup chopped walnuts
½ cup mini marshmallows
whipped cream
fudge sauce

Find your favorite bowl and pile in all these tasty ingredients. Then swirl, swirl, swirl with a gentle hand and a hopeful spirit. You can't go wrong when you whip up this classic. Eating Rocky Road always puts you on the *right* road.

Ice Cream Flavors and the Inner You

The *Inside Scoop* isn't the only source that claims there's a link between personality and ice cream flavor preferences. A study in ice cream "flavorology" was actually conducted by a neurologist named Dr. Alan R. Hirsch, director of the Smell & Taste Treatment and Research Foundation in Chicago. The results suggest that distinct personalities do gravitate toward certain flavors when we step up to the ice cream counter. So skip the horoscopes and the fortune-tellers. Allow ice cream to be your guiding light on the path to self-awareness!

So what does *your* favorite ice cream flavor reveal about you?

Chocolate: You are creative, lively, and flirtatious. You also like being the center of attention and become bored with the same old routine.

Vanilla: Don't believe the myth. The vanilla lover's choice is *never* boring—you're colorful, impulsive, expressive, and a risk taker.

Mint chocolate chip: You have strong morals and you always fight for what you believe in. You are ambitious and confident too—and, truth be told, a little stubborn.

Butter pecan: You are devoted, orderly, respectful, and fiscally conservative. Odds are high that you make your bed every day and never have a messy desk.

Chocolate chip: You've got a competitive streak and you work very hard. You're also generous with time and money.

Coffee: You thrive on the passion of the moment and you throw yourself into all that you do. Friends know you as adventuresome and dramatic, but you tend to overcommit yourself.

Strawberry: Thoughtful and logical, that's you. You deliberate long and hard before making decisions. You can also be introverted and shy, but always a loyal friend.

Banana: You are easygoing, well adjusted, honest, and empathetic.

Rocky Road: You present a balanced mixture of charm and practicality. You are outgoing and goal-oriented, and you appreciate the finer things in life.

Tasty Afterthoughts

Writing a story set in an ice cream shop brings out the sweet in people. Many generous individuals have added flavor to *Rocky Road*. I am grateful to you all. Any errors, of course, I have served up by myself.

An extra scoop of thanks, with all the toppings, to:

Michele Burke, an editor who is as talented as she is fun and supportive. I knew we were simpatico when I discovered she loves coffee ice cream too. And a tip of the soda jerk's paper hat to all at Knopf who helped transform this story from manuscript to book.

Emily Sylvan Kim, superagent, who always believes in me and tells it like it is. Lucky me to have her on my team.

Kim Dergosits and Susan Rothchild, for guidance with American Sign Language and insight into the world of the deaf.

Camille Freedner and the peer mediators at Chatham Middle School in Chatham, New York, for explaining and enacting peer mediation. I intentionally choose an I-statement in declaring, "I feel that you are all terrific."

My local writer friends Nancy Castaldo, Liza Frenette, Lois Miner Huey, Eric Luper, Helen Mesick, Coleen Paratore, and Kyra Téis, who always give helpful feedback and keep good writer company. A special shout-out to Girl Scout leader Nancy for her crafty insight into T-shirt design.

Pat Reilly Giff, inspiring mentor, across the years and miles. And Ann Haywood Leal, talented author-buddy, who goes back with me to those SCBWI conferences where we scribbled notes to each other and wondered when we would get to check "author" on registration forms.

Sue Bucher, a San Antonio gal born and bred, for offering straight-shooting advice on all things Texas.

Al Roland, for the author photo, and Annie Roland, for fielding random research questions.

Michelle Camuglia, always my first reader and always a good friend.

Abby Curro, for her thorough explanation on installing curtains. (And for installing curtains at my house over the years!)

In tribute to Mr. Ed Berko and Dave Berko. I will always cherish the memory of our visit to an ice cream shop in Annapolis during my first trip to the Naval Academy. Go, Navy!

All the kids in our blended brood—Tae, Rhiannon, Kellyrose, Liam, Connor, and Theresa—for cheering on *Rocky Road* and putting up with my distracted self when Tess's troubles were on my mind. An extra heap of sprinkles goes to Kelly for reading the story early on and offering many valuable suggestions.

Frank Capra, posthumously, for creating a movie that always reminds me that we make the world a better place simply by the way we treat each other.

Janet Hutchison, smart and spirited owner of the Open

Door Bookstore, and the epitome of what brings out the best in Schenectady. And the sisters at Civitello's Italian Pastries. I put your shop in *Rocky Road*, changing the location, however, because your story inspired me—and I love your lemon ice. And to all in the Schenectady community who have worked so hard to bring this fine city back.

All the readers who have written and e-mailed and encouraged another book after reading *Kimchi & Calamari*, and all the teachers and librarians who have put my book in the hands of students and onto state lists.

My parents and extended family and friends, who cheered me on. And special kudos to my niece, Regina Kent, and my nephew, Matthew Beckwith, who often turned to me at family gatherings and asked, "So, whatcha writing now, Aunt Rose?"

To Tom, skilled mapmaker, patient partner, and Spanish translator. *Tú eres mi héroe. Siempre con cariño.*

Finally, to every person who has ever scooped a cone, whipped up a shake, or dressed up an ice cream sundae, and served it with a smile. You never know what that customer on the other side of the counter really needs. This story is for you.

About the Author

Rose Kent, a former naval officer, lives in Niskayuna, New York, just east of Schenectady, with her husband and children in a house with a dozen ice cream scoops. She is an ardent believer in the redemptive power of a sundae.

Her first book, *Kimchi & Calamari*, was nominated for several state library awards. Visit her at www.rosekent.com.